THE
TURNBULL
MURDERS

THE TURNBULL MURDERS

A Historic Homes Mystery

R.J. KORETO

LEVEL
BEST BOOKS

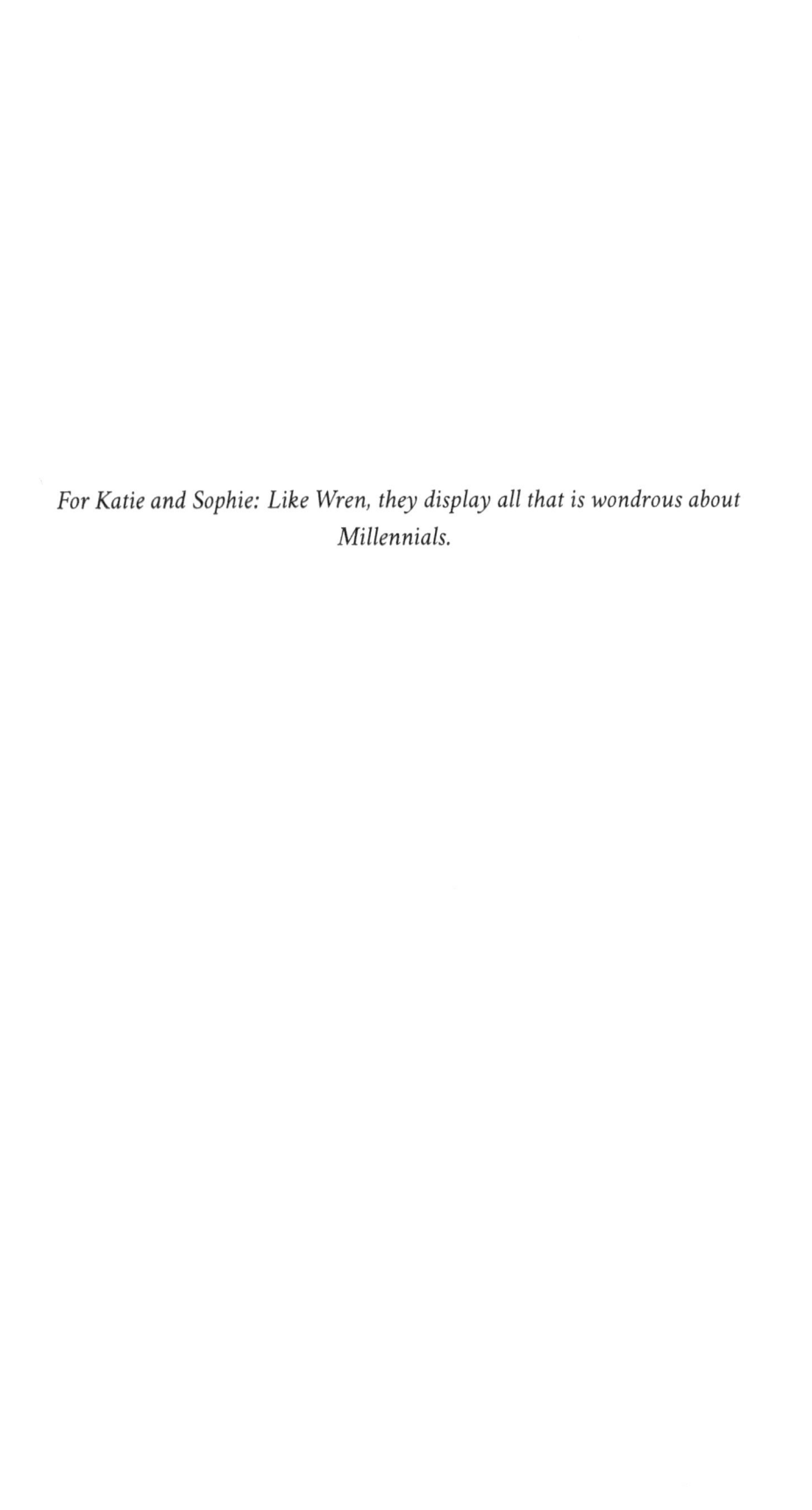

For Katie and Sophie: Like Wren, they display all that is wondrous about Millennials.

Praise for the First Historic Homes Mystery

"A delightful who-done-it in which the house is as engaging as the wonderful heroine. Readers will want to get lost in these rooms and these pages."—Cate Holahan, *USA Today* bestselling author of *Her Three Lives*

"If you love houses and puzzles - which I do - you will be captivated by *The Greenleaf Murders*, the first in Richard Koreto's new series. Equally surefooted in the gilded age of the mansion's heyday and the contemporary world of its decline, Koreto has woven a pretzel of a plot, introduced a charming new heroine, and whetted appetites for more grave deeds and grandeur."—Catriona McPherson, multi-award-winning author of the Dandy Gilver series

"I believe I was secretly born to be an architect, which is probably why I so enjoyed this mystery of a stately NYC mansion and its role in murders both past and present."—Lisa Black, *NYT* bestselling author of *Every Kind of Wicked*

"*The Greenleaf Murders* mixes a modern suspense mystery with the love of old-world mansions and iconic High Society. Buried secrets threaten a family clinging to their former glory as two murders surface, a century apart. Koreto weaves a story that creates the perfect tension between the beauty of the golden era and the fear of a killer in plain sight."—L.A. Chandlar, national bestselling author of the Art Deco Mystery series

Chapter One

January

"The home should be the treasure chest of living." If it were up to Wren, she'd have that quotation from the great architect Le Corbusier put on a plaque in every home she worked on. It always led her to reflect on the people who had lived in each home she renovated. Most architects who designed homes had the luxury of knowing the people who would live there, but as she worked only on old homes, all she had was her imagination. She looked over the restored kitchen, the stone, and steel, the imported tiles. But she wanted to see beyond it, to those who lived here originally, to a family that loved this house—and perhaps loved each other? For some reason, she had been thinking more about that recently. *No, not some reason. For an actual one.*

As if on cue, she heard a rap on the kitchen door, and then Hadley tumbled in, cheeks red from the cold, bags swinging from both hands. The kitchen light bounced off her blond hair, and her green eyes seemed to glow. There was always so much *color* about her.

"I knew I'd find you here, Little Bird," she said. "It always comes down to the kitchen, doesn't it?'

Wren still felt the little thrill when she saw Hadley, had wondered how long that would last, and was beginning to realize that it might go on forever. She had always thought herself plain, but Hadley had made her feel beautiful for the first time in her life. As beautiful as the houses she worked on.

Hadley put her bags on the table, then placed a cool hand on Wren's cheek and gave her a kiss.

"You're right. But I don't know why it should. Yes, we still think of home and hearth, but when this brownstone was built, you'd only find servants in the kitchen."

"Things change. Look at me. I'm a Vanderwerf. We were a power in this city when it was still New Amsterdam. And yet here I am, entering through the servants' entrance. Anyway, maybe that's why the people who built these houses are gone—they didn't realize that the kitchen was the center all along."

Hadley was right. And as beautiful as Wren had made this kitchen, it would be the people who made it warm. It had taken her a while to realize that, but she knew it now. She hoped as rich as they were, her client's family would spend time down here.

"I'd love to cook something here," said Hadley looking around. "You did an amazing job. But for now, I brought some food from last night's job, and some unbelievable news for both of us."

From the bags, she unpacked Rubbermaids full of stew and brown bread. "I was catering the album release of some folk music group. Not my jam, but they're better-behaved than the metal crowd. I figured a nice peasant dish would go over well with that set on a winter's day. With polenta—just a couple minutes in the microwave."

Soon, they were sitting at the handsome oak table. Wren closed her eyes and sighed with pleasure.

"My God, this is perfect."

Hadley flushed a little, then reached over and grabbed Wren's hand. "Thank you. But onto the big news. First, you'll never guess who showed up at the event last night. Apparently, he's a big folk music fan, even sponsors some festival out west. He showed up without announcement, to avoid a scene." Hadley dramatically waved her arms. "Nicky Tallon."

"No! Did you meet him?"

"We had quite a talk. First, you know how they say movie stars are never as handsome in person as they are on screen? Well, that's not true. He was amazing. And rather quiet spoken, almost shy. I mean, he had a whole posse with him, but he seemed—I don't know, unsure about it. Anyway, we had a nice talk. I think he was tickled to meet me—I was one of the few women he's met who didn't want to get him into bed." They both laughed.

"So a couple of things. First, he'll be shooting a movie this spring, partly in New York. He seemed to like my food, so I told him I was available to cater movie shoots, and he said he'd make it happen, even told one of his people. It's not something the star generally decides, but when someone like Nicky Tallon makes a request...."

"I'm so happy for you, sweetie." Wren squeezed her girlfriend's hand. "You've worked so hard—you'll be great."

"Thank you. But there's more. One of the reasons he wants the New York shoot, aside from the fact that it takes place partly in New York, is that he's bought a house here. A very old house, and they'll want to film onsite. He said it needs major renovations. And, of course I told him I knew an absolutely fantastic architect who specializes in historic renovations."

Wren's first thought was about her father—being able to tell him that she had landed a big client on her own.

Hadley, as usual, read her mind. "That will thrill your father, won't it? His little girl, landing a big fish. Anyway, I took the liberty of saying you could make it Thursday morning. I'll be coming too to look over the site for providing catering."

"Nothing I can't rearrange. Thank you, my sweet! What did he tell you about the house? I want to be prepared."

"Ah. I know how much you hate winging things, but you might have to. Nicky looked a little embarrassed and said he couldn't tell us anything until we signed nondisclosure agreements. We're meeting downtown at the Millennium at nine and then straight to the house. Understand that these people are in their own special world, Wren. I know you've dealt with lots of rich people, but these are rich *and* famous, surrounded by people who tell them how wonderful they are every waking moment. It's going to be quite a trip."

"You're saying they're crazy creative people? I'm an architect. I can be crazy and creative right back at them."

"That's the spirit, Little Bird. I'm glad about this. We'll sort of be working together, you working on the house while I'm catering. Listen, I have some people to see, but we can meet for a late dinner? I have some lovely veal."

"I'll pay you back with breakfast out," said Wren. Staying over wasn't automatic—it was something they still danced around, and Wren was thinking maybe if they lived together, it would be easier...should she bring it up now? But as she was aware, winging it wasn't her strong suit. She still lived in the Brooklyn townhouse she had grown up in, telling herself her widowed father needed her company even while realizing that was just an excuse.

Hadley gathered up her dishes and kissed Wren. "See you later, my love."

Yes, it was time to move forward with Hadley. She made a note on her tablet to call her father's old friend and colleague Doris, queen of New York Realtors. For now, though, it was time to think about Nicky Tallon's house.

The first clue was the hotel. The Millennium was a fine hotel but not the very best. It was all the way downtown, practical only if you worked on Wall Street. Did he want to be close to his new house? She couldn't think of any residence a movie star might want down there.

She opened her laptop and brought up a map of Manhattan, hoping the street names would jog her memory of a great home, but nothing relevant. She pulled back for a wider view.

Oh...could it be? She couldn't imagine that was even for sale. But it was easy enough to check. City property records were online and public. This was going to be tricky to look up, but she knew how the system worked, and a few minutes later, she leaned back in the kitchen chair, feeling smug. Her second thought was how proud her father would be of her. The third was how she was a grown woman and a licensed architect and should stop concerning herself with what her father would think of her, even if he was also her boss.

She was going to do a lot of research before meeting Nicky. For now, she began gathering her papers and thought of the evening ahead with Hadley. She'd have to tell her to dress warmly Thursday morning.

* * *

On Wednesday afternoon, a phone call gave Wren a taste of what it was going to be like working for Nicky Tallon.

"Ms. Fontaine? This is Cal O'Reilly, personal assistant to Mr. Tallon. I am confirming our meeting tomorrow at the Millennium. I will be in the lobby to escort you up."

"I'll be there."

"We'll be traveling to Mr. Tallon's house and preparing coffee for everyone. How do you like yours, Ms. Fontaine?"

"Oh…just a little milk, no sugar."

"We have specialty coffees, if you like. Absolutely anything you want." Did he think architects had special coffee requirements? Anyway, Hadley loved unusual coffee drinks.

"Thank you, but a little milk, no sugar, will be fine."

"Very good. Until tomorrow." There was a crispness to his tone, as if he were *playing* the role of personal assistant.

The wealthy were capable of extending great personal service. But they expected it in return.

Wren decided to tell her father only that she was pursuing a lead and nothing more. Most didn't pan out anyway, and no need to excite him with such a lucrative commission until it was further along. On Thursday morning, she put on one of her better suits—pants over nice but warm boots and her dressy navy-blue winter coat. She took the subway from their Brooklyn townhouse, and although she was early, an excited Hadley was already waiting for her, standing out in a bright pink parka. She loved her girlfriend's ability to just wear a bright pink parka instead of a sober grown-up coat. Should she buy a brightly colored parka too?

"I can't believe you figured it out," Hadley said. "You're so clever—but don't worry, I won't spoil your big reveal. It'll create some logistical issues, but I've already been brainstorming on it."

"I'm going to pretend I didn't figure it out; I just knew about the house. Actually, I did have some knowledge—it's very unusual. Anyway, my father always says we have to make it clear we're a step ahead of our clients." She linked her arm with Hadley's. "We're meeting big shots, but we'll show them we're big shots too."

They asked for Nicky Tallon at the reception desk, and a moment later, a young man greeted them.

"Wren? Hadley? Cal O'Reilly." He extended his hand. Wren took him in quickly. *A bit of a peacock.* A burgundy blazer with a sharply contrasting shirt and purple-rimmed eyeglasses. "We've spoken on the phone. I'm Nicky Tallon's personal assistant. Please follow me." They followed him to the elevator. "We have the entire floor for security. You can imagine Nicky's need for privacy." He presented that as if he were imparting sacred knowledge. As he turned, Wren and Hadley looked at each other, and Hadley rolled her eyes.

A security guard by the elevator on Nicky's floor waved them on, and Cal let them into a suite.

Wren hadn't expected such a large group, but then again, weren't movie stars always pictured as having an entourage? They were on their phones or talking in groups and helping themselves from a tray of coffee and Danishes. Nicky Tallon was talking in a corner with a fifty-something man in a sober suit—the only one who, like Wren, wore traditional business clothes.

Cal hung up their coats, got them some coffee, and then introduced them to Nicky and his companion.

"Nicky—Wren Fontaine and Hadley Vanderwerf."

Nicky smiled. It wasn't that he was handsome, realized Wren—he was perfect, like some sort of artwork.

"Great to see you again, Hadley, and a pleasure to meet you, Wren," he said, extending his hand. "Thank you so much for coming. This is Zach Landau, my business manager." Perhaps it was because she knew he was an actor, but everything about him seemed rehearsed, from that studied greeting to his clothes—so much money spent to look casual. Was it him, or had he been "designed" the way she designed homes?

"I'm so glad you could both come today," said Zach. Wren didn't see much behind Nicky's eyes, but Zach gave both of them a shrewd look. "I'll give you the full story, but first, we have NDAs to sign. Why don't the four of us step into the next room for a little quiet?" They followed Zach through a connecting door into the next room, where the papers were waiting for them on a table.

Zach reached into his jacket pocket and pulled out business cards. Wren looked at the old-fashioned typeface and design, which would've been familiar to Charles Dickens. It was no accident. Zachery Landau, JD, CPA, wanted everyone to know that in the entertainment world, he was the grown-up.

Wren handed her card—modern yet timeless, as her father said. He should know—he designed it himself. Hadley's was full color and glossy. Wren was impressed that Zach took the time to actually read the cards carefully before pocketing them.

"You'll find these pretty standard. I'm sure you're both used to them in your respective professions." They were, indeed. They both signed, and Zach put them back in the folders. He leaned back and gave an indulgent look at Nicky, who seemed as pleased as a child that his time had come.

"There's an island in the harbor…" he started. Hadley caught Wren's eye: *you were right.* "It has a fantastic old house on it. And I've bought it from the government, the house, the whole island. We're going to film there. Wren, I want you to fix it up. I want you to make it perfect, like it was when it was built. I want to live there, in that incredible house on my own island in the middle of the greatest city on earth."

Oh, nothing rehearsed there! Wren's heart warmed, and she had to stop herself from leaning over the table and kissing Nicky: someone else who had fallen in love with a house.

"And I want to renovate it for you. We're talking about Turnbull Island, aren't we? It's the only possible island in the harbor you could be talking about."

Nicky leaned back and laughed, then slapped Zach on the shoulder. "We got the right one. I told you, Zach. Thank you, Hadley. Anyone who could make a stew like that would know what's what."

Hadley beamed and squeezed Wren's hand, but Zach didn't smile.

"Taking a somewhat more *objective* approach, I did a search on you, Wren. Your firm is world class, and you personally are becoming the go-to architect for historic homes."

Wren fought a blush. Her father always said modesty had no place in architecture.

"We've worked on a wide variety of houses of all ages in New York, and I'm sure we can handle this one."

"Well, that's just great!" said Nicky. He leaned over the table, and now it was Wren's turn for a slap on the shoulder. "I knew you could do it."

"Of course, there's a lot to do before we actually get to work. I have to view the house, and bring out our contractor, and then submit a proposal. It's an involved process, especially with a landmark building like the Turnbull House."

"Paperwork," said Nicky. "I'm sure we can work around that. Now, Hadley, we're going to have a big crew there, so I'll be counting on you to provide the food."

Hadley grinned. "Like Wren said, I have to view the area and submit an estimate, but I'm sure we can work something out."

"That's great." Hadley got the third shoulder slap. "Look, I want to talk to you about the food. We'll let these two go over the paperwork stuff. We're leaving for the house soon anyway."

Hadley gave Wren a thumb's up, slipped her arm into Nicky's, and then left Wren alone with Zach. He folded his arms across his chest.

"You see what I'm dealing with?" he asked.

"He won't be my first challenging client," said Wren.

"Yes…well, that's what we need to discuss. Yes, Nicky may become your client. But I'm his business manager." He smiled wryly. "Let's say I provide a certain audit function here. Nicky has a lot of money but not an infinite amount. This island purchase of his is a toy. There are limits to what we can spend on that house."

Wren often felt she didn't know where she stood with people. But she knew where she stood with houses.

"I offer only one level of service. The complete and perfect renovation of that house. I don't do anything less. I do it right or not at all."

She watched Zach start to speak several times and stop. Then he spread out his hands.

"Naturally," he finally said. "We'll go over the details after you submit your proposal." Wren had no doubt he'd go over every single line. "I guess after dealing with my Hollywood clients, it'll be refreshing to deal with a fellow adult. In that spirit, I'll give you one more thing: It won't have escaped you that there are lots of people around Nicky—agents, publicists, all sorts of people from the studio. Not all of them are thrilled with the idea of someone of his stature planning to hide himself on an island, even temporarily."

"Does that include you?" asked Wren.

"I'm just the money man. Anyway, I'm looking forward to your proposal." No backslapping for him—he reached across the table and gave Wren a firm handshake.

Back in the main suite, Wren found Hadley talking with Nicky and a young woman dressed in plain blue jeans, orange high-top sneakers, and a turtleneck. Nicky had his arm around her.

"Wren—this is Saffron Scott. Saffron, Wren is going to fix up that house for us."

"It's nice to meet you," Saffron said with a shy smile. "I haven't even seen it myself yet, but I saw photos, and it looks so great. Nicky says it's unbelievable, and it'll be so cool to live on an island."

Saffron looked just out of high school, a good twenty years younger than Nicky. She glanced at Hadley, who gave Wren a barely perceptible shrug. *Yeah, that's the way it works.*

Cal came around and asked if anyone wanted anything. They said they were fine.

"You're sure, Saffron?" Cal asked. "I have that hazelnut coffee you like."

"You are SO sweet," she said and touched his hand. He turned red. "But I'm okay for now."

"Anyway, I made sure there will be more on the boat."

Nicky didn't seem to mind that his girlfriend and assistant were flirting. But this was not the time to reflect on her client's love life. At this point,

Wren knew her father would have an amusing and relevant anecdote to bond with the client. She had already prepared something that might appeal to Nicky and Saffron.

"Do you know anything about the house?" she asked.

"No. I mean, I know it's very old," said Saffron. "The thing is that it's far enough away. Nicky had an idea of finding a place far from…everything."

"Yes, somewhere quiet. And, what's more quiet than a private island?" said Nicky.

Time to build a connection, like her father advised her to do. "I understand you like folk music," she said to Nicky.

"Oh yes! We both do. We met at a concert, where he heard me play," said Saffron.

"So you probably know the song 'The Captain's House.'"

"Of course!" said Saffron. "It's so sad. He lives in a house with his wife and sister, and although they try so hard to make a welcoming home for him, he's called away by the East and leaves forever."

"The house you just bought, Nicky. It's the house in the song."

"You're kidding!" said Nicky. Saffron's eyes got even bigger.

"The man who built that house was one Captain Turnbull. He was a successful trader and actually owned multiple ships. It was assumed he'd settle down and raise a family and let others captain his ships. He was a well-known figure in post-Revolution America. But then he disappears from the record. His wife and sister presumably stayed in the house—but again, nothing is mentioned until property records show another owner had it many years later. Who knows if the folk song is right? Like with most folk songs, its origins are obscure, but whoever wrote it knew that house and the island—the descriptions are precise."

Wren had hoped at this point Nicky and Saffron would tell her how clever she was and ask more about the house. Like when her father tossed off an anecdote. But as she watched, tears started to flow down Saffron's cheeks.

While she was struggling with how to respond, a sharply dressed man laid a hand on Nicky's shoulder. "Can you give me a minute?"

"What?" Nicky looked annoyed.

"I need a minute. It has to be now. Come on, Los Angeles is busting my balls—"

Nicky rolled his eyes and stepped away, leaving the teary-eyed Saffron with Wren and Hadley.

"The home Nicky just bought...that's where the women lived alone for the rest of their lives?"

"Well, yes..." said Wren. "We don't exactly have all the details. It was a long time ago—"

"So we have to move there," said Saffron, her voice wavering. "We have to make it *home* again, for the family's sake, to make it *whole* again..." and she threw herself at Wren, hugging her tightly. Wren had no idea what to do. When her father finished a story, everyone would laugh, and someone would get out the scotch. She looked over Saffron to Hadley. *I told you, Little Bird, these people were different.*

Wren didn't know what to do or say, so she lightly held the crying girl. But she could hear Nicky, and the man who pulled him away, and they were getting louder, above the background buzz of everyone talking.

"...the studio doesn't want you hiding away..."

"I'm not hiding away. I'm buying a damn home..."

"You have a home in California..."

"It's just a stage they stick me on to meet people every damned day. I mean a home, a real home, for me and Saffron...."

"But we're counting on the publicity tour...."

"I'll do the damn tour, then I'm going to my new home, and I don't want to talk about it anymore."

"But Nicky—"

"Don't—" Wren saw Nicky take a step forward. He wasn't just perfectly handsome; he was tall and broad, and the man he was arguing with retreated. "Just...don't. I'm not kidding."

The man put up his hands in surrender, but they kept talking, only quietly now.

Hadley had produced some tissues meanwhile and gave them to Saffron, who cleaned herself up.

"Thank you...I'm sorry. That song is so sad, and the thought of those women...all alone in their home, wondering where their husband and brother went...that's something I know about...." She shook her head, as if to dismiss the subject.

"Saffron, who is the man Nicky is talking with?" asked Wren, trying to change the subject.

"Oh...that's Beebee Jenkins. He's with the studio. Nicky's always fighting with him. He doesn't want Nicky to buy the house...they want to keep him in California." Wren thought about what Zach said—not everyone was onboard with the island house.

Saffron looked up at her, and with her red-rimmed eyes, she looked even more waif-like.

"Wren—do you think you can find out what really happened while you work on the house? What drove the Captain away? If we're going to live there, that's very important."

Chapter Two

L ike a hummingbird, Nicky's assistant Cal had been running from one group to another, making sure everyone had what they wanted. He kept an eye on his watch and then clapped his hands.

"Okay—everyone! We're leaving from the lobby in five minutes. There are limos downstairs to take us to the pier, and if you gave me your coffee order earlier, you'll have it for the island."

Wren, Hadley, and the other guests began getting their coats from the rack by the door. Cal handed Nicky his coat, Wren saw, but helped Saffron with hers. She beamed at him as thanks, her recent outburst forgotten.

"The prom king and his queen," snickered Hadley.

"What's going on here?"

"Junior has a crush on the boss's girlfriend. But look at her—she dresses like a teenager. She'd probably be happier with Cal than with Nicky, never mind his millions."

"She's pretty enough, but not stunning and a little odd. I imagine guys like Nicky can get anyone. Why her?"

"Oh, Wren, it's not always about beauty and glamour for guys like that. It's about worship. And someone young like that won't just love him, she'll worship him."

"Okay. I think I'll have my work cut out for me," said Wren. She watched everyone else get ready. Beebee, the studio man who had fought with Nicky, got his coat. He looked sour about the whole thing. Zach was coming too, but his face gave away nothing.

As they walked through the lobby, Wren was amused to see everyone look at Nicky—and then look again. Nicky didn't seem to notice. Several stretch limos waited for the group, and Wren and Hadley were ushered into one with Nicky, Cal, Zach, and Saffron—who was carrying what looked like a small guitar case.

"The other cars are for the studio people. I spend enough time with them. It's a few minutes' ride to the boat. Or maybe longer—I can't get used to city traffic."

"You grew up in rural Idaho, didn't you?" asked Hadley.

"In a town you won't find on a map," he said. "Just kinda fell into this—wandered down to L.A. and got a job as a limo driver, then picked up by a modeling agency, which led to guest spots on TV until I became everyone's favorite doctor for six seasons on 'Surgical Suite,' and then some movies, and here I am." He looked a little embarrassed about the whole thing, as if he couldn't believe what had happened, couldn't figure it out, and wasn't necessarily happy about it. Saffron patted him on his leg. He smiled at her and squeezed her hand.

"So Nicky—have you given any thought to what you want out of the house?" asked Wren. "We have time to plan it after I've seen it, but have you thought about what you want the house for?"

Nicky frowned. "Well…we're going to live there. Get away from all the people in L.A. I mean, I got a nice place in California, but everyone is there all the time, you know. I want a real home. Is that what you mean?"

This was going to be interesting. Most of the firm's clients were captains of industry, with strong ideas about what they wanted from their houses… about what they wanted from everything.

"Well…yes. But more specific. The Turnbull house has about twenty-five thousand square feet—that's a very large house with a lot of possibilities. Do you see it as a family home, a place to entertain close friends and family, a venue to throw parties?"

That seemed to stump Nicky, and Wren wondered if her question would start Saffron on another crying jag. But she just smiled gently. "We just want to live there together. Just us and people we love." Nicky gave her an affectionate look.

"Yeah, you said it," he said.

"Cal, of course, too. Nicky depends on you. You'll live there, right?"

"Oh…sure," he said.

"And Thalia—naturally," said Saffron. *Who was Thalia?*

Nicky looked uncomfortable at that. "I'm sure everyone doesn't want to know all the details," said Nicky. He turned back to Wren. "As you said, we have a lot of room. We will need to think about what to do with it. We'll want a home theater, of course."

"Of course," said Wren.

Nicky nodded and then changed the subject to something he felt more comfortable with.

"So Hadley, you think you could get a barbecue going there?"

"Oh yeah. I've got a chicken glaze that'll knock your socks off…."

Fears of traffic aside, they made good time to a marina on the west side, where they all got out. The Captain, in a blue coat, came down the gangway.

"Ready any time, Mr. Tallon."

"As soon as we're all onboard," he said.

"Why does he want a house?" asked Hadley. "You could just live on that."

"Nicky doesn't want just a house. He wants a home," said Wren, and Hadley nodded. "He probably leases this to live on while he reviews the island—I doubt if that house is in a condition to live in."

The Captain led them into a large room with easy chairs, couches, and tables.

"This is the main salon," he said. "We'll be there in about thirty minutes. Make yourselves comfortable."

They cast off soon, and Wren watched lower Manhattan pass by them as they sailed into the upper bay. She looked around the yacht. Hadley had a point, it could be a home, it was designed like a home. *Wherever people go, they create a home, one way or another, even if it's on the water.*

The parties chatted among themselves, and Cal set himself behind a small bar near where Wren and Hadley were sitting, dispensing coffee, juice, and bottled water. Saffron was staring out the windows with childlike wonder, going back and forth from one side to another for the different views. Cal carried a coffee and Danish to Saffron, who rewarded him with another bright smile.

And Beebee had again cornered Nicky. They were quiet, but Wren could see the tension in Nicky's shoulders. Finally, Beebee got up and, shaking his head, made his way to the bar.

"Kid—do you have some vodka to go with that orange juice."

"No, I don't," said Cal.

"You're telling me there's no vodka on this boat?"

"I'm telling you, I don't have any available."

"Maybe you could find some if you weren't so busy trying to screw Saffron."

"Up yours, Beebee."

Beebee turned red. He hadn't expected that.

"I'm a studio executive. You'll call me *sir*."

"Up yours, *sir*."

You could see him struggling to respond to that and looked around. Other people had heard the exchange, even if they were pretending they hadn't. There was nothing he could do, at least today. He took his vodka-less juice to a corner and sulked.

"Can Cal get away with that?" Wren asked Hadley. "At the end of the day, he's a servant. Beebee seems to be a studio big shot."

"Ha! Servant, yes, technically. But as a personal assistant, he's a very senior one. You see, it's a complex pecking order. Yes, Beebee technically outranks Cal, but Cal works directly for Nicky, and as long as people buy tickets to see Nicky's movies, Nicky outranks everyone. You can always hire a new executive, but there's only one Nicky Tallon. Getting yourself involved in Hollywood gossip?"

"Just interested in how this will affect my work. How much pressure will the studio put on Nicky about it? How much say is Saffron going to have, especially if Nicky starts noticing his assistant adores her. My father once designed a house for a hedge fund manager with a trophy wife younger than his children—and believe me, she called the shots."

"So you'd be okay taking instructions from a teenaged girl wearing orange high-tops?" Her tone was teasing, but Wren didn't smile.

"Saffron will have ideas for the house, I'm willing to bet. She knows how important a home is. I can work with anyone like that." Hadley didn't respond to that right away. "I know. I just came across as really pompous, didn't I." She didn't have her father's gift for casual conversation.

"No, Little Bird. You came across as wise." And she kissed Wren's cheek.

An elegant-looking woman of about fifty slid in next to them. Wren had seen her briefly at the hotel suite. She knew her right away, of course, but couldn't think of a pretext to introduce herself.

"So the architect and the caterer—Nicky pointed you out to me. I'm looking to speak to someone new. I'm—"

"Oh! Did you think we wouldn't recognize Veronica Selwyn," said Hadley. Veronica seemed pleased with that. "A pleasure to meet you. You're in this movie?"

"For my sins, yes."

"I'm Hadley Vanderwerf, and this is Wren Fontaine. I loved you as Captain Blake in 'Bronx Precinct.'"

"Thank you. As TV shows go, it wasn't the worst, and those five seasons plus occasional movie roles like this give me freedom to do theater. So, Wren, you're going to create the private palace for Nicky?"

"A manor house," said Wren. *Oh God, correcting people....*

"You're literal. I guess you have to be in your line of work. I'm along for the ride today—I like to see the site before filming, even though we're some months away. And I admit I want to see that house. Nicky hasn't shut up about it. He's so excited. He's really a sweet boy. Anyway, you two are an item, as the kids say? Nice to work together." Wren didn't know how to respond to that, but Veronica didn't seem to expect anything. "Say—your name is Fontaine. I once met an architect named Ezra Fontaine—a relation?"

"My father."

"How funny! He designed an extraordinary house for a friend of mine two years ago in Wilton, and we met at the housewarming. A few more seasons of Bronx Precinct, and I might be able to afford him myself."

"I know the house you mean. It is extraordinary. My father doesn't suffer from false modesty in pricing his services. And neither do I."

Veronica laughed. "There's no false modesty in performing arts either." She looked around, then leaned in and lowered her voice. "Listen, you two seem nice, and we're all girls together here. A few things to know if you're going to be working around us. We've already started filming. And I can tell you that Nicky is a very nice boy, and remarkably modest for someone that famous, but—how to put it—he's not a deep thinker. Still, he's authentic, and that's rare around here. As for that funny little girlfriend of his—she comes from another planet. And I saw you watching Beebee's little encounter—keep away from him. I've already had to tell him twice to keep his hand off my ass, and let's face it, ladies, I'm past my sell-by date. I'm fifty, but I get to play Nicky's mother. He's forty. It's not easy to be an aging actress."

"I hope I look half as good as you when I'm fifty," said Hadley.

"You're sweet."

"And thank you for the tips. That's nice of you," said Wren. "Much appreciated. But one more thing—Saffron mentioned someone Nicky is apparently close with. Someone named Thalia. Do you know who she is?"

"Oh yeah. *Another* Nicky girlfriend. At that level, men get to have different women for different moods. I can't say I know how it all works. I don't even want to know. You will get to see her, no doubt. Saffron may be legally insane—they may have some weird daddy-daughter thing going on—I don't want to know. Thalia is just your garden-variety bitch."

"Speaking of Saffron, I noticed Nicky seems to have a rival—Cal appears to be interested in her," said Hadley.

"Oh God, yes," said Veronica. "Give the boy credit for ambition, trying to steal a girl from Nicky Tallon. It's ludicrous, but most of the men would try it with Thalia, so he gets additional credit for originality. He's pretty sharp, our Cal, does a nice job of running Nicky's life, so we'll excuse him for being silly over Saffron. Oddly, she would probably be happier with Cal than with Nicky. There is something very…off there. Anyway, great meeting you. See you inside." And she left them alone again.

"I'm feeling more and more like Dorothy landing in Oz," said Wren.

"Oh yeah."

Looking out the window, they could see Turnbull Island coming into view. Wren wasn't a naval architect, but she guessed the pier they were approaching went back to the 1940s, the last time the island was important. The house was just visible at the top of the high ground, and Wren felt her heart beating the way it always did the first time she saw a home. This was especially exciting, a house that had been closed up and inaccessible for decades.

The Captain announced that they'd be docking shortly. They stood and put on their coats and saw Cal with a tray of labeled travel mugs. "Everyone is getting the coffee they requested," he announced. "It's a five-minute walk to the house, and the heating inside is minimal."

They each grabbed a mug as they headed down the gangway. Nicky and Saffron fell in with them.

"Excited?" asked Nicky.

"Yes. I like seeing a house for the first time. I guess it's like when you're given a script to read for the first time?"

Nicky laughed, but there wasn't much humor. "I don't read them much. I have all kinds of people around me who say, 'This is good for you, Nicky,' or 'This isn't right for you, Nicky.' Anyway, this will be my usual bit, the open, honest working man in a world of evil rich people." He sounded half amused, half resigned.

The path was narrow, and they walked in a line up the hill until they came up to the side of the house, and Wren had to restrain herself from running to see it from the front.

Oh, it was nice, thought Wren. It was *very* nice. There weren't many photos of the house, and none recently, so it was a revelation to her. Whether it was the architect or the Captain himself, someone knew their business—the lines, the proportions. If it was that good outside, it was probably like that inside too, and whatever had happened in the last two hundred years was fixable. It could be brought back. *She* could bring it back.

A two-story portico protected the front door, and Wren admired the fanlight and side lights flanking the door—they had been replaced with cheap glass at some point, but she could get new, better panes. As they gathered under it while Cal got out the keys, Wren touched the side of the house—wooden clapboard, strong and traditional, and apparently still in good condition. She held her breath as Cal opened the door, and everyone filed in.

It was going to be okay. Years of tenants had left their mark on the house, and it was long overdue for a painting, but its fundamentals seemed still good, with no obvious signs of rot. The entranceway, bright and welcoming, led to a staircase that soared to the second floor. The ornamentation on the walls—garland and urns—were still present and could be touched up.

And even Wren, who had been prepared, felt her heart skip a beat at the great room, a perfect oval. Everyone just looked around, speechless, and Wren found it entertaining to watch their faces. They had never seen anything like this. They probably never would again. They had all doubtless dined in the houses of the wealthy in California, but no modern house could possibly radiate the perfect graciousness, the elegance, of this design. She thought about the argument she could have about that with her father.

For now, she thought about the beautiful fireplace. No doubt the flue had been plugged up decades ago, but she'd have it opened again, bring out each perfect point. They'd remove that sloppy door, probably installed in the 1930s to create some privacy and restore the archway that complemented the room with perfect balance. She could see it now, with the well-tooled wooden furniture, silver tea service, and the Turnbull family relaxing there, as the Georgian fashions gave way....

No. Stop it, Wren. She could bring back the house, but not the people.

For now, the fireplace was empty. An outdoor generator kept the house moderately warm year-round to prevent weather damage, but after the walk, everyone was glad for their coffee.

Nicky looked thrilled, his eyes roving over his new purchase. Wren could see he was still amazed even though this was not his first visit. He knew in his heart what Wren knew intellectually—there was nothing like this.

The crowd gradually dispersed among the various spaces, and Wren did a quick accounting of the downstairs rooms. Yes, she saw more temporary walls, damaged floors, water stains—but again, nothing she couldn't fix. The house remained.

Back in the entranceway, however, she found Saffron was looking a little surprised—even disappointed.

"What do you think?" prompted Wren.

"I thought it would be…fancier," she said. "Like a castle."

Of course. Wren was guessing Saffron had no context for a great house and was probably thinking of Disney World.

She glanced up—Nicky was waiting for her response. Then suddenly, he put his fingers in his mouth and whistled loudly. The group came back, and he addressed them in his best actor's voice. "Everyone—architect Wren is going to give us a description and history of this house. She's in charge here and knows the whole story."

She realized he was right as she fought down a momentary panic. Wren was used to explaining houses to clients, but not so early in the process and not to a large audience. Still, she was glad she had figured out earlier where they were going. She caught Hadley's eye and got a smile and wink. Wren organized her thoughts and took a breath.

"This house is done in what's called Federal style, which was popular around 1800 when it was built." She looked at Saffron. Again, she needed context. "This was not long after the American Revolution. John Adams was president. This house was built for a wealthy family, but this wasn't a palace." Everyone looked at her expectantly while she paused. How to explain without boring everyone? Her father was good at this. She wasn't.

"There was a family of architects in Britain—a father and sons—named Adam, in the late eighteenth century. They studied ancient buildings in Italy and mixed what they found with traditional English homes. The result was bright and handsome, with lively pastel colors and often sophisticated curves like you see in this room. In England, this was the time of Jane Austen—Pride and Prejudice." She saw understanding nods. "The Americans admired the Adam ideals, and over here it became Federal style, named after the new Federal government, and you can find homes like this up and down the East Coast." Was she overdoing it? She caught Hadley's eye and got an encouraging thumbs up. "With houses like this, everything went together—the architecture, the floors, and ceilings, the decorations. It was all of a part—everything worked in concert for beauty. What you are seeing here is the perfect mix of design and proportion. You are seeing *harmony*."

"So, like a movie set? Only real," said Veronica. "Actors, script, setting, and costumes all go together?"

"Yes," said Wren, grateful for the intelligent insight. "Exactly. And we're going to bring it back. We're going to rebuild it like when the Turnbulls lived here, with modern conveniences but the original design and accents. It will be…amazing. It will be astonishing. It will be worthy of this room and all the other rooms." The group looked around, imagining it. This was a group, Wren assumed, with a good imagination.

"Getting specific to this house, it was designed by John McComb, Jr., who also designed Gracie Mansion, the official residence of the mayor, and Alexander Hamilton's house in Manhattan, both of which you can still visit."

"Ooh…you mean the Hamilton like in the musical?" asked Saffron.

"Exactly," said Wren, delighted she had reached her. "Anyway, it passed from the Turnbull family—" stepping past the mystery for now "—and was eventually bought by the federal government. Over the years, various government departments used it—the navy, the coast guard. During the height of immigration, extra personnel worked out of here processing those who came through Ellis Island. After World War II, the feds gave it to the state of New York, and there were various plans for it, but nothing happened—and then it seems Nicky took it off their hands. The good news about all of this is that after a quick look, it doesn't seem that any of the tenants were here long enough to care about, or have the funds, to make major changes, so again, we can bring it back to its original splendor."

Nicky rewarded her by clapping his hands and laughing. "Well, that's terrific!" Wren's eyes darted to Zach, who gave her a wry look, and everyone politely applauded and slapped Nicky on the back. She looked for Beebee but didn't see him. "So, how do we get started?"

"There's quite a bit to do. Plans, permissions. I need to bring my contractor out here, and we have to go over everything in detail to make a deeper examination of the house's condition. I'll put together a proposal. If everything goes according to plan, we might be able to start work in June. And then it'll take some months."

"Not till then? We'll be filming here in the spring…is that going to be a problem?"

"It shouldn't be, Nicky. It'll be mostly outdoor, using exterior shots only," said one of the film people. "If we can, we'll dress up this entranceway."

Wren's first inclination was to say her job site was off-limits, but then she heard her father: it was all right to be inflexible in artistic integrity and safety, but you still needed to make allowances for clients' quirks. The old proverb: "With the rich, always a little patience."

"I'm sure we can work something out," she said.

"Okay then. Saffron, why don't you, Wren, and I have a look upstairs and go over the bedrooms. Hadley, if you don't mind the cold, we have our location scout here, and we'll check out some places to film and where you can set up. Wander around, folks."

Hadley left with some of the film people while others fanned out around the downstairs rooms.

"Can I join you folks?" asked Veronica.

"Of course," said Nicky.

Saffron grabbed Wren's hand. "Let's see the rooms! I can pick out mine." She pulled Wren along like a child promised a meeting with Santa. They practically ran up the stairs. Wren looked over her shoulder—Nicky and Veronica were following at a more sedate pace and were talking too softly for her to hear.

"Look," Wren said, restraining Saffron for a moment. "If you're going to live in this house, you have to learn to appreciate it. Look back—see how it flows, the stairs, the room, the landing. Everything works together." Saffron blinked.

"You make it sound like a living thing," she said.

"It is," said Wren. "You were…emotional about the family that lived here. Houses take on the personalities of the people who lived there. And the houses themselves affect the people."

Saffron thought about that for a moment. "I like that," she said.

They walked to the bedroom at the end of the hall.

"This is the largest bedroom. And it's on a corner, so it has windows on two sides."

"It's a beautiful view," said Saffron, looking over the bay. "You don't get sea views in Idaho." *Ah...just a coincidence that Nicky paired up with someone from his home state? Or had he known her before?*

"Oh...this is a great room," Veronica said. "You'll be very happy here."

Saffron frowned. "But I always thought I'd live in a castle, somewhere very...safe. I don't suppose you can make this a castle."

"It wouldn't be *right*," said Wren. She had been down this road before, explaining to clients with more money than sense why a Victorian house couldn't be made to look like a chateau in the Loire Valley. You had to find a metaphor that worked.

"You wear orange high-top sneakers," said Wren. "Why aren't you wearing, say, a low-cut leather boot with those jeans?"

"That wouldn't be right for me," said Saffron.

"And you have to think what is right for this house," said Wren.

"I see. The house is a person," said Saffron with great solemnity.

"Of course, we can still make changes that harmonize with the house. We can add a bathroom here, for example," said Wren. Saffron nodded absently.

"Was this the room Captain and Mrs. Turnbull had?" asked Nicky.

"It must be. From its position, it must be the best room," said Veronica.

"Yes, I'm sure you're right," said Wren.

"You can be very happy here," said Veronica. "You will need to dress this place."

"Do you think they'd mind us living there? I mean, what you said about personalities. I guess it's like their ghosts are here. I mean, not really, but sort of..."

Wren was going to laugh at that, but stopped when she saw how serious Saffron was.

"Yes. That's what I said. The houses I work on are all old, with many families who had lived there over the years. I live in an old house myself.

When I was a girl, I thought about them. I like to think they were happy there, and they like seeing me happy there." Saffron nodded again and kept looking around the room, as if she expected to see the Turnbulls.

"Then it's important that we'll be happy here," she said. "How about the kitchen? Could I see that?"

"I'm curious myself. Kitchens are always a fun challenge in an old house. You want them modern, of course, but still reflecting the spirit of the house." They started walking down the stairs. Wren saw Veronica had slipped her arm through Nicky's.

"Would the Captain's wife and sister have cooked there?" asked Saffron.

"The Captain was a wealthy man, and he would've had servants. But in the winter, the kitchen would be the warmest room. I could see everyone gathering there over coffee—even the master and mistress, if they wanted to stay warm."

"Nicky, this could be splendid," said Veronica. "I hope you're going to give young Saffron here a budget and free hand furnishing and decorating this place. With Wren's advice, of course."

"Absolutely," said Nicky. He looked a little shy, then turned to Veronica and said, "Thank you."

"We'll talk more about that as we proceed," said Wren. "We have a lot of options to make this house both beautiful and comfortable."

"I want it like when the Turnbulls lived here, when it was their home."

They had the kitchen to themselves. Whatever modern kitchen equipment had been installed, the final inhabitants had ripped out when they left. Wren could see traces of what had been a beautiful stone hearth, most of which had been covered over by some easily removed boards.

"This is the original hearth—essentially a huge fireplace where they cooked. It's still here."

"You'll leave it here, won't you?" asked Saffron.

"Of course. That's my job. To modernize the house while leaving what makes it special. We'll merge a modern range into the hearth and get period-style furniture here."

"So it will be like when the Turnbulls were here?"

Wren was about to point out that the Turnbulls didn't have recessed lighting, electric ovens, and gas ranges. And Wren could explain in great detail the unpleasant realities of not having indoor plumbing. But again, Saffron was so serious...

"Yes. It will be just like the Turnbulls—even better."

"It'll be lovely. Have some faith in Wren, sweetie," said Veronica. "She'll make you a nice home here," She gently stroked Saffron's shoulder.

"I'm glad," Saffron said. "Will Hadley be able to cook here? You two can come here, and Hadley will cook that great stew for us."

"Oh...ah...I'm sure. You know...some people make their kitchen the center of the house. We can expand this room...as I said, you and Nicky have a lot of choices."

"This is going to be wonderful!" said Saffron—and hugged Wren again. She began to wonder how much hugging this renovation would involve.

Saffron disengaged herself. "I know we have to leave soon, but I want to play 'The Captain's House' here." She shrugged the case off her back and opened it—it was a mandolin. "Isn't it beautiful? I had an old one, but Nicky bought me this new one, such a lovely maple." It was a work of art by itself.

Saffron may have come across as ditzy, but her fingers were deft as she started to pluck it—and then she started to sing. Wren was surprised by her contralto voice, lower than her speaking voice, and at the assured playing. Saffron suddenly seemed much older as she sang the mournful story of the Captain who disappeared. She didn't cry when she was done, but Wren thought she might herself, her singing was so affecting.

"That was wonderful," said Wren. "You're very talented." Saffron smiled shyly. "Maybe you want a room dedicated for your music here. The Turnbulls might well have had a piano—the ladies may have played to entertain themselves."

They heard a whistle upstairs.

"We need to go now, but I'll make some notes, and we'll talk again soon." Wren felt like she had taken control. Saffron was the one who cared, and she was going to be reasonable. Nicky was going to indulge her—he just wanted a place to get away from it all. And Veronica was going to back the

26

plan with some well-needed common sense. Wren knew how to proceed. She'd write a proposal, dicker with Zach for a bit, and bring this Federal masterpiece back to life.

Her father would be proud.

Everyone was gathering in the entranceway. Hadley looked pleased with herself and was chatting with Nicky. She saw Wren and gave her a thumb's up. Wren gave her one in return.

Cal was doing a headcount. "Okay—I think we're all here. Except for Beebee." He grimaced. "Anyone seen him?"

Someone said he had been looking around the house, someone else that he had wandered off to go scouting around the island.

"I didn't see him," said Nicky.

Cal sighed. "He's keeping us waiting. All right. Everyone stay here—he probably came back to the house at some point and is in one of the rooms." He stalked off, and Wren and Saffron joined Nicky and Hadley.

"Like the house, sweetie?" asked Nicky.

"I picked out a room, and we saw the kitchen. Wren is going to give us a great kitchen so Hadley can cook her stew there."

"Hun, I'm not sure Hadley wants to be our personal chef."

"I don't know—" said Hadley. "Once Wren gets done with this place, being the live-in chef here could be a pretty sweet gig."

Cal came back, but instead of his confident walk, he was almost staggering.

"I found Beebee." His face was completely drained of color.

Wren looked at Hadley and walked to where Cal had come from. Others followed. They saw Beebee on the floor, his coffee spilled into a puddle.

Wren smelled the hazelnut.

Chapter Three

June

Wren had made multiple visits to Turnbull Island with her contractor, Bobby Fiore, and other professionals who would bring the house into the twenty-first century. But today was the day they would actually start work on the house. She shared the breakfast table with her firm's senior partner and father. Ezra asked various questions about the processes and the corresponding costs, and she felt like a student again, answering questions from a professor.

"Oh…and that unfortunate matter of that dead studio employee—has that been settled?"

"Mostly," Wren said. She suspected her father would not accept that, and she was not disappointed.

"Do you want to elaborate?" he asked.

"The initial conclusion was that it was an accidental overdose, but I got a call a few days ago from a Lieutenant Howard, who is with the homicide squad, so we can draw our own conclusions. She said that they were taking a fresh look and to make ourselves available for more interviews and visits. Others who were there also got calls. It's kid gloves for the rich and famous."

"I hope this won't delay the job."

"I don't see how. We were told the scene was available to us now. There is nothing left to examine."

"Keep an eye on it and let me know if there are any problems. Also, make sure those actors don't wander casually into the house—even our client. Imagine the fuss if one of them gets hurt."

"The worksite is sacred. I learned that from you. I don't expect they'll have the time anyway. There will be a few scenes shot in rooms we're not working on."

"Who else besides our client is in the film?"

"Oh my!" said Wren, grinning. "You're star-struck and want to see whom you can meet."

"Don't be silly. These are people who may need our services."

"You don't have to remind me. I got us this job."

"Wren Fontaine, Architect to the Stars."

"I don't have a cast list, but I met Veronica Selwyn back in January, and she says she remembers meeting you at that Wilton house you designed two years ago."

"Oh, really?" Ezra stopped in mid-sip. "How nice she remembers. Her Amanda in 'Glass Menagerie' was extraordinary. She won a Tony, you know." He pondered the basket of croissants and decided to have another one with the thick-cut marmalade he liked. "I'll have to come out soon to look over the site."

"To check on my work?" said Wren. "Really?"

"You don't think you need any supervision? You've become quite arrogant."

"Oh, Father, that's the nicest compliment you've ever paid me."

"Sarcasm doesn't suit you."

"I'm not being sarcastic." Ezra just grimaced and said nothing. "But this isn't about checking up on me. It's about you wanting to meet your celebrity crush."

Ezra looked at his watch. "I'm going to be late. So are you." He stood up.

"You've always told me to make clients wait for me."

He raised an eyebrow and then smiled at her. "Okay, you win this one. I agree there's no other architect in the city who could handle this project—even me. Have a good day, Wren," he said as he walked out of the kitchen. Wren felt very pleased with herself.

* * *

A flotilla of comfortable launches had replaced the super yacht to quickly ferry all the film and construction staff. The actors had to show up with the morning sun, but Bobby and his workers, along with Wren and Hadley, were showing up later. Hadley had engaged staff to serve breakfast, and usually showed up later most days to oversee other meals.

Bobby was looking a little dubious.

"Afraid you'll be seasick?" asked Wren.

"I'm afraid the materials won't make it over."

"The barge company seemed reliable. It'll be fine."

"I suppose. But this is a new one on me, a job site on an island." He turned to Hadley. "You're ready to give us lunch?" Because the workers wouldn't be able to take their breaks in a neighborhood, Bobby and Wren had negotiated for Nicky to foot the bill for lunch—provided by Hadley.

"You'll love it," she said.

"You're not going to give them what those actors are getting, are you? My people aren't big on kale and radicchio."

"Because they've never had them cooked right—but don't worry. Stick-to-your-ribs food for hardworking men and women. Without busting the budget. Or waistlines. You and your crew need to watch your cholesterol intake."

Bobby smiled. "We'll see. Anyway, despite the special situation here, I'm looking forward to getting started. This is the oldest house I've worked on. Plenty of things to do with electricity and plumbing, but the simplicity of the design makes it easier." He fixed a look on Wren. "You agree, boss?"

"The house, perhaps. But the people who lived there more than two centuries ago—what were they like?"

"You mean that mystery—the Captain and his wife and sister?"

"Well, yes. But even besides that, you need to understand the people who lived here. They made it a home, and I'm making it a home again. The people and the home must be understood together."

Bobby shook his head. "You're so like your father."

"Even better," said Hadley. "Ezra just has to deal with modern clients. Wren has to get into the head of clients who died years ago."

Wren smiled at the compliment and looked at the house on the hill as they approached the island. Captain Turnbull had been away on his ship a lot. What was it like for those two women on that island? Did they fill those rooms with guests? If so, who? Or did they mostly sit by their fires with books and needlework as the days drifted into each other? Nicky would have a home theater and was talking about creating a helipad. But it was still an island—would he and Saffron (and the mysterious Thalia!) end up the same way....

The launch docked, and they disembarked. Bobby and his crew turned an appraising eye on the house as they walked along the path up the hill. Hadley waved goodbye as she headed toward the filming location.

Once at the house, Bobby was pleased to see their supplies and materials had arrived. He watched Wren with an amused eye. She had been in the house again and again since January, but every time she walked in, it was the same: looking up and around, immersing herself in the surroundings.

"Imagining the men walking through here in their tricorn hats and powdered wigs?" he asked.

"They were both going out of style by the time this house was built," said Wren absently.

"You'd know," said Bobby. He found an outlet for his portable stereo system, and soon music was filling the room. Bobby liked working with opera in the background. "Okay, boss. Where do we start?"

* * *

They had a good morning, working on the essential if less glamorous parts of their job, going over the roof and masonry. Water was the biggest enemy, two centuries of thunderstorms, sleet, snow.

"But well protected from the waves, on the highest point on the island," said Bobby.

"Yes. There was no flood insurance in 1800. Your only protection was a hill," said Wren. "I am sure a sea Captain like Turnbull, facing danger every day, would know something about risk mitigation."

Wren looked down on the movie set—it was like a village. The island probably had never hosted as many people at once in its entire history.

She saw Hadley and some assistants making their way up the hill with insulated boxes. Bobby's crew gathered around when they arrived, looking dubious. This was not a group that liked being disappointed with their food. The assistants set up the boxes on stands, and Hadley stepped over to Wren.

"How's it going down there?" asked Wren.

"As expected. Gluten-free, high-protein, free-range, low-carb, vegan—and I'm getting everyone what they want. Oh, and that police lieutenant arrived. She's been talking to the film people, but now she wants to talk to us—we're the outsiders." She looked at the workers—they were smiling, even Bobby.

"There doesn't seem to be a palate you can't please," said Wren. "I'll grab something for the road, and we'll see the detective."

"The filming is going well?"

"As far as I can tell. They've been here two weeks, and it could be a few weeks more, at least."

"Is the movie going to be any good?"

"Ha! If I knew that, I'd be rich. But I'll tell you something, just watching. Veronica is a real actress. She's terrific. Now, Nicky, on the other hand..." she shook her head. "I watched some of the filming. He's no Al Pacino. But Veronica is really stepping up. She takes him aside and gives him some help, quietly, and he's clearly grateful. It's kinda sweet, actually. At the end of the day, Nicky is who he is. Cheerful and sweet and handsome. Nicky excels at being Nicky."

"But who is Nicky? We don't really know about him—a small-town boy from nowhere, Idaho. Are we really seeing him? Is his whole life an act? We don't really know him, do we?"

"Ooh, that's pretty heavy. And you say you're not a people person," said Hadley.

"It's like houses. I once wrangled a tour of one of the most magnificent postmodern houses in the country, and inside, it looked like the owners had pulled the furniture from the set of *Father Knows Best*. Pleasant, shabby-comfortable."

"If you have a cutting-edge house, why not cutting-edge furniture?"

"He was a Midwest boy who made a mint developing shopping centers," said Wren. "He built a stunning ten million dollar house to impress his associates and competitors. He furnished it like the house he grew up in to feel comfortable."

"That's a very nice metaphor. But are people as easy to understand as houses?"

"If only," said Wren, and she laughed.

It was lunchtime on the set as well, and the actors and crew were milling about.

"That's her over there," said Hadley, pointing to a woman in a casual suit who was strolling around and viewing the scene. "She seemed eager to talk to us."

The lieutenant turned to them as they approached, and Wren felt those brown eyes take her in quickly.

"You must be the architect, Wren Fontaine? Lieutenant Arlene Howard, NYPD. I've never met an architect before, but I thought you'd be all in black with round steel-rimmed glasses. But as a detective, I shouldn't be making assumptions, should I?"

"As long as we're making bad assumptions, I thought you'd be male, fat, and stuffing your face with donuts."

After a moment, Howard laughed. "All right, we're both guilty. I didn't know architects had a sense of humor. Anyway, additional investigations have led us to reclassify this as a homicide.

"So you think it was something other than accidental overdose, as reported?" asked Wren. Howard didn't answer, just smiled thinly.

"The pair of you are of particular interest to me. You're the only ones there who were outsiders—not part of the film community. It's a rather tightly knit group."

"You should see a group of architects," said Wren. Howard laughed. Wren was pleased with herself.

"Or a group of cops. I suppose every profession draws an inside-outside line. Anyway, that's why I want your opinions. I have the original statements you gave at the time. Now, Wren, if I may...." She pulled a tablet out of her bag. "I see you said you smelled hazelnut. You were sure about that? Hadley is a chef—I expected that. But an architect?"

"I use all my senses when restoring a house," said Wren. Howard looked as if she was going to laugh but changed her mind when she saw Wren's solemn expression. Unlike Howard's response to Wren's "group of architects" remark, this was the response she was used to getting when she spoke.

"You know, they found fentanyl in the coffee, and it was assumed that he dissolved pills to drink it. It's not a common way of doing it, but he had a history—so it was assumed...." She shrugged. "Anyway, did you smell hazelnut anywhere else? I know the assistant—Cal—kept a list, but no one asked at the time, and no one remembers."

"I didn't smell it," said Wren. "But I heard it. At the hotel, I remember Cal asked Saffron specifically if she wanted a hazelnut coffee. I can't remember the exact words, but something about giving her the hazelnut coffee that she liked. But she said no."

"Okay. But that wouldn't have been the same as the cups prepared after everyone departed the boat."

"I don't think so," said Wren.

"Did he walk around and offer drinks to other people?"

"Yes, but he seemed especially attentive to Saffron." Howard raised an eyebrow.

"It's obvious he's hot for her," said Hadley. Now, Howard laughed.

"Trying to steal a girl away from Nicky Tallon! I wish him luck. So, did anyone else, as far as you know, have hazelnut coffee?" They both said they didn't know.

"I know that Beebee Jenkins had...arguments with both Nicky and Cal. Did you see him argue with anyone else?" Again, they both said no.

"All right then. Thank you both. I'm sure we'll be talking again." She nodded and left.

"So what was that about?" asked Hadley.

"She was fixated on the coffee, as if someone else had hazelnut. But there was no one else in the room with Beebee. And even if Saffron had hazelnut, she was with us."

"Someone else may have had hazelnut. Only Cal would know. He either doesn't remember or is lying. Look, maybe he did drop his fentanyl into the coffee. But I'm telling you, it wasn't Saffron's coffee. Saffron is not taking fentanyl or other heavy drugs. Believe me, I'd know by now."

Wren reached for Hadley's hand and squeezed it. Hadley had been in recovery for years.

"Look, I know the lieutenant said we were outsiders, but you've had many performing arts clients, just not this crowd. You've said these people are high-strung and always squabbling. But they don't kill each other, do they?" said Wren.

"No, it's fight, kiss and make up, fight again."

"But someone probably killed him anyway, if the police are bothering to open the case again. And not just because of the heat of passion. They planned it." Wren and Hadley looked over the actors as they gathered to film another scene. "But maybe no one was killing Beebee?"

"So you think they got it right the first time—accidental overdose?"

"Oh, no, I think it was murder. I think the lieutenant truly believes it was murder. But she was asking about the hazelnut. I wondered why. It's like when you see something odd about a home's construction, you want to know the reason, and Howard wasn't sharing it with us. So let's say she knew Beebee and Saffron were the only two who had hazelnut coffee. That's why she was so interested if I had noticed the hazelnut. In all these weeks, they haven't found a reason for anyone to murder Beebee." Wren looked at Hadley. "Am I crazy? You see where I'm going with this?"

"Someone poisoned that cup. But they got the wrong hazelnut cup. They meant to kill Saffron."

Chapter Four

"The lieutenant knows this," said Wren. "You can see what happened. They couldn't make a case for accidental overdose and couldn't find anyone who hated him enough to plan a murder like that. So they're wondering if someone wanted to kill Saffron."

"Who would want to kill Saffron? It would be like killing a Muppet," said Hadley.

"We don't really know much about her, though, do we? But maybe this is more about Nicky. She's his girlfriend."

"I guess so," said Hadley. "It's a weird relationship, though. Some older guys like girlfriends young and innocent—almost like a daughter."

"What is she doing on the set?"

"Looking bored, mostly. She doesn't have anything to do. She listens to music and plays her mandolin. I asked her if she wanted to see Manhattan—she sounds interested, but I think she's a little afraid of going around by herself."

"She showed a lot of interest when we were going over the plans. It's early in the process, but maybe if I could bring her into the house, away from the rest of the cast and crew. She'd be safer, and we could find out more about her."

"Oh yeah, surrounded by Bobby and his crew. It doesn't get safer than that. Let's grab her. I want to see how lunch went over with the crew anyway."

They found Saffron perched on a folding chair, overlooking the water, and idly plucking on her mandolin.

"Oh! Hello! I didn't hear you. Just looking at the sea—I lose track of everything else. In California too. Sometimes I get up at dawn and just sit on the beach."

"Idaho has some nice lakes, I believe," said Wren.

"Yes, but lakes *end*. Oceans go on forever. That's what I like about this island. You're...you're safe but not locked in."

"That's...an interesting way to look at it," said Hadley.

"Would you like to come up to the house for a while?" asked Wren. "It'll be some time before we can paint and move in furniture, but you seemed so interested during the planning, you can come up now, and we can talk in more detail about what you might want to do."

"Really! We can start on that! I've been looking online. I'm so excited about what we might want to do." Then she looked uncertain. "Do you think we need to ask Nicky?"

"I've been doing this for a while. Men are not interested in details like this." That was a lie; plenty of men obsessed over the shape of each sconce, the wood grain on each piece of furniture. But she didn't think Nicky was one of them. It was true that, like Saffron, he loved the concept of the house, but he didn't have her imagination.

"Yes, I think you're right, Wren. Nicky always lets me have my way." *Doesn't he!*

She carefully put away her mandolin, slung it over her shoulder, and eagerly set off in her orange sneakers.

"It's her ten million dollar Barbie Dream House," whispered Hadley. "Did you have one as a little girl?"

"A well-meaning aunt bought me one. I found the proportions awkward and the layout simplistic. I spent Christmas Day fixing it. Father was so proud." Hadley just shook her head and smiled.

Saffron headed straight upstairs, but Wren saw the crew was finishing up their lunch, and Bobby was frowning.

"What?" asked Hadley. "What was wrong with my lunch?"

"Not a damn thing. That was the trouble. The crew liked it so much they want you to become the permanent caterer."

"That's super," said Hadley.

"Okay then. Wren, you can explain to your father why free food is going to be part of any future contracts. That basil chicken was a wonder, Hadley, and they aren't going to work without it."

"I think Frank Lloyd Wright would've loved your basil chicken," said Wren.

"I'm sure. Anyway, I've got some calls to make, and they're going to want dinner eventually. You kids have fun," said Hadley and gave Wren a quick kiss.

Wren found Saffron in the corner bedroom.

"This is going to be mine," she said. "I already told Nicky. I like the view so much. Pale yellow walls, and a ceiling fan, and—oh—what do you call them again—canopy beds."

"Yes. This room probably had one originally. The idea was to have curtains on the side to keep warm."

"That's good to know. I want it like when the Captain lived here. I guess they had those old-fashioned lamps?"

"Yes, those and candles. They used whale oil back then."

"Can we have those too? Instead of electric lights, at least in this room?"

"That's the thing. It sounds fun to have a home like that, like it was when people lived there. But without electricity and plumbing and central heating…." Saffron looked disappointed. Wren had been here before with old houses, with people who expected a level of reality they couldn't handle. "It sounds silly, but the Captain and his family really did live in a different world. We can't go back."

"Really?" asked Saffron, without any trace of sarcasm.

Wren started to say, "When I was your age…" but she was only about ten years older. Still, she felt she was old enough to be Saffron's mother.

Wren took a deep breath. "When I was a girl, I didn't have many friends. I wanted to live in a big nineteenth-century house with servants to take care of things. I read a lot of books, and I understood those times. At least, I thought I did. I knew I didn't understand the world I was born into. But that wasn't an option. I was stuck where I was. I had to learn. Am I making sense?"

Saffron nodded solemnly and looked very sad.

"Look—we can do some wonderful things here, I promise."

"It's just that…we can't get away from the past, can we?" That seemed unusually ponderous coming from Saffron. But then, Wren realized she didn't know anything about Saffron's past. She had assumed that Saffron had had little formal education, but she was a performer. Perhaps it was an act—what her wealthy boyfriend expected.

"I can give you the best of past and present."

"I know, you're *fantastic*, Wren. Let's look at Nicky's room." So, separate rooms. *Whose idea was that?*

The next room was going to be Nicky's.

"I know these rooms are small. The idea of large bedrooms is a modern one. Bedrooms were long thought of as just places to sleep. I could add a connecting door, if you want."

"Okay," said Saffron, but didn't seem concerned with that, or the size. "I think Nicky would like a masculine room here."

"Yes, another four-poster, simple and strong designs in wood. But we weren't planning another bathroom in this room—it would make it too small."

"Men don't care about things like that. But he'll want some big wardrobes for his clothes. They don't seem to have closets here."

"No, closets came later. What you want is a wardrobe, or chifforobe."

"Okay. I don't suppose there's any original furniture from when the house was new."

"Actually, we found a few pieces that are likely original. They were stuck out of the way and forgotten, and no one in later years realized how valuable they were. They're Nicky's now. Would you like a look?"

Saffron eagerly nodded, and Wren took her to a small upstairs room where they were temporarily storing them. A few chairs, a wardrobe, and a linen press—a large mahogany affair for storing blankets and quilts.

"They're beautiful," said Saffron.

"I think they were likely designed and built by John McComb, Jr., the architect who built this house. Many architects also worked as furniture designers. They would have a vision of what worked for a house and would design items for the specific needs of the owners."

"Could I have that wardrobe in my room?"

"Of course. We'll wait until all the work and painting is done and we'll find a suitable place to put it. Here—let's have a look. Careful, as these pieces are very old. I know an excellent restorer who can make these perfect again."

They slowly opened the wardrobe and then the linen press.

"So these were used every day?"

"Yes. Probably mostly by the servants, who would be in charge of clothes."

"And this you said was a linen press?"

"Yes, it was designed to store bedding. The linen press was probably exclusively for the servants—the ladies of the house wouldn't bother themselves with it. They probably had quilts here—heating in these old homes was difficult. This is an especially large one." Saffron stood on tiptoes to see into the high shelves, long emptied of their contents. It was so massive, the shelves so high, even Wren initially had to get a stepladder to examine it thoroughly.

"You can decide what to do with this, but keep in mind the rooms aren't very large. We could turn the room on the other side of yours, which is also small, into a walk-in closet, even a sort of dressing room, as it has a window with natural light. It depends on how many guest rooms you want. How much entertaining will you do?"

"Not much. This is supposed to be for us. Anyway, I think we'll spend most of our time in the kitchen."

"Something else that changes. The kitchen now becomes the center. But there's a beautiful dining room and parlor here, and of course, the magnificent oval great room. They all have fireplaces. We'll make sure they're in working order." Saffron thought that over. "Your home in California—don't you eat in the dining room there?"

"We eat out. Or there's a catered party. Or everyone just snacks by the pool."

"How about when you were a child," Wren said, trying to force a casualness into her voice. "What did you do growing up? That helps me decide what may make clients comfortable." She watched Saffron closely and could see the wheels turn inside her head. "Nicky and I like to look forward, not backward," she finally said. "Let's look at the kitchen again. I'd like a big table there."

"All right. I'll show you some trestle tables, heavy wood. It will match nicely and give you plenty of room if you want to eat there." They started to walk downstairs.

"By the way, who is Thalia?"

"A friend of Nicky's. She's unbelievably beautiful. She'll be around later.

Say, you and Hadley are very close, aren't you? I mean, you're a couple… right?"

"I…yes," said Wren. "We've been together for a while now."

"I once heard her call you 'Little Bird.' Is that because your name is Wren?" *Sharp ears. Hadley only called her that when they were alone.*

"Yes, but I'm not named for the bird. My father is an architect too, and there was a famous architect in the seventeenth century named Christopher Wren, whom my father admires, so I was named after him."

"That's very funny. Your mother was okay with that?"

"My mother liked to humor my father."

"She must love him very much."

"She did."

"But not anymore?" Saffron stopped suddenly.

"She died when I was nineteen."

"That is so sad!"

"Saffron is an interesting name, too," said Wren. "Did your mother name you for the spice?"

"Oh no. I picked that name later. I heard it, and I liked it. I don't think of my old name anymore—we like looking forward."

Bobby and a couple of his crew were already at work in the kitchen, and the stereo was pouring opera into the room.

"Bobby—I don't think you met one of our clients, Saffron Scott." Saffron's name wasn't on any paperwork, but she was becoming the de facto liaison on the renovation. "Bobby Fiore is our top contractor. We don't do any serious renovation without him. Bobby, Saffron, and I are going to start

41

talking about accents, colors, and furniture."

Bobby took in this woman, barely out of her teens, with her careless ponytail and high-top sneakers. *Better you than me,* his look said.

"Pleased to meet you, Saffron," said Bobby. "I know you have a lot of decisions to make, but no client who has listened to Wren's advice has regretted it."

Saffron took that comment seriously, cocked her head, and looked at Wren. "So you know how to make this a home?"

Wren wondered if that was just an accident or if Saffron realized how shrewd a question that was. Most clients asked Wren if they could *renovate a house.* Saffron asked if they could *make her a home.*

"Yes, I do," said Wren, and Saffron nodded before turning back to Bobby. "What are you listening to?" she asked.

"Opera—and it's my job to educate Wren." He gave her a mischievous smile. "Can you name it?"

Wren closed her eyes. "It's German—that's not like you. You usually go for Italian. This is Wagner, but I can't tell which one."

"Think of the setting. Think of who built this house."

"Oh! Of course, Der fliegende Holländer, the Flying Dutchman." Bobby laughed.

"Very good. A sea Captain story to get us in the mood. Saffron—if I'm right, that's a mandolin case you're carrying, so you're musical. Do you listen to opera?"

"No—I never have. What is the story?"

"The Flying Dutchman was an old legend. A sea Captain invoked the devil, so he is cursed with his crew to sail forever, but every seven years, he has a chance to see if a woman will love him, breaking the curse."

"Oh! How sad." She closed her eyes. "Is it okay if I stay and listen?"

Bobby was thrilled—an opera convert! "Absolutely. I have an English libretto in my truck. You can follow along. And if you like it—I'll bring some Verdi in tomorrow."

"I'll leave you both to it, then," said Wren. She realized she hadn't really learned anything about Saffron's past—except that Saffron didn't want to talk about it.

Which said something too.

Chapter Five

"She cried over the opera," Bobby told Wren the next morning in the kitchen. "I'm playing Traviata today. She's in the living room brooding over it."

"Yes—our Saffron keeps her emotions close to the surface."

"I'm no expert, but I can tell she's a talented musician—I've listened to her pluck away at that mandolin. Also asks bright questions about the opera. And just like you can tell if someone really loves a house, I can tell if someone really loves classical music, the look on her face. She's sensitive to it. Anyway, she told me she asked Nicky to take her to the opera when he visited earlier, while they were setting up. He said he would but didn't look thrilled about it."

"Yeah, not really his scene, I imagine."

"What we do for wives and girlfriends," said Bobby.

"Yeah...I'm wondering about that," said Wren. "Apparently, there's another girlfriend, someone named Thalia."

"No telling with actors," said Bobby, with a shrug.

Wren stepped into the living room and saw Saffron lying on the floor and intently following along in the libretto.

"Oh, hello, Wren. I came early with Nicky. This music is...something. I wonder if there's any mandolins in any opera? I tried last night to pick out some tunes."

"That's good. Listen, you're always welcome here, but if you're bored, it's a big city. There are things you could do around town. Hadley and I have lived in New York all our lives. We could point you to places to go." It would

44

not only get her away from the set where someone might want to hurt her but keep her from getting bored. Did Lieutenant Howard also wonder if Saffron was the target? Wren realized she couldn't keep Saffron occupied on renovation work all day, every day, and how much opera could she listen to?

"Maybe," said Saffron. "Thank you. It's just that there are so many *people* in New York. I don't like being around so many *people*. It's like L.A. I stay in the house. It's just...." She frowned and just let it trail off. "I like being in this house. Nicky said we could stay away here. But I wish I knew what happened to Captain Turnbull and his family. It would make this house...I mean, it would *heal* it, you know? Could we find that out?"

You don't know what you're asking. This isn't something you can just Google. Can you even imagine what kind of person it would take to solve a mystery whose main clue was embedded in a folk song. No, you couldn't possibly, Saffron. But ohh...I know the one person who could...

"It could be very difficult—but just maybe I can help. I went to Columbia University, here in New York, and one of my professors is a historian specializing in this city's history. She likes a mystery. I bet she'll have some ideas."

Saffron smiled. "That sounds wonderful! I'm sure Nicky would be happy to pay her whatever she wants."

"Don't worry about that. There may be some small research expenses, but if my friend agrees to do it, she'll do it for her own amusement, not money." Saffron looked confused. Wren wondered again what kind of bubble she had been raised in. "She'll see it as a puzzle, for fun—look, you play your mandolin even when you're not paid to do it, right?"

"Oh, I see. Okay. Thanks, that sounds so great. So she was a teacher and is now a friend?"

"Yes, exactly."

"Okay. That makes me feel a lot better. If we're going to make our home here, we have to be at peace with Captain Turnbull and his family."

Wren didn't know how to respond to that and was about to make some sort of excuse and join Bobby in the kitchen when Hadley walked just ahead of Nicky and another woman.

"Hey, folks," said Hadley. "I brought some friends."

"Oh! Thalia!" said Saffron. She leapt up and flung herself at the woman, who seemed a little overwhelmed, and gave a resigned smile while gently holding the girl. Nicky looked on indulgently. He was dressed as an eighteenth-century gentleman, in a dark red frock coat and ruffled shirt. He looked a little awkward in it, but it suited him—like Mr. Darcy. No. Nicky was Mr. Bingley—cheerful and open.

Hadley stepped over to Wren.

"She caught one of the launches, apparently, to surprise Nicky. Now that is what a movie star's girlfriend should look like." Thalia had extricated herself from Saffron, and Wren could see just how stunning she was.

"You could cut your fingers on those cheekbones," whispered Wren, and Hadley giggled. "So she's the girlfriend?"

"Nicky certainly greeted her as one. I still don't know what the hell is going on. I've seen a thing or two, Little Bird, but this one has me stumped."

"I wonder…" said Wren softly, and Hadley glanced at her, but didn't say anything as the trio approached them.

"And this is Wren Fontaine, who's putting this place back together," said Nicky. "Wren, my…special friend Thalia." Wren heard the slight pause, saw his faint blush. Nicky wasn't sharp enough to come up with a phrase like "special friend." But she could quickly see a certain shrewdness in Thalia's hazel eyes as the model extended a manicured hand.

"A pleasure, Wren. Nicky and Saffron have told me so much about this. We're all so excited about it."

"Why don't you give Thalia a tour," said Hadley. "Nicky and Saffron have seen it enough already, and I wanted to talk to them about the menu for a special dinner I promised them here next week." A quick wink. *You get to talk to Thalia alone. Maybe she'll open up to you in private.*

"I'd love to see it, if you have a moment," said Thalia. "But first, one thing, Nicky. A cop came around asking about Beebee. I had to confirm I had to slap him at that party in L.A."

"Don't worry about it. They're talking to everyone. And you weren't even on the island when he died."

"They found I was at a shoot around the corner from the hotel before you left. They seem to think I could've somehow slipped in and poisoned the coffee. I don't need this."

"It's a short-term thing. They're talking to everyone, and everyone hated him."

"Nicky will have Zach make it go away," said Saffron with absolute certainty. "See the house. It's fantastic—look it over, and then we'll talk more." Thalia blew her a kiss and followed Wren upstairs.

"Architects always love talking about the houses they're working on," said Wren. "This was built around 1800...." She watched Thalia as she discussed moldings and room proportions. Wren knew when people were just humoring her—but Thalia wasn't. She definitely was listening and showed curiosity. When they got to the corner room that Saffron had picked for herself, she showed only brief interest, however, and moved quickly to Nicky's room.

"Rather small," she said.

"As I explained to Saffron, bedrooms were just used for sleeping then, even for rich people."

"But the next room—could that be turned into a sort of dressing room."

"Yes—that was exactly my idea too."

Thalia rewarded her with a brilliant smile. "I'm rather proud I thought of it then. Perhaps our jobs are not so different. You're concerned with the beauty and decoration of a house, and I'm concerned with the beauty and decoration of the human body. However, you no doubt studied for years, and my career is just a fortunate genetic accident."

Wren couldn't think of any response that didn't sound patronizing. *My father would know what to say. He always did.*

"Saffron is very excited about living here," she eventually said.

"I know. Her personal dollhouse." That's what Hadley had said—Saffron's own Barbie dream house.

"She's been interested in all the details. I've been working more closely with her than with Nicky."

"I'm not surprised. Nicky is a sweet, loving man. What you see is what you get, and that's not common around here. But he's not the most imaginative man. Now, Saffron—she has more than enough imagination for both of them." She looked around. "They didn't believe in closets back then, did they?"

"People didn't own that many clothes. I imagine as a model you have lots of clothes. I can do something very nice with that dressing room, add plenty of closet space while still maintaining the spirit of the house."

"I'm sure you could. But I don't know how much time I'll really be spending here, playing house with Saffron. Don't get me wrong, like Nicky, she's very sweet. It's flattering the way she looks up to me, and I really do like helping her. But spending my life here…I have plans. My modeling career is going to be on a downward slope soon. This is a young woman's game."

Did plans include being Mrs. Nicky Tallon? Or a transition into acting with his help and connections? At least Wren was beginning to get a handle on what was going on.

"It's a big house. The three of you can be very comfortable here."

Thalia gave her a look that Wren thought was almost pitying, then kept looking around the room.

"I'm sorry you've been bothered about Beebee's death," said Wren. "I know what that's like. Hadley and I are not part of the film group, and yet we've been questioned too."

"Like Nicky said, everyone hated him. It didn't matter. I was with Nicky. He got all handsy with me."

"I think he was pressuring Nicky to give up this house."

"Yeah, well, can't blame him for that. It's kind of a toy, but Nicky is really a little boy. Wait—do you think Nicky killed Beebee? That's ridiculous. He's a teddy bear. He gets angry, but he wouldn't kill."

"I'm not accusing anyone," said Wren. "My only concern with this is making sure nothing stops work on this house."

"You're like the studio in that. They don't want anything shutting down the production. Look, I know a little about these people. They fuss and fight like children, but they don't kill each other."

"I was wondering about that," said Wren. She was looking closely at Thalia. "I'm thinking the police have come back because they came to the same conclusion."

"That someone not connected killed Beebee? But it was on the island. No one else was here."

"But they seem to think it was poisoned coffee. Maybe there was a mistake. They wanted to kill someone else. He and Saffron both had hazelnut coffee that morning."

That didn't upset Thalia. It amused her. "That's ridiculous. The girl can be a little…odd, even annoying. But kill her? You know what, Wren? " Her smile turned nasty. "Have you spoken with Veronica Selwyn? She really hated Beebee. And she has a short temper. Anyway, thank you for the tour. It's a beautiful house, and I'm sure it will be spectacular when you're done with it."

Downstairs, Hadley was still talking with Nicky and Saffron, and Cal had joined them. He was standing so close to Saffron that she couldn't believe the girl was comfortable, but she didn't show any sign of even noticing.

But Thalia did.

"Cal! So good to see you again. By the way, most women don't need an additional shadow." He turned a little red.

"Hello, Thalia," he said with no enthusiasm. "Just came by to say they needed Nicky back."

"Isn't the house fantastic?" asked Saffron.

"It is, in fact, fantastic, sweetie," said Thalia.

"We're going to stay here forever. Our own house on our own island."

"Look, sweetie. It's going to be fun to stay here for a few weeks at a time, but you can't shut yourself away here forever."

Saffron frowned. "But it's so beautiful here. It can just be us." Thalia just shook her head at the silliness of this little child. "Veronica likes it a lot."

"I'm sure she does. She's a past-her-prime actress looking for a comfortable place to retire, not a young woman with her life ahead of her."

Saffron wrinkled her nose. "You mean me?"

"I mean both of us. You know, Nicky, I'm blaming you for this. Don't you know how to show a girl a good time? If you gave her some fun, she wouldn't want to shut herself away here."

Oh, but how great to be able to shut yourself away here, thought Wren.

"Listen, a week from this Saturday, we're going out. It's going to be amazing," said Thalia.

"The club…thing," said Nicky, less than enthused. "I'm not even sure Saffron is old enough to get in."

"For God's sake. Do you think anyone is going to question someone in Nicky Tallon's entourage?"

"But still—"

"Don't worry, Nicky. I'll keep a close eye on Saffron all evening," said Cal.

"Of course, you will," said Thalia with a sly smile. "Come on, Nicky, settle down. It's time for Saffron to grow up and spread her wings a little."

"It'll be great," said Saffron. "Wren, Hadley—you come too. Meanwhile, there's a dinner this Saturday—some people are coming from L.A. and we'll all be there. You all have to come, and then next Saturday again, at a party at a really hot club."

Wren froze. Dinner with actors and studio execs would be hard enough, but an event at a *club*…she didn't expect she'd enjoy the same kind of parties Thalia did. Still, it would be good to oblige her client's friend, and her father had pointed out all the irritating things he had to put up with to keep clients happy.

She caught Hadley's eye, who winked. This sounded more like her scene.

"We'd love to," said Wren, forcing enthusiasm.

"It's still secret, but I have called the right people," said Cal.

"I hope so," said Thalia. "And be sure to arrange the transportation."

"Okay," said Nicky. "That sounds great then." He gave Thalia a quick kiss. "Come on, Cal, back to the set before they start screaming. You ladies enjoy the rest of the day."

He had sent his two supposed girlfriends off together without a fuss or regret and seemed fine with Cal's interest in Saffron. Did he just not realize it, wondered Wren. Or did he just not care?

"Come on, sweetie, let's grab the next boat out of here," said Thalia. "Nicky gave you your own card, right? We need to get you some clothes." She took in Saffron's worn jeans and orange high tops. "Yeah, lots of new clothes."

"Oh, okay," she said. And, like an obedient child, followed Thalia out.

"So…a party," said Wren. "The last time I really enjoyed a party, I had hot dogs, lemonade and cake, and a magician."

"I had the opposite problem. I had too much fun at parties. I've avoided them since getting sober. Look, we'll go together. I'll make sure you have fun, and you'll make sure I don't have too much fun. And like Saffron, I'll see you're properly dressed." Wren suspected she didn't have anything in her closet suitable for a party attended by models.

"I'd know how to dress for when this house was built—but not for today. So I'll put myself under your care."

"Super. I've got to get back to the set myself."

Wren put the party in the back of her mind and resumed work to the strains of Verdi. She and Bobby worked quietly until the afternoon when Veronica sauntered in. She looked a lot less self-conscious in her period dress than Nicky had, Wren realized.

"Hello! They don't need me on the set for a bit, so I thought I'd come to see if I could have another look at the house. That cop that questioned me knew I hated Beebee, but everyone did, so she's going to be busy. But if you don't want actors wandering through your workplace any more than we want architects strolling through our set, just tell me, and I won't take offense."

"It's quite all right. It's one of the finest examples of Federal style left in New York, and I saw how much you appreciated it at our original walk-through."

"Ha! You have some growing up to do. You're still young enough to be nice, but I heard your father was like a German Shepherd guarding his site."

Wren laughed. "Yes, I've been on enough sites with him. That's him all over."

"I just want to take another look at the kitchen. I like kitchens, and that delightful girlfriend of yours—who's a fantastic cook, by the way—says the kitchen is worth another look. I only got a few moments at it last time."

"Yes, she is good. And, of course, you can look at the kitchen. I don't even cook, and I like kitchens. To me, it says family." Veronica cocked her head at that. *Did I just overshare? I'm trying to be friendly, but I often get it wrong.*

"I like that, Wren. You know, I want to see the kitchen because I do like to cook, but I see your point about family. I don't have children. I've run through three husbands. Well, four, if you count the first one when I was seventeen. But I like the idea of family." She paused. "Look, it seems you took that funny little sprite of Nicky's under your wing, you and Hadley. That's nice of you. I don't know what's going on there. You know, Nicky'll never be Laurence Olivier, but he shows up on time, has his lines memorized, and does what the director tells him—those rural boys were raised to do what they were told. I like working with him, but sometimes I wonder if anyone could be as simple as he is."

"You said 'simple,' not 'stupid.'"

Veronica laughed. "Oh yeah. You're a smart cookie. I figured an architect at your level would listen carefully to words. I meet plenty of stupid people, but Nicky is *simple*. It's like he can't figure out how this happened, how he fell into the life of a top box-office draw." She took a deep breath. "I think I got off topic. Look, we can be a silly bunch, but at the risk of sounding trite, we can be like a family. He and Saffron are a lost pair in this world."

"They seem to have Thalia."

"Oh yeah. She's into Nicky for whatever she can get. Her idea is to keep Nicky and Saffron apart from everyone. Thalia doesn't like anyone else around. She isn't happy Nicky and I get along well on the set. I suppose I should be flattered I'm still making other women jealous. Anyway, she and I had…have had words, as my mother used to say. Bitch." Before Wren could say anything about that, Veronica waved the subject away. "But why I'm really here—Nicky and Saffron seem to like and trust you—that is, you and Hadley. Anything you could do to keep an eye on Saffron, especially with this mess over Beebee, I'd appreciate it. And I'm sure Nicky would too. It's a busy set, and meanwhile, she seems to like you and Hadley."

"Of course," said Wren. "In fact, Saffron seemed interested in the history of this island, and I was planning to introduce her to a friend who can help her. Give her something to do, and away from…well, away."

"You're a dear," said Veronica and kissed Wren on the cheek. "And now, I'm really going to have a look at your kitchen. I have some ideas I can share with Saffron and Nicky." *Do you, now?*

"Just tell my contractor, Bobby Fiore, I gave you my okay. But prepare yourself for some fawning. 'Bronx Precinct' was a favorite show among the crew, and they're going to be thrilled at meeting Captain Blake."

"That's why I always carry a pen and a bag of glossies. The price of fame, Wren."

* * *

The next day, Wren's father wore his professorial tweed jacket, a good sign that he was just going to make a quick review and not go crawling around the house. Still, she had to fight to remember she was now an experienced architect, not a student.

"Despite the breezes, I can see this being hot in the summer."

"I'm not adding just air conditioning, but a central dehumidifier."

"And in the winter, everyone just gathers around the hearth?" He smiled.

"Now you're teasing me. Central heating too. Neatly hidden behind these beautiful walls. But we're also rebuilding the fireplaces."

"I remember when you wouldn't have changed anything. You would have insisted that everyone live here now the way they did back then."

"I was sixteen. I like to think I grew up. I like to think I live in the real world now."

"That's not entirely true, Wren. If you lived entirely in the real world, you would want to tear this old place down and put up something new—"

"Father!" she said. "How can you say that? It's a work of art…oh…you're teasing me again." She was embarrassed to have fallen for it.

"I'm sorry," he said. She doubted he was, but she would have a bit of her own back.

"You're just jealous because there is nothing modern that can touch the perfection of this house, the magnificence of that curved room—"

"'Nothing modern,'" said Ezra. "Meaning my houses, too?"

Wren patted her father on his cheek. "Your houses are wonderful, Father. It isn't your fault that you can't go back in time to something like…this."

"Are you *patronizing* me, daughter?" Wren just smiled. "You know that bit about history cuts both ways. Don't get lost in the past. You will never figure out what went through the minds of the people who built this house." Wren suppressed a shiver—he always could read her mind.

"I don't live in a fantasy world," she said, sharper than she meant.

"We all do, all of us architects. We don't live entirely in the real world. There's something about what we do in creating fantasies for the people who hire us. All the more important in that you're working on this house for people who are in the fantasy business." She studied him. It was true he was an artist, an artist who created buildings that were works of art as much as this one was. But he rarely spoke that way. "Speaking of which, I think I'll have a look at the movie set." He headed for the door, then turned. "Nice job, Wren. This indeed will be magnificent when you're done."

And the compliment pleased her more than she wanted to admit.

* * *

Freed from actors and fathers, she got a good morning's work done with Bobby. At lunchtime, Hadley joined her, and Wren noticed an amused look on her face.

"What's happening?"

"Oh, you should see your father in action. Ezra has made himself very popular on the set, turned the charm up to ten—especially with Miss Selwyn. But it's okay. He's well-behaved. No need to be embarrassed."

"I'm not embarrassed. I'm jealous."

"You can be just as charming as your father. You just don't like it. Come on down with me."

The crew was setting up a shot while the two principals, Veronica and Nicky, chatted with her father. He looked up as they approached.

"Hadley, thank you for dragging my workaholic daughter away from the house for a few minutes." It was the first time Wren had heard him describe workaholism as a bad thing—but he was full of bonhomie today. "I was telling Veronica and Nicky about the housewarming for the Channing House I did on Martha's Vineyard, and William Styron and I were talking…."

Wren could tell that Veronica was amused and impressed. It was equally obvious that Nicky had no idea who William Styron was. Veronica saw that, too, even if her father didn't.

"He wrote the book Sophie's Choice was based on," said Veronica, and that helped.

"Oh, great movie. I didn't know it was a book first. I'd love to be in a movie with Meryl Streep. I told my agent I'd do a role with her for free."

"Oh, sweetie, don't say things like that in public. Someone might hear you and believe it." She laughed, and so did Ezra.

"So Nicky, where is that elfin friend of yours?"

"She's been enjoying spending time in the room she's picked out for herself," said Wren. "She dragged a chair up there, and she either plays her mandolin or listens to our contractor's opera recordings."

"What's he listening to today?" asked Ezra.

"Traviata this morning. Saffron seemed to really like it. Romantic and glamorous with a tragic ending—she really connected with it."

"I'm sure," said Veronica. "Young girls always love Traviata. Nicky, you really have to help that caged bird fly a little."

"I know," he said, looking a little embarrassed. "Wren and Hadley are going to involve her in some historical research on this house. And then they're all going out to some party with Thalia." Veronica rolled her eyes. "Glad Saffron is being kept busy, but Thalia isn't entirely—well, my mother used to use the word 'wholesome.' I don't suppose that word is much in use anymore."

"It is with me," said Ezra. "I know precisely what you mean."

"Architects are precise, I'm sure," she said with a wink. Another man might've blushed at that, but not Ezra Fontaine. He just returned the compliment with a mock bow.

"I think they want us back, my dear," said Veronica. She linked her arm with Nicky's, then glanced over her shoulder. "If we're talking opera, Ezra, I'm more of a Tosca girl," she said.

"It's very melodramatic," said Ezra.

"Isn't it," she said.

Chapter Six

The studio had taken a private room at the restaurant, and a pair of well-built men in leather jackets stood at the door to make sure it stayed private. They admitted Hadley, Wren, and Saffron with a nod, and Nicky waved them over to a group with Thalia and other actors and studio people.

"Oh, we're in the group with Nicky," said Hadley. "Everyone will know how important we are. The architect and the caterer to the stars."

Wren squeezed Hadley's hand. Then she gave a quick glance at her outfit and at what the other women were wearing. Tonight was casual—she was all right. But did she have anything suitable for the club next week?

Nicky wore a light blue jacket, nicely cut for his broad frame. Some-one—Thalia?—had no doubt orchestrated his clothes. Thalia's sapphire blue dress showed off her fair complexion and perfect figure.

"She really is magnificent," murmured Wren.

"Clothes and confidence," said Hadley. "That's what it comes down to."

"I may be terrible with clothes, but I know something about visuals. She is simply beautifully made, confidence and clothes aside."

"You and I are going shopping tomorrow," said Hadley.

Saffron had meanwhile embraced and kissed Thalia, who indulgently hugged the girl back. Saffron then curled up under Nicky's arm. He kissed the top of her head.

"I'm still trying to figure that one out," said Hadley. "He treats her like a little girl—but that's not my reading of Nicky's…predilections. And for all her teenager clothes, she's not a child. She's a young woman."

"I wonder…" said Wren. "Maybe we're overthinking this."

"That trio is still beyond me, and I've seen more of life than you, Little Bird."

"Ah, but as the Marquis de Montcalm said, '*Mon innocence est ma forteresse.*' My innocence is my strength."

Hadley just looked at her in amazement, then kissed her on the cheek. "Is it any wonder I love you?"

Thalia and Nicky seemed pleased to see them. Cal stood just behind Nicky and smiled at Saffron's arrival.

"So glad the pair of you could come tonight. The three of you have a good time running around the city?"

"Oh yes," said Saffron. "We went to some fantastic stores for shopping in Greenwich Village—Hadley knows all the best places. And Wren knew about this great mansion that belonged to this very rich man named Frick, and now it's a museum, and I have all kinds of ideas now."

"Super," said Nicky. "Thanks to both of you for showing Saffron a good time."

A waitress came around with a tray of drinks. "We are featuring specialty martinis tonight. We can make more of these or get you anything else from our bar."

"What is that one?" asked Saffron.

"That's a chocolate martini," said the waitress, and handed it to Saffron as her face lit up. "Our bartender's own recipe, and light on the alcohol."

"Didn't see that one coming," said Hadley.

"Indeed. Good thing they're not carding here. No one of legal drinking age ever ordered a chocolate martini."

Wren didn't much like martinis herself but could hear her father telling her to fit in, so took a classic martini with an olive, something she could briefly sip and then put aside. Thalia took a martini with a pearl onion. Wren watched Nicky frown and whisper something to Cal, who quickly scooted away and came back with a tall glass of beer for his boss.

"What bottled water do you have?" asked Hadley.

"Ice-7, distilled from arctic icebergs," she said. "I'll have it for you momentarily."

"Oh, you don't want one of these fun drinks?" asked Saffron.

"I'm sure I would. Too much. I used to drink a lot and almost destroyed my life. So now I can't drink at all. I haven't had a drink in about five years."

She nodded, and Hadley and Wren could see the wheels turning in her head. "You must've been very strong," she finally said and kissed Hadley on her cheek. "I want to be as strong as you." And even Hadley didn't know what to say to that.

The martinis quickly relaxed everyone. Saffron seemed delighted with her chocolate concoction. It was, in fact, a childish drink, but Saffron wasn't holding it like a child. She held it properly, just like a sophisticated lady. And she sipped it smoothly too. Saffron may not have been raised knowing about martinis, but she had clearly observed.

Cal slipped next to her. Today's blazer was ochre; Wren wondered how many jackets Cal had in his closet. She supposed that if you're going to work for Nicky Tallon, you need something to help you stand out.

Hadley linked arms with the cinematographer. "If you want to take the next step, I have a rock band client that needs a video director," Wren heard her say. She winked at Wren and went off with her new business contact. Nicky clinked glasses with the director, who put a fatherly arm around his star and whispered something to him. She saw Nicky roll his eyes and watched as they stepped away. Wren remembered what Nicky had said about people always fighting for some of his time and wanting that island to get away from it all.

"Uh, Saffron," said Cal. "They put out some hors d'oeuvres in the next room."

"Ooh...do they have those little quiches? I love them SO much." Cal nodded happily, and they went off together, leaving Wren and Thalia alone.

"It must be so nice to be that happy about quiche," said Thalia. "Anyway, I'm so glad you and Hadley came. I'm sick of just being with film people. But that's the price of being with Nicky."

"I'm getting a sense that it's the price Nicky pays for being Nicky."

Thalia raised an eyebrow. "I've never met an architect before, but I'm betting they don't miss much. He's a little boy, really, and his sweetness is what makes him attractive. Sometimes I wonder if he's genuinely like that or just too stupid to realize that modesty is not a useful trait in this business."

"Maybe it's just that he knows what he wants," said Wren. "He wants that house on his private island."

Thalia gave her a wry look. She wanted to be on the arm of a famous movie star at the best parties, and the best restaurants, not stuck on some empty island where she could only *look* at Manhattan. It may have been enough for the Captain's wife and sister, but not for her.

"I think Saffron would be happy there," ventured Wren. A slow smile spread across Thalia's perfect face.

"I'm sure she'd be delighted to be there, cut from the same cloth, as my grandmother would say." Wren heard a little laughter in her voice. *She's telling me something. If I understood people as well as houses, I'd figure it out.*

"I don't see Veronica," said Wren, looking around."

"She's not here tonight. Our Veronica is working on landing husband number five. Coy looks while talking on the phone. Let everyone know that she's being taken to Ashton's tonight."

"That's a fine steakhouse...but not the most fashionable place," said Wren. "Mostly aging lawyers and stockbrokers who like roast beef and mashed potatoes."

"That would suit her. A wealthy geriatric who can ease her way into retirement. Anyway, she said she'll stop by later—if she's not otherwise occupied."

"I've never met her before, of course, but I think she is still beautiful," said Wren. Thalia gave her a pitying look.

"I remember saying that our jobs were similar, but there is a big difference: You work on houses that become more valuable the older they get. Actresses and models get less valuable." So Veronica's next husband would be her retirement plan. And Nicky would be Thalia's plan when her modeling career wound down.

Saffron and Cal returned with plates of quiches and mozzarella sticks. Cal looked like a love struck sixteen-year-old, watching Saffron with a mix of pride and adoration. Wren wondered again about this young man trying to steal a world-famous movie star's girlfriend. *Unless I have it wrong. Unless we all have it wrong...*

Thalia didn't seem upset at all. Indeed, she looked fondly at the young couple. "You two would make the cutest prom king and queen. Let me guess, Cal. At your prom, you wore a powder-blue tuxedo with a ruffled shirt, right?"

Cal didn't like that, but unlike Beebee, he couldn't tell Thalia to go to hell. He just smoldered until Saffron, happily munching on her food, broke in.

"I've never been to a prom," she said.

"Proms haven't crossed the Snake River yet?"

"Oh, I know about them. It's just that—"

"Thalia. Stop it," said Cal. Saffron looked surprised. Thalia looked like she was going to say something, but then just smiled and continued drinking. They stood in uncomfortable silence until Nicky returned, pleased at being back. The maître d showed up at his elbow.

"If you're ready, Mr. Tallon, everyone can take their seats."

"That's great, thanks." Hadley returned and gave Wren's hand a squeeze, and Nicky motioned them to a table with Saffron, Thalia, and Cal. Just the six of them, no other film people.

"We're sitting at the cool kids' table," said Hadley.

"Yes," said Thalia. "And it's not the children's table. Saffron—you're really going to drink that...chocolate thing?"

"It's so good!" said Saffron. "And Nicky isn't having a martini either. He's drinking beer."

"And you can have a beer if you want, but adults at adult parties order adult drinks, not glorified chocolate milk."

Saffron pouted. Cal and Nicky wisely buried their faces in the menus, but Wren was fascinated by this bizarre variation on "eat your vegetables."

"Look, sweetie," said Thalia, forcing a patient tone. "We're eventually going back to California. Yes, we can visit that lovely house Wren is fixing for us, but we can't make a long-term home there. You have to grow up."

Saffron looked so crushed that Wren wanted to get up and give the poor girl a hug.

"And what are you drinking, Cal? A *daiquiri?* Dear God."

Men like Cal don't like to have their manhood questioned. Wren knew that much. And she couldn't figure out Thalia's angle—Saffron and Cal were just so happy together? Why the cruelty?

Thalia waved over a waiter. "These two will have martinis, please, wet, with a pearl onion." She turned back to the couple. "You'll love them, kids."

"Okay," said Nicky, heavily, drawing a line under it. "What's good here? We have some real New Yorkers here. Heck, we have a chef. Hadley, what should we eat here?"

Hadley sketched out the specialties as the waiter came around with more drinks, and everyone was ready to order. Nicky ordered the porterhouse quickly, as if he had been thinking about it all day. He had been stuck with sushi the previous day, Wren remembered. Thalia ordered the Dover sole.

"Lamb chops—there are four of them. I don't think I can eat four lamb chops," said Saffron. Thalia rolled her eyes.

"There's a fridge in your room," said Nicky. "They will wrap up whatever you can't eat, and you can have it later." That seemed to please her. She closed her menu, tried her martini, and made a face. Cal clearly missed his daiquiri but wasn't going to show it. Thalia watched both of them and shook her head.

As everyone had ordered, people came around from other tables to talk to Nicky or just to bask in his presence. Wren found it claustrophobic, surrounded by all those people, and she was only at the edge. She couldn't imagine how Nicky could put up with it, and again, she understood his wish for a private house. A house, it seemed, only one of his girlfriends wanted.

Everyone gradually wandered back to their tables for more gossip and drinking, and Cal cleared his throat. "Uh, Nicky, since you hardly need me while we're filming, and Saffron is getting a little bored hanging around the island, I thought I'd take her around the city one day, myself, since Saffron seems to like it so much. Maybe get some lunch...." The tone was halfway between a statement and a question.

"But we have to solve the mystery," said Saffron. "We have to figure out

62

why everything went wrong for his family."

Cal looked crushed, and Wren felt he needed rescuing.

"There's plenty of time," Wren said. "We'll work with my good friend Professor Lavinia Suisse. Anyway, tomorrow is Sunday, Hadley and I are off, and I promise we won't do any mystery-solving without you." Aside from helping Cal, Wren wanted a break from babysitting. Saffron looked dubious. "Here's an idea—you two should go to the Metropolitan Museum of Art. There is an American Wing there, where you can find art from this time period, which will give you a sense of the Turnbull world. It's even more appropriate than the Frick. You'll need to know about that going forward."

"That's a good idea. Cal, let's do that—we'll see the museum and all the paintings."

"If it's nice, Central Park is across the street," said Wren, "and you can visit the Whitney too—it's a collection of American art. You can get some ideas for decorating your house."

"This is going to be fun," said Saffron and gave Cal a kiss on his cheek, which turned him scarlet. Thalia seemed amused, and Nicky—relieved? "Wren is right. We need to see more of the city."

"And we could get a cab to Chinatown for lunch," said Cal.

"I'll text you a name of a Chinese restaurant I know. The chef is a friend, and you'll be well taken care of," said Hadley.

"Great ideas. Wren, Hadley, you're lifesavers," said Nicky. "You have the credit card, Saffron. Cal, you'll take care of her, right?"

"No worries, Nicky. I know New York."

Talk turned to Hollywood gossip, which left Wren and Hadley feeling a bit lost. Under the table, Wren squeezed Hadley's hand, who squeezed back for reassurance. After all, her father's clients tended to be Wall Street titans, and he had had to sit through many a dinner pretending to be interested in investing strategies.

Saffron jumped on her lamb chops with enthusiasm and delighted in the restaurant's signature jumbo onion ring. Wren saw Thalia give Saffron a glance, but there was some affection there for the younger woman's thrill at the food. Yes—younger, but probably by only four or five years. Still, it might've been decades measured by sophistication: Thalia's dress came from a top designer. Saffron wore a denim skirt—a concession to the formality of the occasion—and a checkered top. Didn't Thalia want to help Saffron dress appropriately? Was that just too exhausting, considering the fight over cocktails?

Or maybe Nicky liked Saffron that way.

For dessert, most chose fruit. Cal had key lime pie. Saffron ordered the waffle sundae.

"Thalia looks unhappy again," whispered Hadley.

"Jealousy? Waffle sundaes aren't compatible with a size four," said Wren.

The lights were low, so it was especially startling when flashes began sweeping over the table.

"What's that?" asked Saffron.

"Looks like police or an ambulance outside," said Thalia.

"Do you think anything is wrong?"

"Sweetie, this city has about six times as many people as all of Idaho. It's busy. There's always something wrong somewhere."

The waiter came around to pour more coffee.

"Is everything all right?" asked Saffron.

"One of the kitchen staff became ill, but it doesn't seem to be serious," he said.

"Oh!" said Saffron. "I hope everyone is okay."

"We were assured she would be fine. They're taking her to the hospital just to be safe. Now, can I interest anyone in one of our extensive selections of brandy?"

As the evening wound up, more people came to have a few words with Nicky, which he bore with as much goodwill as he could. It was late, and it had been a long day on the set. Cal said he'd text everyone with the details for next Saturday's event.

"Can you tell us where?" asked Hadley.

"Steele Primus," he said proudly.

"Good boy," said Thalia, but Cal was too focused on Saffron to notice how patronizing she was.

"That's a good place?" asked Saffron.

"Oh, sweet Saffron," said Thalia, "Oh...." She smiled and shook her head.

"All right, then," said Nicky, getting up. "Looking forward to it. Say, did Veronica come around? I thought she said she'd look in."

"Probably already asleep. When you reach a certain age, you need to get to bed early," said Thalia. "Anyway, goodnight, everyone."

Saffron was not so casual, however. She insisted on giving Wren and Hadley a kiss and a hug goodbye. "It is going to be SO great at the party next week," she said.

"Thank you for dinner," said Wren.

"And thank you for joining us," said Nicky.

Wren saw Cal lean over to give Saffron a kiss. It appeared that he was going to kiss her lips, chickened out, and caught her cheek. Well, it was right in front of Nicky.

Hadley took Wren's hand, and they walked through the restaurant to the lobby, where the doorman showed them into a cab. They headed up to Hadley's studio apartment in Hell's Kitchen, where Wren was spending more and more time.

"I know," she said.

"You know what, Little Bird?"

"I know we should move in together and get an apartment where we can make a home."

Hadley squeezed Wren's hand. "I would like that. But I won't push you."

"You don't have to. I'm much too old to be living with my father. And he's much too young for me to say he needs someone to take care of him. I dashed an email off to Doris—the Realtor we talked about. She's gathering some listings even now." She looked into Hadley's eyes. "I don't want you to think this has ever been about doubting us. It's just me being silly."

"Wren, silly? Perish the thought! Anyway, someday you'll design a house where we can live together, with a super kitchen, and I will cook my sole meunière for you every week."

Wren squeezed her hand back.

"Meanwhile," she said. "Any thoughts on that weird trio with Saffron,

Thalia, and Nicky?"

"Straight people can be very strange, my dear." They laughed. "But look, Nicky may like that 'just a simple country boy' act, but he's been big in Hollywood for some fifteen years now. I've watched him on the set—the director doesn't like him very much, and it's beginning to bother Nicky, who I think is realizing just how out of his depth he is. Veronica has stepped in, again and again, to play peacemaker and keep everything going."

"Really? She seems—hard."

"She is. But she's a pro and has a good rapport with Nicky. I think they genuinely like each other, and she can often be counted on to handle Nicky. He's not openly difficult or arrogant. He really works as best he can. He knows she's a serious actress and respects her."

"That's fortunate. But is it more than professional? You don't think—"

"She's hot for him? Why not? No one says anything if a man falls for a girl ten years younger.

Wren nodded. "True. It reminds me of an old saying I heard—'a beautiful woman attracts a man, but a sympathetic one gets him.'"

"Yeah. I can see that working in a heteronormative paradigm." They laughed.

"Anyway, for now," said Hadley, "Thalia's got her eye on the prize, but I don't think she's half as clever as Veronica. And Saffron? She's the joker in the pack. Sometimes men like Nicky never get tired of the worship."

"Unless Cal carries her off," said Wren. "He adores her."

"But how much is it reciprocated?" At that point, Hadley giggled. "Imagine being Cal and taking Saffron home to meet Mom and Dad. Do you think orange sneakers are all she owns?"

"We'll see at the club," said Wren.

"Yes. And speaking of clothes, I'm taking you shopping. You need something suitable for clubbing."

"I have something, I'm sure."

"I'm sure you don't."

"Oh, all right. We'll go shopping. But I have to pick up some stuff at home anyway tomorrow morning."

Hadley kept her studio tidy, but it was simply too small for two people long-term, even for two people in love. It was time to be a grown-up and move things forward.

They got ready for bed: Hadley's robe was covered in Chinese characters, Wren's in geometric patterns.

Wren's phone started ringing.

"Who's calling you this late?" asked Hadley. "You know only respectable people call before nine."

"Hello, Ms. Fontaine? It's Lieutenant Howard. Do you have a few minutes to talk?"

"Oh…sure."

"Would it be convenient to talk in person? Where are you?"

"I'm…in Manhattan with Hadley." *Why should she still be embarrassed to say that out loud?* "Not another death?" asked Wren.

"No, but…something we should discuss now. I have your address and can be there in ten minutes. Would that be okay?" Wren muted the phone. "Lieutenant Howard wants to talk to me—here. Okay?"

"Fine with me. Not the first time I've had cops come to my house. But the first time, I didn't have to race to clean everything up."

"Very funny." She switched the phone back on. "We're in our robes, but happy to meet."

"Thanks. See you in ten."

"So, what's this about?" asked Hadley.

Wren frowned. "No details. But remember, someone was sick at the restaurant."

"Have you ever been in a busy restaurant kitchen? Heat, boiling water, sizzling oil, running, stress, sharp blades. It's a wonder more people don't end up hospitalized. And what could we have seen anyway?"

"I'll make coffee. I think cops always want coffee."

Lieutenant Howard showed up, looking tired.

"Christ, what a way to end the day. With a walkup."

"We have coffee."

"God bless you." They all took chairs, and Howard took a deep sip. "Well, thanks for seeing me this late. I understand you were out to dinner tonight with Nicky Tallon and his entourage."

"And one of the kitchen staff got sick," said Wren.

Howard looked surprised. And then smiled. "Good one. I bet you were always the kid with the answer in school, and the teacher said, 'Someone beside Wren.'"

"You got her number," said Hadley. Wren turned a little red, and Hadley kissed her cheek.

"Yeah, well, you're right again," said Howard. "That's why I'm here. At the end of a long evening, the kitchen staff decided to finish some of the cocktails cleared from the tables. One of them got very sick after sipping a drink. It turned out it was laced with fentanyl, and it was from a martini with a pearl onion. Sound familiar?"

Chapter Seven

"It was from our table?" Wren finally said.

"No doubt about that. You had a private room with waitstaff exclusive to your party. It took a lot of questioning and research, but martinis with pearl onions were limited to your table. Three people were drinking them, according to the waitstaff—Thalia, Saffron, and Cal. One of them didn't 'take the bait', and it ended up back in the kitchen where a dishwasher was cleaning things up."

"Is she okay?" asked Wren.

"Fortunately, yes, she didn't take much, and the EMTs came quickly. She told us it was definitely one of three glasses that came back with pearl onions."

"Can't you tell from fingerprints?" asked Hadley.

"She had her drink, which she said was from only one of the glasses, then dumped the liquid, rinsed it, and put it in the dishwasher before the drug took effect. We were able to find a bit of the fentanyl in one glass, but we can't tell whose. You two are the outsiders, so I'm starting with you. Did you see anything happening among those drinks that night?"

"Thalia took the first one—and she may have had a second," recalled Wren. "The waiters were just replacing drinks as they emptied, but I don't know if she finished more than one. She may have had one just sitting there."

"Models usually don't drink too much," said Hadley. "Too many calories, and it damages your complexion."

"I'll make a note of that," said Howard drily.

"There was one funny thing," said Wren, and she told Howard about Thalia pushing the martinis onto Cal and Saffron.

"Did they drink them?"

"They sipped them—I wasn't really paying attention. People hovered, waitstaff came and went," said Wren. Hadley nodded.

"So…if I understand you: There were three people with martinis, as the waitstaff said. But you don't know if everyone drank them."

"I don't even know if someone drank someone else's drink," said Wren. "Did Thalia take Saffron's unfinished drink? Or Cal's? The table was small, and it would've been easy to get confused."

"Never mind who is the poisoner, we don't even know who the supposed victim was," said Howard, more to herself. "Christ."

"Have you decided if Beebee was the target last time, or an accident, a mix-up in the drinks?"

Howard thought that over. "No, we haven't made a decision. There was nothing else this evening that showed any hidden conflicts?" Wren and Hadley shook their heads.

"Nothing beyond that weird drink argument," said Wren.

"Yes…what is that relationship about? Some sort of Hollywood three-some?"

"I've worked with people like that before, and even so, I can't tell," said Hadley.

"I'm wondering…" said Howard. She stopped and smiled. "Saffron seems close to Thalia, but Thalia didn't seem to reciprocate as much when we spoke to them. Are they the real couple here?"

Wren blinked. Hadley giggled. "So we're now special LGBTQ consultants to the police department?" she asked.

"I'll print you a certificate," said Howard. "Just throwing that out there."

"I'm well-known for my highly sensitive gaydar," said Hadley, still laughing. "And I'm not getting that from either of them."

"Thank you. And what about you, Wren? You look like you disagree."

Wren frowned. It seems so obvious, but it was at the same time ludicrous, and she didn't have enough pieces to be sure. She thought carefully about what she wanted to say. Hadley was sensitive enough, and Howard was wise enough, to give her time.

"There are patterns in both houses and the people who live in them. We like to think everything is new, but we really do repeat. The Turnbull family who lived in that house and Nicky and his—menage—who are planning to live in it today, are really not that different. What I mean is that I think that despite fame and other trappings, Saffron, Thalia, and Nicky are actually rather ordinary people for whom something went wrong."

She felt bad that was all she had, as Howard looked at her expectantly.

"I appreciate that, but where does that get us?"

"I really don't know. Just that I think the answer is somewhat...blander than we imagine. I agree it's an odd little threesome, but...anyway, I wish I had more. All I can tell you is that we'll be at a party at Steele Primus next Saturday, and maybe I'll see something."

Howard nodded. "Fair enough. I'm going to tell everyone to be careful with their drinks. I'd rather the whole thing was canceled, but it's going to be impossible to protect everyone from each other for the entire length of the film shoot." She sighed and stood.

"Oh, one more thing. What about Veronica Selwyn?" asked Howard. "She was the only principal actor not there this evening. We heard she skipped the event to have dinner with someone, but we don't know who. It was at Ashton's. The owner recognized her but said he didn't know her dinner companion. I'm sure he's lying, but I don't have a lever to get it out of him. We haven't reached her yet, but I imagine she'll tell us."

"The food is very traditional there, but people go because the tables are far apart, and you can count on discretion for business or romantic meetings," said Wren.

"How do you know this?" asked Howard.

"It's a favorite place of the people who can afford to hire my father to design their homes."

"Ha! That makes sense. Anyway, Ms. Selwyn seems to resent a lot of people, and Ashton's isn't far from the Millennium. Your dinner was early, and if hers was late...." Howard shook her head. "I'm just wandering. Thanks for your time, insights, and coffee. Please keep this discussion confidential, at least for tonight. I'm sure what happened will be all over the Internet by morning. Good night."

Hadley showed her out.

"So, what do you think now, Little Bird?" asked Hadley.

"Hollywood is looking less and less glamorous," said Wren. They pulled down Hadley's Murphy bed and slipped under the sheets.

"I know the perfect place to find you a dress."

Wren gathered her courage.

"I'm not sure I'll be going to the club after all. I did the schmooze-with-the-client thing tonight, and club parties are not really...I mean, they don't show me to my best advantage." She looked into those green eyes, pleased that there was no anger, only sympathy. "Of course, there's no reason you can't go, you like those things, and I know you make lots of contacts..."

"And you'd bond further with your new client and maybe meet more rich people who've bought old houses. So tell me: Do you just not *want* to go, or are you *afraid* to go?" Wren didn't want to answer that. "Because I'm afraid, Little Bird. Dinner at a respectable restaurant is hard enough, but at a club like that, alcohol everywhere and drugs all over the place...people I'd like to meet, I should meet, but I don't know if I can do it without you."

"I have faith you'll be fine. More than five years sober."

"I know I'm not a mess anymore. But I'm still afraid. And you're not the unpopular high school math geek anymore. But you're still afraid. Here I am running a business, and you are fixing homes for multimillionaires, both of us afraid."

"One of the best parts of being with you is not having to be afraid," said Wren. So many years of being afraid of people. "When I first met you, I was afraid of you, because you reminded me of the girls I envied in high school and college."

"That was very silly of you," said Hadley. "Everyone has fears. You don't think even Thalia is afraid of turning thirty and losing modeling jobs to seventeen-year-olds?"

Wren rolled over and kissed Hadley. "I'll probably need some shoes, too. And I'm going to start writing a presentation. I'm going to deliver it myself to a bunch of actors."

"You'll be great."

Yes. Because it was about the house—not people.

* * *

They got up early the next morning, and Hadley made them omelets. Wren called an Uber and said she'd come back soon and then go shopping. Secretly, she still hoped she'd find something appropriate in her closet but deep down knew that was a lost cause.

There was little traffic, and soon she was at their Brooklyn townhouse. *Yes, the family home. I'm a little girl still living with my Daddy. I need to grow up and get a place with Hadley. Yes, I'm a coward.*

Her father was always an early riser too and was no doubt in his study, sketching or poring over plans.

But when Wren entered, she heard a woman singing—"My heart belongs to Daddy...." That was odd—their housekeeper, Ada, didn't work on weekends and certainly didn't sing. It was coming from the kitchen. Wren walked in and quickly found that "stunned speechless" could be an actual thing. Her father was in one of his dressing robes sitting at the table, drinking coffee, and looking very pleased with himself. At the stove, standing over pans of bacon and scrambled eggs, was Veronica Selwyn, also dressed in one of her father's robes.

The speechlessness was one-sided, however. Wren was dealing with two masters of savoir-faire.

"Good morning, Wren," said her father.

"I'm making too much. Feel free to join us, my dear," said Veronica. The toaster popped. "Could you get that, Ezra?" Her father put the toast on plates and got out some preserves from the fridge.

"Thank you," said Wren, tonelessly. "I already had a big breakfast."

"Of course, that lovely chef girlfriend of yours," said Veronica. She slid the bacon and eggs onto plates and sat down. "I made fresh coffee," she said. "I learned to cook as a struggling young actress and thought breakfast was a fair way of paying your father back for that hideously expensive dinner at Ashton's he took me to. Dinner at eight, like all civilized people."

Wren fell into a chair, still not knowing what to say. Then Veronica gave her a sympathetic look and put an arm around Wren's shoulders.

"I know it's a shock, and although I hope you and I can become good friends, I won't expect you to call me 'mom.'" They just looked at each other for a few moments.

"That's a joke," said Wren, finally. "It is, right?"

Veronica grinned, and her father laughed. "I had you going for a moment, didn't I? I earned my Tony, kiddo. But I need to apologize. It's startling, and I'm not being nice. Don't worry."

Wren took a breath. "I'm not. My father does very well for himself, but I imagine he'd have to be a lot richer to get you to take a fifth walk down the aisle." Veronica laughed. "Oh, good one! I had that coming." Her father met Wren's eye and smiled.

"Anyway," said Wren, "I'm just stopping by to pick up some clothes. Veronica—are you coming to the, ah, event at Steele Primus next Saturday?"

"That club thing? I'm a bit long in the tooth for that. You kids have a good time."

"Clubbing, Wren? Something new for you," said Ezra.

"It's just because it's a client event," she said.

"How did the dinner go last night?" asked Veronica.

"That's an interesting question," said Wren. "You wouldn't have heard yet, but someone was poisoned last night at dinner. It hasn't been made public yet, but it will be soon. Killed with fentanyl, just like Beebee Jenkins." She received a pleasurable jolt. *It's their turn to be surprised.*

"My God—who? Is someone dead?" asked Veronica.

"No. A dishwasher sampled a martini after our table was cleared and got sick, but they caught it in time, and she's okay. But the point is that one of the martinis on our table was poisoned. The police don't know who did it or even who it was meant for."

"Wren. I'm very concerned about this," said Ezra.

"Don't worry. This won't affect our schedule."

"I don't mean the schedule. I mean you. People are more important than buildings."

"Be careful, father. Talk like that can get your architecture license revoked. But I appreciate it." She gave him a kiss on the cheek. "No one wants to kill me."

"You're probably right. This has all the hallmarks of actors. We're vain and selfish and petty," said Veronica.

"But murder?" asked Ezra.

"Yes. Normally I'd say murder was out of bounds for us. But that's the thing about actors. We're all so insane that a true sociopath can wander among us unnoticed...Ezra, I do like a man who has good coffee in his own home."

"A sociopath. That's...wonderful," said Wren.

"I'll tell you who to keep an eye on. That odd assistant of Nicky's, Cal. We talked about him, Wren, trying to steal that wood sprite Saffron from Nicky—it's been said often enough among actors, but Nicky is old enough to be her father. Anyway, Cal is in a funny place in the world of the rich and famous—working with them but not entirely one of them, and that can twist people. And he can be weirdly protective of Nicky, too. It's hard to get by Cal to meet with Nicky."

"Why do you want to meet with Nicky?" asked Wren.

Veronica sighed. "It's all about age in this business. Men get a longer lifeline but not infinite. He's about forty and can't do these macho roles forever. He's surrounded by idiots. I want to help him start thinking about a transition." She looked a little embarrassed. "Yes, I know I said we were awful, but not all of us, and not all the time. Some people helped me, and I want to pay it forward."

"That's very sweet," said Ezra, and kissed her. Wren thought it was time to make an exit. She stood.

"Anyway, the police are questioning everyone and will probably want to talk to you, even though you weren't there. No stone unturned. I'm just grabbing some stuff and will see you Monday."

"Sure thing, Sweetie. And love to Hadley."

Wren packed what she needed and gave a half-hearted look through her wardrobe for something suitable for Steele Primus, but no. Plenty for a fundraising reception at the Museum of Modern Art, but that was it.

She grabbed a few items, called an Uber. Veronica and her father were still exchanging fond looks over the table when she came downstairs again. Wren slipped out quietly.

* * *

Hadley was working on her laptop when Wren came in.

"That was quick. Plenty of time to shop for next week, if you want."

"I'm going to need a rest." She sat down. "I found out who the enigmatic Veronica was dining with last night. My father."

"Ooh, what a slyboots he is, as my mother would say. But was it a late dinner?"

"Dinner at eight, she said."

"Veronica is a great actress, could've disguised herself, slipped into our private dining room beforehand to poison someone."

"What a horrible thought, that Veronica is a murderer. I suppose Lieutenant Howard will consider her, untangling the motives, considering she's friendly with Nicky. But frankly, I don't even want to think about any of that. Howard will find out about Veronica as soon as they connect. You see, I found all this out because when I showed up this morning, she was making them breakfast."

Hadley just stared for a moment, then started to laugh. "Oh...wow! Your father got a Tony winner, and on the first date. Good for him!"

"It isn't funny."

"I once spent the night with a Grammy winner, but a *Tony* winner, that's a whole 'nother class."

"Hadley! This is my father."

"Yes, and he's a grown-up. He's been single for more than a decade. This can't be the first woman since your mother died."

"Well, no. But it's been a little more...discreet."

"My love, what is really upsetting you? That she's using him?"

"As you said, he's a grown-up. I don't think he's out shopping for an engagement ring. And he isn't wealthy enough for her."

"Ooh…Wren being nasty. I love it. But is it the other way around? You're disappointed because he is using her? She's just a notch on his bedpost?"

"His bed is nineteenth-century mahogany. He wouldn't dare notch it. No, it's just that…it made me feel ridiculous. Because I wouldn't walk in on my father if I had my own place. No, *our* own place. Everyone is moving on. I need to as well. With you."

"Oh, Wren…we're going to be so happy." Hadley was almost crying. "With your perfect eye, you'll make whatever we find terrific. And I'll cook for you every night."

"It'll be wonderful," said Wren, and she suddenly realized she was excited, just excited, not worried after all. They sat in happy silence for a few moments, imagining their new life.

"Really," Wren finally said. "A Grammy winner? Who?"

With an exaggerated look around, Hadley whispered a name in Wren's ear.

"Wow…I had no idea."

"I know, right?"

Chapter Eight

Wren wished she could see the city through Saffron's eyes. Everything was new to her. Everything caught her attention. Born in the city, Wren had always taken it for granted—it couldn't be helped—but she remembered so well her astonishment at Prague, Budapest, Paris, Athens, York, Istanbul, seeing again and again the different ways people continually reinvented the city.

Nicky had once again provided them with a stretch Cadillac for their expedition, and Wren signed off early so she, Hadley, and Saffron could drive up to Columbia. They picked up the car right off the boat, and Saffron quickly rolled down the window to stick her head out and watch the city go by. Wren watched her, as she had on their previous outing: She's taking it in. She may have grown up rural, but she got the city, and that was unusual. Wren was inclined to think Saffron had more on the ball than she first realized.

"What are you thinking about?" asked Wren.

"Oh!" said Saffron, surprised by the question.

"My parents took me to cities all over the world. My father always asked me what I was thinking about as I saw each new city."

"The people," said Saffron. "So many *people*, how do they live here? I don't know if I could—I mean, even in L.A., we're outside the city, and I think that's crowded. And yet, looked at another way, it's more people to meet and to make friends with."

"I like that way of looking at it," said Wren. "New York City has more than eight million people. You could fit all the people in Idaho in this city four times."

Saffron frowned. "Is that why Captain Turnbull built a house on the island? So he could get away from all those people?"

"That is what we hope to find out," said Wren. She slipped into her teacher mode. "If you're going to understand Captain Turnbull and his family, you're going to have to understand something about this city." They were running early—why not? She turned to the driver.

"We're going to do a little site-seeing—I'll give you directions," she said.

"No problem, ma'am. I grew up in Queens, so I know the city well."

"Great! Now, Saffron, we're in lower Manhattan. We didn't see this area last time. It's among the oldest parts of the city," said Wren. "You've heard of Wall Street?" Saffron nodded.

"Yes, the neighborhood where they handle all the money. Zach is always talking to Nicky about what's happening on Wall Street."

"Yes. And it's not just a neighborhood. It's a real street, and there was an actual wall there in the late 1600s. This is when the city was a Dutch colony."

"Right! Someone told me it was called New Amsterdam back then."

"Exactly. And then more people came. New York was always about business and opportunity, for centuries." They drove along Wall Street. "That's 40 Wall Street. It was briefly the tallest building in the world."

"It looks like…a very big church, like the old churches I saw pictures of…." Her voice trailed off as if she was afraid Wren and Hadley would make fun of her.

"That's very observant of you." Saffron was pleased at the compliment. She may have been uneducated and unsophisticated, but she wasn't stupid. She knew Neo-Gothic when she saw it, even if she didn't know the term. "The men who built that nearly one hundred years ago wanted everyone to think that," said Wren. "They would be very happy to know that was your reaction."

Wren caught Hadley's eye—she was surprised too. Saffron nodded solemnly.

They went up Madison Avenue, and Saffron's eyes grew wide looking at the high-end shops.

"Are these the kinds of stores where Thalia's clothes come from?" she asked.

Hadley laughed. "You learn fast," she said. "I bet those are the stores she'll take you to." Saffron considered that in silence.

Back down Fifth Avenue, and Saffron took in the grand buildings but was more impressed with Central Park.

"That's the city's jewel," said Wren. "We saw it briefly the other day. It's one of the greatest urban parks in the world."

"And if you live on Fifth Avenue, you can see it and go there all the time? That would be the best part of living there."

"It is. I grew up on Fifth Avenue," said Hadley.

Saffron's eyes got big. "You were very lucky," she said.

As they cut across to the West Side, Saffron lit up at a building on West 72nd.

"What is that? It's not like that other churchy building, but it's... something."

"That's the Dakota. Probably the most famous residence in the city," said Hadley.

"Oh...that's where John Lennon lived. I can see why. Wren—what do you call that?"

"The Dakota is a mix of things. That other building, 40 Wall Street, was Gothic Revival, looking back to the Middle Ages—knights and armor and all that. This largely looks back at the Renaissance, a later period. The overall idea is grand houses in France."

"It was also the model for the apartment house in a classic horror movie called *Rosemary's Baby*," said Hadley.

Saffron nodded. "I can see that. It's what you said, Wren. People affect houses, and houses affect people. But we haven't seen anything like our house."

"There aren't many left—it's very old—and few of them were as extraordinary as the Turnbull House."

They continued uptown. "This is Columbia University, one of the oldest schools in the country," said Wren.

"And one of the best," said Hadley. "Wren went here because she's so smart."

"Not that smart," said Wren.

"Oh yes, I can see that," said Saffron, with that same unnerving solemnity. "I can see you're smart."

"Anyway," continued Wren. "We're meeting Professor Lavinia Suisse. She really is extremely smart. She was my professor when I was here and then became a friend." She flushed a little. "She knows more about this city's history than anyone, and she lives in a great apartment near here with her wife."

"Oh! Her *wife*." She paused. "So she helped you be who you are?"

"She didn't make me who I already was," said Wren. Hadley raised an eyebrow.

"Oh—I know *that*. I mean, she helped you...find out who you were? Is that right?"

"Yes, that's right," said Wren. "Lavinia gave me the courage to be who I was, and that was no small thing."

"Yes," said Saffron. "I can see that."

They pulled up in front of Lavinia's building, a grand university apartment house that counted some of Columbia's most distinguished academics as its residents.

"This looks nice," said Saffron, but she turned to Wren for confirmation.

"Wait until you see the inside," said Wren.

Lavinia was waiting for them at her door.

"Dear Wren, you interrupt me grading papers—for which I thank you profoundly." She gave Wren and Hadley kisses and brought all of them into her living room, where every surface was piled with books and papers.

"Sorry, folks. Busy time of year."

"Lavinia—this room hasn't changed in the decade I've known you."

"Dear, sweet Wren," said Lavinia. "I've always loved how your commitment to truth is completely untempered by tact. Now, introduce me to your friend."

"Lavinia—this is Saffron Scott. As I told you, she's a friend of Nicky

Tallon's, whose house I'm restoring on Turnbull Island. Saffron, this is Professor Lavinia Suisse."

"I'm glad to meet you, professor," said Saffron. "Wren told me you're the smartest person ever." Lavinia laughed.

"It's a mistake to flatter academics. They believe it too easily. And call me Lavinia. A pleasure to meet you too. Let me get some coffee."

"I brought cookies," said Wren, producing a tin from her bag.

"Christ, Wren, you don't have to bring a present every time you come. Angela is on me about my eating habits, anyway, but if I'm going to hell, I might as well do it with macadamia nuts. Angela sends her love, by the way—she's performing a bypass today."

Lavinia moved some of the papers, and soon everyone was sitting around the cookie tin with their mugs. Saffron's eyes kept raking over the floor-to-ceiling bookshelves.

"It's like living in a library," said Saffron.

"I know. Isn't that great?"

Saffron's eyes swept around the room before landing on a photograph. "Oh—Wren, that's you, isn't it?"

Lavinia laughed. "Yes, that's me and Angela on our wedding day. And Wren was our bridesmaid."

"You are so sweet, Wren." She had been twenty, and looked fifteen in a flowered dress with a matching bouquet. Saffron's eyes got wet. "You are all so lucky."

"I suppose we are," said Lavinia. "Now, onto why we're here. So, my dear, you want to know about Captain Turnbull and his family. Wren told me about the house, so I've been doing a little research. An interesting man, our Captain, and I was able to find out a bit about him. Came from a modest Brooklyn family and went to sea when he was about fourteen." She paused. Her mouth curved into a smile. "This is when people usually say, 'My God, he was only fourteen!'"

"Oh, I can see that," said Saffron. "Idaho isn't on the ocean, but I could see wanting to do that."

"That is...interesting," said Lavinia, turning her sharp teacher's eyes onto

Saffron. "I always see if my students can identify with figures out of history. And, in fact, this will be easier if you can connect with Captain Turnbull. So as I said, he started at sea and quickly rose. It was a dangerous profession, but there was money to be made for the daring and the lucky. He became part owner of a ship and continued to prosper. Now where's my laptop?" She found it under a pile of scholarly journals. "This is the seal of New York City," she said, showing the screen to Saffron. "The Native American is a Lenape, Manhattan's original inhabitants. Much of the rest of the seal speaks about Captain Turnbull. That's a sailor, like the Captain—New York was an important port from the beginning. Look what's in the middle—a windmill used to grind grain and barrels of flour."

"And beavers?" asked Saffron. "I didn't know you had beavers here."

"To be honest, I'm not sure we will do, but it's the official New York state mammal. One of the original trading businesses here was fur, including beaver fur. Captain Turnbull traded fur, and grain, among other things, and made a lot of money. By the time he bought the island, he was becoming as much a businessman as a sailor. That's why he bought this island and built this house—to run his shipping interests. This was a city based on commerce in a new country based on commerce. And he was going to take his place among the leaders. Records are sketchy—he may have gone to the Ottoman Empire, what we call Turkey today—or even the Far East. He seems to have come back wealthy."

"But his wife and sister—" said Saffron. "Like in the song. Why did he leave again? The song suggests he couldn't settle down. What happened to him?"

Lavinia bestowed one of her superior smiles on Saffron. Wren had seen that look on her face many times,

"You don't ask a lot, do you, dear?" she said with a touch of sarcasm." The romantic answer is that he fell in love with the East, even with a particular woman there. Tracking what happened to Captain Turnbull after all this time to foreign ports—it would probably be impossible to find a trace of him. But even so, I was able to find a few bits and pieces. But you do need to understand that this is real history—not a storybook. Although I was able to put some things together, you may not be able to draw conclusions. At least, not the conclusions you want."

"People often aren't the way you want them," said Saffron, as serious as Lavinia.

"All right then," said Lavinia. "Let me show you what I have. First, I managed to find a portrait of the Captain and his family." She turned around the laptop again.

Wren had always thought that old sea Captains wore beards—Thomas Turnbull was clean-shaven, but he might've been advised to grow one. He needed something to soften that hard jaw. Still, it was proportionate to the rest of him, the broad shoulders and chest. He wore a dark suit, and it fit him well, but Wren thought he didn't look comfortable in it.

The women flanking him were a different story. They wore well-tailored but simple dresses, and their hair was done up in neat braids. One was clearly his sister—a similar jawline and broad figure, although she imagined the painter had tempered both of them. The other woman was no doubt the wife, with an exotic beauty. Wren could see a pout around the mouth—was the artist amused at painting that?

"Oh," said Saffron. "Oh my."

"It took some work to find this," said Lavinia. "I figured he'd have commissioned a portrait, and I hoped it didn't end up destroyed over the years. An art historian friend with a portraiture obsession found it with a private collector in Chicago who was pleased to forward this photo, taken for his insurer. The canvas has the artist's and subjects' names on the back. This is Captain Thomas Turnbull. On his left is his sister, and on his right is his wife."

"Why are the women standing and the Captain sitting?" asked Saffron.

"If he was much taller—and I suspect he was—it's easier to fit them all neatly together," said Wren. "Also, it gives the women a chance to show off their dresses."

"They aren't very fancy dresses," said Saffron. "Wouldn't they have worn their fanciest dresses for a painting?"

"It was a big change from the earlier period," said Wren. "Dresses became simpler, with a high waist and fitted bodice, influenced by the dress of ancient Greece and Rome. There had been a revolution in France, which led the world in elaborate dress, and many of the wealthy were killed, so overly elaborate dress became unfashionable." She paused. "It's my favorite time."

"And while we're looking at old photos, take a look at the one by the window." Wren groaned inwardly. "Wren and I are wearing the dress of that time period."

"Oh wow," said Saffron. "What was this—Halloween?"

"Wren and I belong to a club devoted to honoring and appreciating the past. We dress in period clothes."

"Oh, but you'll have to have a party at Turnbull House when it's done. We'll all dress up. Hadley—can you make the food they had then?"

"Sounds like fun," said Hadley.

"Delightful," said Lavinia. "I'm sure we'll love it."

"We'll have such a great party!" said Saffron.

Yes, thought Wren, *in your very own period Barbie House.*

"Now, you may have noticed that Mrs. Turnbull here doesn't look Anglo-American," continued Lavinia. "In fact, I discovered, she was Russian—her father was a trading partner of the Captain's."

"She's stunning," said Hadley. Wren agreed—her exotic beauty had clearly won over the Captain.

"Men and their trophy wives—nothing really changes," said Lavinia.

At that, Wren glanced at Saffron, but if she got the reference, she didn't react.

"Anyway, "her name was Katya Volkov. The Captain moved into this house in August of 1800 with his new wife and his sister, who was, in the vocabulary of the day, a spinster, that is, unmarried. Her name was Verity."

"The Captain ran his business," continued Lavinia. "He was getting on in years, and seafaring is a young man's game, so he was more a prosperous businessman now than a sea captain, although he kept the title."

"But what about the song. It says love dragged him away—but he already had a beautiful wife. And Russia is in the East, right? I mean, he already had a beautiful wife from the East. "

"I won't dismiss songs out of hand. They can tell us a lot, but not necessarily what we want to know. That song probably wasn't written until long after this happened, after Verity and Katya were dead, based on stories people told, and changed, over and over again. It said what people wanted to hear, a song about lost love and mystery. We can't assume it's an exact history of what really happened."

"But…but…we have to find out what happened. What happened to the Captain? What did his family do after he was gone? The song makes it seem there's a *real answer* if we can find it." She sounded frustrated and looked like she was about to cry. "I need to know."

Chapter Nine

Wren meanwhile watched Lavinia. She expected she'd have something up her sleeve. Lavinia was a phenomenal historian, and her students knew she *always* had something up her sleeve. She opened her leather-bound notebook.

"History is sneaky, but occasionally we get a break. I was able to find an old record. Actually, 'record' is probably too formal. 'Case notes' is more like it, stuck into a folder and forgotten for centuries, eventually scanned into a poorly indexed database a few years back. It's all we have, but it's something. Anyway, there was no formal police force in the city back then—what we had was a 'coroner,' a city official whose job it was to look into deaths." She looked at her notebook. "On June 12, 1805, Manhattan coroner Richard Bedlow wrote that he was rowed over to Turnbull Island, summoned by a note from Mrs. Turnbull, the Captain's wife. Upon arrival, he was greeted by 'Abigail—a servant.' She told him that one of the male servants on the island, Jack Llewelyn, had died in a fight with the Captain.

"Bedlow asked for further details. Abigail told him that Miss Verity, the Captain's sister, had formed a friendship with Jack. The Captain apparently was unaware—no doubt absorbed in his business affairs. At any rate, the friendship developed. As Bedlow reports, Abigail said she and Miss Verity used to make trips alone—Jack would take them in a boat, and they often spent the night in Manhattan, with Jack returning the next day. But during one of those trips, said Abigail, Miss Verity married Jack with Abigail as a witness."

"Ooh, married beneath her," said Hadley with a laugh. "That happened more than once among the Vanderwerfs, and the family was not happy, I can tell you."

"I'm sure. Some things don't change," said Lavinia. "And this time, it apparently ended in tragedy. We are fortunate that this Mr. Bedlow seemed very serious about his job. He pressed for the details—"

"Is it like the song?" asked Saffron.

Lavinia smiled. "Yes…and no. I think whoever wrote the song knew this story and just took some liberties with it. It's a shame no one found this account earlier. But maybe someone did and decided just to leave it alone for the sake of the song. But let's see what we have now. Abigail told Coroner Bedlow that on hearing this, the Captain became deeply angered. The Captain found Jack in the house, and they fought—Jack was subdued before anyone could interfere, and when they found him, he was dead. The body was stored in an outbuilding."

"Oh!" said Saffron. "He just died? I mean, the Captain killed him, and that was it? The man his sister loved?" Her eyes got wet.

"The Captain was likely a hard man to become wealthy in such a dangerous profession. Bedlow notes that Abigail told him the Captain had a year ago raised a hand against his wife—her arm was broken, 'and if Coroner Bedlow didn't believe her, there was a doctor in the city who could give evidence he had set her arm.' But whether murder or spousal abuse, there was no real police force back then anyway to stop his behavior. But we have more on the story."

"Okay. I just thought…" She fished for a tissue and let Lavinia continue.

"Coroner Bedlow asked to speak to Miss Verity—technically, Mrs. Llewelyn now—and Mrs. Turnbull, but Abigail said that the two women were mourning. And that Katya Turnbull was especially affected as she was with child."

"How sad! But who could blame them for wanting to be alone," said Hadley. "Two sisters-in-law, one's husband making the other a widow and child without a father. As you said—a classic tragedy."

"Indeed. You would hardly believe it," said Wren. Lavinia gave her former student a surprised look, then smiled and resumed. Wren saw that Saffron was listening with rapt attention.

"Anyway, Abigail said she could provide any information to the coroner and could show him Jack's body, which he had to view as a matter of law. Bedlow noted that he spoke to Abigail on the way, asked her if she had seen the fight, as the ladies hadn't. She said she had seen it only at the end—it was over quickly. She said even with his limp, from a long-ago accident at sea, the Captain finished the fight with just a few blows. He was over six feet tall, very big, and Jack, although taller than the ladies, was shorter than the Captain and slightly built."

"Oh!" said Saffron. "Really? She said what happened? So we really know?"

"My dear, wait a moment," said Lavinia. "When we look into the past, we never really know everything. You can't get into someone's mind. This isn't a time machine." She held up her hand to forestall further questions. "But let's finish Mr. Bedlow's account. It is going to get a little grim—"

"Oh, I've seen grim things," said Saffron with a heavy solemnity.

"Have you, my dear?" asked Lavinia. Wren wondered again where this girl came from. "We'll skip it anyway and just say for now that if you want to pursue this, there are medical experts who can help you. But there are still some interesting details about the much-battered body. Bedlow asked if Jack was wearing the clothes he had died in, and Miss Verity told him the clothes had been torn and bloodied where, in her words, 'it wouldn't be decent' to be buried in. Abigail had stripped Jack, washed the body, and dressed him in fresh clothes."

"Oh—she did it herself?" asked Saffron.

"Of course. In those days, illness and birth, and death were immediate, with few professionals protecting people from the messy details. Anyway, our coroner was sharp-eyed. He writes that Jack's shirt was too small—could not be buttoned across his chest. And the pants left his ankles bare. I hear some disdain in his writing. Abigail explained that Jack had no other suitable clothes, and they had to use some clothes that had been left by a sailor who had served under the Captain."

Saffron frowned. "No other clothes?"

"It does seem odd. But even wealthy people didn't have a lot of clothes, and a servant like Jack even less. Dressing a corpse is no fun, and Abigail may have just grabbed what was convenient."

"Bedlow wanted to question the Captain, of course. He had killed Jack, even if it was by accident. But apparently, the Captain, again according to Miss Verity, was worried about being charged in Jack's death. He said he would sail away—but not on one of his ships, where he could be traced. That should've been it. The Captain wasn't around to face questioning, and there would be no finding him—not back then. God knows where he went. But we are fortunate that Bedlow was both diligent and curious. He had more words with Abigail—"

"Oh!" said Saffron, who then felt Lavinia's laser-beam eyes. She turned a little red. "I'm sorry. I just want so much for them...."

"I know, my dear. Let's complete the story. It seems that Bedlow asked Abigail if it had been clear for some time that Miss Verity and Jack were forming an attachment. She said it had been, and they all had been nervous about the Captain's reaction. The Captain had said Miss Verity's presence would save him the cost of a nanny, and she'd been needed to run the household on her own with Mrs. Turnbull indisposed. Abigail said that Miss Verity was very excited about becoming an aunt and had been very caring for her sister-in-law. And the Captain—he was no doubt excited about becoming a father? Abigail didn't know—the Captain obviously did not discuss his feelings with her. However, she did reveal that once or twice, when angry, the Captain accused his wife of infidelity, wondering if the child was his. Anyway, he was often ashore on business—Mr. Bedlow could ask his friends in town what he thought. Men and women. Bedlow asked if the Captain had a mistress. Abigail said he was sure she didn't know, but apparently couldn't help adding that she wouldn't be surprised. And then—and I'm going to quote Coroner Bedlow exactly—'Abigail told me the Captain was violent in his love and his life, and I took note of the look of utter disgust on her face.' Anyway, Abigail told the coroner she worked mostly for Miss Verity and Mrs. Turnbull and found both of them pleasing and generous mistresses to work for and assured the coroner they were chaste."

"Violent in love," repeated Saffron. "Does that mean he hurt, even raped, his wife? That he also hurt his sister?"

"That's exactly what it means," said Lavinia.

"I think of the house as a..." she struggled "...a *sanctuary*. That's the right word, isn't it?

"That's exactly the right word," said Wren. "Do you think Turnbull House should be a sanctuary?"

"Yes. A house must be a place of safety. And I'm sad it wasn't then. And isn't now. We had one death in the house and an almost death at the dinner."

"We will think about creating a house for you, a house free of its...bad history," said Wren.

"Thank you," said Saffron.

Wren saw a wry smile on Lavinia's face.

"Anyway, Mr. Bedlow noted that Miss Verity was still young enough to have children, and there was no law against a marriage between her and a man ten years younger. He reported Abigail was annoyed by his question—was it any of his business? But the coroner was not put off and asked Abigail if she was jealous. After all, Jack was no doubt about her age. Had she been interested in him? Miss Verity—an aging spinster—had stolen her sweetheart, which was bad enough, but because of her selfish and inappropriate attachment, he was dead at the Captain's hands."

"That sounds pretty mean of him," said Saffron. "Abigail was right. People's relationships are no one else's business."

Wren thought that, a perfectly timed observation. More and more, she was realizing how that odd little Thalia-Nicky-Saffron triangle worked.

"You're right," said Lavinia. "Bedlow may have been nosy, but he wasn't stupid. He no doubt knew he had provoked her. Abigail told him he had no right to make such accusations; she was a good girl, and chaste, and went by boat to St. Mark's in town every Sunday. She had no attachment to Jack, and if men treated wives the way the Captain treated his, she'd happily live her life as a spinster. In his exact words, 'So outraged was the girl, I feared she would strike me.'"

"I'm rather growing to like Abigail," said Hadley. "If that was the situation

91

back then, I don't blame her for not wanting a man in her life."

"I like her too," said Wren. "I'm thinking that whatever her title was, she was more than a simple maid. She helped with provisions. And managed to set herself up as family spokeswoman to an important official like the coroner. More of a housekeeper, really."

"Well-reasoned," said Lavinia. "I imagine she cowed our Coroner Bedlow. But in his accounts, he wonders if there was jealousy of another kind. Jack, a former servant, would have a life of ease after marrying a Turnbull, while Abigail would continue to work. 'I feared more wrath, but felt I had to put this to her. I expected more rage and denial. At first, she seemed surprised, as if she didn't understand the question, but then gave me a sly smile and said she was more than satisfied with her lot in life. And so the matter was concluded.'"

"That's it?" asked Saffron.

"That's all we have. We have no information the Captain ever returned. Did he want to escape the law? Perhaps. But he was a rich man who could no doubt defend himself as merely protecting the ladies from Jack's seduction, as he would have put it. This just may have been an excuse for the Captain to take off. We don't really know the details. Did he feel betrayed by his wife or sister? By both? Wanderlust may have been too strong even when he had such a magnificent house."

"Nothing changes, does it?" asked Saffron. "People wanted the same things back then as they do now. Love and comfort. I mean, that's all I want." She seemed shy at that and then flamed as Lavinia laughed.

"Oh no, my dear, I'm not laughing at you. It's just the joy at your conclusion. You're absolutely right. The world was very different then, but the emotions were the same."

"So what does that tell you?" Wren asked Saffron.

"Well...that maybe it's harder to have a home and family than I thought. Things can get in the way. I'll have to work hard to make sure we have a safe place where we can live forever."

Yes, thought Wren. She got that right.

"We'll see it through together," said Hadley, laying a reassuring hand on the girl's shoulder.

Lavinia gave her listeners a knowing smile and continued. "We know by 1870 the house and island had new owners—purchased from Alexander Turnbull, son of the late Captain Turnbull—and that his aunt and mother were buried on the island. We have a death certificate for him in 1890, aged eighty-five, resident of the County of New York. No mention of Abigail."

Saffron looked crushed. "This is all so sad. Jealousy and anger. Two women losing their husbands, a boy growing up without his father, and Abigail...I bet she really liked Jack. She wouldn't have gotten so angry if she didn't."

For all her naiveté, Wren saw Saffron could be shrewd about people. She might well have been right.

"We only have the facts we have," said Wren. "And not even those, not entirely. We just have Abigail's accounts. Or more precisely, Bedlow's report of Abigail's account."

Saffron screwed up her face. "Okay. So maybe we have it wrong, then. Let's say Katya was having an affair with Jack, and the Captain thought the child was really Jack's, and that's why he killed him. But either way, their child grew up without a father." She slipped into herself for a moment.

"You've been hanging around movie sets too much, my dear," said Lavinia. "As I said, history just...is. We don't always get the answers we want. Or even any answers at all. Maybe with the indefatigable Wren and Hadley helping you, you will find more. I wish you luck."

Wren didn't think Saffron entirely grasped that, but she knew this was important. "I see," she said. "I just want to find...the family story, I guess."

"Why?"

"Because they were part of the house...it's like they're haunting it, and I want it to be perfect for us to live there, to be happy there, with the spirits of the Captain and his wife and sister."

Wren thought Lavinia's head might explode at that, but the professor just nodded and seemed to consider that for a while.

"Never mind movie sets, you've been hanging around Wren too long," said Lavinia. "Anyway, I'm going to text my information to Wren, and as this has piqued my curiosity, I'm going to see if I can find some Census records. Who knows—I may get more information, and I could get an article out of it."

"Something went very wrong on the island, in that lovely house," said Saffron. "I just want to know why all this happened."

Lavinia raised an eyebrow. "I don't know if you realized it, but that was very astute. You didn't ask *what* happened, which we may never know, but *why*, and with some luck, you may be able to figure that out. Just keep an open mind."

"Oh yes! We'll keep at it, and we'll bring peace to the island, to the house. Lavinia, you are the *best*." It was too late for Wren to warn Lavinia that Saffron was a hugger, and all she could do was watch in horror as Saffron launched herself.

"There, there," said Lavinia, wriggling free. "Good luck on your...ah... quest."

"Could you tell me where your bathroom is?" Lavinia pointed the way and then shook her head.

"You two have your work cut out for you."

"Sweet and harmless," said Hadley. "She's essentially a puppy."

"She's fey," said Wren.

Lavinia laughed. "I've never known you to use a word incorrectly. Now that's a very old word with many meanings. Do enlighten the class, Miss Fontaine."

She took a breath. "One of its earliest meanings, particularly Scottish, is 'under a spell of doom—fated to die.'"

"Is this about Beebee's murder? That it was really meant for Saffron?" asked Hadley.

"In part..." said Wren. "But more than that, there's a frightening intensity about her—and that's not playing well with a lot of people. She's uneducated, but there's an underlying shrewdness there. I think...she feels rather than thinks, but gets to the right place in the end." She gave a self-deprecating laugh. "The opposite of me, really."

Lavinia laughed. "Yes—it was shrewd of you to notice that."

Hadley nodded. "I agree. Also, there is a volatility about her."

"But you said she was a puppy. How threatening is a puppy?" asked Lavinia.

"Maybe I'm just imagining things," said Wren, "but she has Nicky Tallon's affection and money. She's important. She's more important than she realizes, and that's what frightens me." She blushed a little. "Maybe because I was a…little intense, too."

"You certainly were. All right, at the very least, you'll keep her out of trouble. It's actually all very interesting from a historical viewpoint. I look forward to hearing reports of what you find."

"I think Saffron had one thing right," said Wren, looking a little uncertain. "I agree that bit about haunting is nonsense, and maybe it's just my particular point of view, but I think she's right about the house. It says something about the man who built it, the family who lives there. They worshiped at St. Mark's. It was built in 1803 and designed by John McComb Jr., who built Turnbull House and Gracie Mansion. Families affect houses—and houses affect families. There is something there if I can find it—there is more to this story."

"The story?" asked Lavinia. "Abigail's—or Saffron's?"

"Both," said Wren.

"If there is a connection, you'll find it," said Lavinia.

Saffron returned. "This is going to be great! We'll do what we can to bring peace to everyone."

"That's a tall order," said Wren.

"But you're so smart. Can we start tomorrow?"

"I think we can. And now, we'll let Lavinia get back to grading papers. I believe we're meeting everyone for dinner soon?"

"Oh yes! You can come too, Lavinia. Plenty of room, most of the cast and crew will be there—I'll introduce you to Nicky. Do come, you and your wife."

"You're so sweet," said Lavinia. *Her look said I'd rather kill myself.* "But as you just heard, I have papers to grade, and Angela and I are having a quiet dinner out. But you kids have a great evening. Hadley, make sure Wren has

95

fun. You're better at it than she is."

Wren leaned over to give her mentor a kiss goodbye. "Call me if you need more. And be careful with your fey friend, my dear," Lavinia whispered.

Chapter Ten

Wren found a weekend spent thinking about the mystery of Turnbull Island a good way to distract herself from her father romancing a world-renowned actress. What did she know? Two women had died on the island and were buried there. Jack was no doubt buried on the island as well; Wren didn't see Coroner Bedlow dragging a battered body back to Manhattan when there was plenty of room on the island and servants to do the digging.

She thought of Abigail, a young woman with probably little formal education, but no lack of intelligence. There was no stumbling or hysterics in her tale, according to Coroner Bedlow. Wren wondered if she could untangle Abigail's story two centuries later. She justified her task by telling herself that if she made Saffron happy, she'd make Nicky—her client—happy. Her father would think the whole thing loopy but would approve of the goal.

On Monday, she invited Saffron, Nicky, and whoever else wanted to participate, to talk about the "Turnbull Search" when there would be a break in the late afternoon. Before everyone arrived, she made her way to the parlor, where it all started, and looked around again. The Victorians would later build houses that were grander, but none that were more perfect.

Saffron and Hadley showed up first. "We're going to do it. We're going to find out what really happened here and bring peace to the family."

"Remember Abigail's story," said Wren. "Life can be a little more complicated, and this happened a long time ago. We're not sure what we'll find. If anything."

"I know you'll do it!" said Hadley. "Nicky, Cal, and Veronica are coming, but Thalia is at a shoot today." Wren wasn't surprised. It didn't sound like something that would interest her—Thalia looked *forward*.

Veronica and Nicky followed, dressed for the occasion, still in their costumes. The period clothes suited them, Wren observed. Nicky wore a handsome blue coat over white breeches, like a character in a Jane Austen novel, for all the young women to swoon over—when women were still expected to swoon. Veronica wore a rose dress, flattering and well-suited for her age without being matronly. The difference between them was attitude. Nicky looked a little self-conscious, but Veronica moved in her dress as if she had been a Turnbull herself. It wasn't just experience but the difference between a competent actor and a great one.

Wren noticed they were arm in arm. What would they have said about her back in the day? "She's awfully free with her favors." Then she felt the embarrassment wash over her. She had enough to do without worrying about who her father was sleeping with.

Cal followed a few steps behind them. He greeted Saffron with a big smile and sidled up to her.

"Thanks for coming, everyone. I sent all of you a summary of what we have found out about the Turnbull family and the death that led to the Captain's exodus, presumably to the East, as the song says. We're taking some concrete steps to find out more about what really happened. To start with, I've contacted a well-regarded firm that specializes in exhumations. We've used them before—this is an issue with old estates. Perhaps whatever markers they had were lost or destroyed, or maybe the women didn't want anything—just to disappear into the island they had called home. We don't know. But if we can find them, we may learn more about their story."

"Not to dampen your enthusiasm, but this is a big island. How can you find an unmarked grave?" said Veronica. "And how can you just dig it up?"

"Actually, when it comes to graves, it's a small island. Home burials were a lot more common back then, and they knew it wasn't practical to bury them where it was too rocky or where it might interfere with drinkable water. There aren't many ideal spots, and this firm has technologies that can help

98

further narrow it down. As for legal aspects—and I've been through this before—with graves this old, there are no legal obstacles, and we continue to treat any remains with full respect."

"My apologies. I should've known you'd have this in hand," said Veronica, showing plenty of white teeth. Wren forced a smile.

"Thank you. We'll see where, if anywhere, that leads us. But right now, the real reason I brought you here. I wanted to talk about the house. The house itself may be a clue to what we're looking for—the story of the Turnbulls. I know we went over the structure of the house, but now…." She took a breath. "Now we're going to go over the house's *personality*." She looked at the faces. Everyone looked curious, maybe even excited. Hadley gave her a thumbs up, and Veronica arched one of her perfect eyebrows.

"Come with me to the great room." She led them into the oval room. Even after all the days she had spent in this room, it still took her breath away. "This is perfection. The proportions of this room…I could give you the mathematics, but all I need to say is that it's aligned with the way we see the world, and so we get an absolute sense of symmetry. An absolute sense of order. Predictable but not dull. Just look at it and think what it meant to someone like Captain Turnbull, who spent years on violent and unpredictable seas."

"Do we think the Captain built it this way intentionally to give himself a sense of peace as he settled down?" asked Veronica. Nicky looked at her with admiration, impressed by her question. *Oh, she's challenging me,* thought Wren.

"It would be almost impossible to get inside the mind of a man who lived two hundred years ago. Even figuring out the wants and needs of home builders our firm works with is difficult enough—as my father would no doubt tell you." Veronica's mouth curved in admiration—*nicely returned, Miss Fontaine.* Hadley stifled a giggle. "But let's assume he was not an imaginative man. He led a life that required hard work and courage, but not imagination. I'd like to think that the Captain created such an orderly house to give himself a feeling of stability after all his years at sea. But I find it easier to believe he had engaged John McComb Jr. as his architect simply because he was famous and fashionable." *Perhaps the same reason Nicky Tallon hired me,* she thought wryly. "Because the proportions of this room, of this house, are absolute perfection. It says stability. It says order."

She looked over her audience. She had them. Nicky and Saffron were looking at her seriously. If Saffron didn't get it intellectually, she got it emotionally. Cal seemed to understand. And Veronica—she had some secret thoughts rolling through her. Wren realized she may be talking about a two-hundred-year-old house and its long-gone inhabitants, but this was just as much about the present. Could she turn it into a place where Nicky and his cobbled-together family could find the peace they wanted?

"Saffron—you seemed disappointed when we first looked over the house because it wasn't as elaborate as you were expecting. Times had changed. We had a revolution. The French had a revolution. Even in England, the power of the monarchy was fading. Displays of great wealth were out, replaced by what I describe as simple elegance. What makes this house extraordinary is not gold and marble but the shape of the rooms, how everything works together. Look at the delicate carvings where the walls meet the ceiling, the elegant columns that frame the fireplace, and how they reflect the archway at the entrance to the room. See the design of the fanlights over the doors, almost like spiders' webs. Altogether, it can give the residents a sense of peace. In the end, it's all about...harmony."

They may not know about architecture, but they knew about music. Wren thought of Saffron, how those sweet mandolin notes wafted over the island. If anyone knew about harmony, it would be Saffron.

Nicky looked around and nodded. Veronica's perfect mouth curved into a knowing smile.

"So...what does this mean when it comes to the Captain? About what happened to him and his family?" asked Saffron.

"It may mean everything," said Wren. "I want you to try to imagine yourself living here day after day. We decorate our homes. But our homes...decorate us." Was that too much? No, she got a good reaction. "Think of the women living here. Think of being in this room, in this house, the daily harmony... and then there's the Captain."

"Not a man of harmony," said Veronica. "Couldn't the house fix him?"

"Are you planning to live here?" asked Wren. "Are you asking if the house can fix you?"

Veronica looked surprised—but just for a moment. "Oh, good one. I asked for that."

"We're architects. And McComb was among the greatest. But we aren't magicians." Veronica laughed.

"Nicely said," she responded and did her best curtsy.

"I think," said Wren, "that the Captain built a refuge for his wife and sister but, without knowing it, built a prison for himself. The order and perfection could not fix a mind that was itself so disordered. And that left us with a tragedy."

That was enough, she saw. She had gotten them thinking, so she let the silence hang.

"So the house...destroyed the Captain? Made him so crazy he killed Jack?" asked Saffron.

"The Captain? I don't know. He may have already been crazy. We can't begin to imagine what life was like on an eighteenth-century merchant ship. No. The Captain may have built this house. But the women lived here. They made it a home. I want you to think about what they did to this house. And what the house did to them. Think about symmetry. Think about the perfection—of this room in particular, but all of it. Think about *harmony*."

They all looked around the room, studying it. Wren felt a rush of pride. Her father had said it wasn't easy to get everyone to really look at a house, but she had done it. Saffron especially. Wren could tell that much when a client really "got" a house. Saffron saw herself there. She was already placing herself and the others in that home and considering how it would work.

Veronica squeezed Nicky's arm and looked up at him. "I don't know about mysteries. But Wren is right about proportions and perfection. I can't think of a more restful place for an actor to get a sense of self. This house is perfectly arranged, as a play might be." Wren watched Veronica think. "I've been in some of the greatest modern houses around, designed by some great architects—including Ezra Fontaine." Wren felt herself get hot as Veronica winked at her. *Dear lord.* "But nothing like this. This place gives me a sense of calm."

Trying to sound authoritative, Wren responded. "It is grand—a house for a rich man. But McComb gave him a residence that could provide him with a calm world. A world with a sense of order."

"I think that's why all of us like it," she said.

Nicky smiled down at her. "You're right, Ronnie. I'm seeing that more than ever. Hey, Wren, I like what you said about proportions and the rooms. I guess it's important for it to be furnished and decorated along those lines, right?"

"That would be essential. I could advise you—"

But Nicky had already turned back to Veronica. "You'll give me some help with this? You have such a good eye."

Seeing them in the costumes, Wren could imagine Nicky and Veronica setting up house here. Or was it just their costumes? They seemed right for the house, and although Wren couldn't trust her instincts on people—they seemed right for each other.

"Absolutely," said Veronica. "I know some fantastic designers who would kill to work on this space. My first theater work in college was actually in set design. And what is a house except a more permanent set."

You are right, thought Wren. *That's a great conclusion—if you assumed the residents were all actors. And they might be, whether they knew it or not.*

He rubbed her arm, and she squeezed his again.

Saffron was still looking around the room, oblivious to the discussion. She and Cal were holding hands.

"Saffron—have you picked your room out yet?" asked Veronica.

It was clear what room was the master—did Veronica mean that? Or was Saffron getting another room? And what about Thalia? It seemed—ridiculous. But Wren was finally getting a sense of what was really going on here.

"The one with the great view of the bay."

"Okay, but you might want to think about something besides posters of kittens and puppies." Cal flashed a look at Veronica, then reassured Saffron.

"Nicky will give you money for decorating. We'll go together, find some great furniture, all set up for your music." That seemed to please Saffron. Veronica just rolled her eyes.

And then Thalia came in. Wren didn't know much about clothes, but she knew about color and form. Thalia knew how to decorate herself—but not for Turnbull House. She didn't belong in this house. She belonged in a mid-century penthouse with floor-to-ceiling windows and plenty of chrome.

"Another house tour? Hello, Nicky." She spared a glare for Veronica and then gave Nicky a kiss.

"Wren has given us so much here—about its...personality," he said. "She's made me realize more than ever how I can make a home here."

Thalia sighed. "You're still serious about this place? This is a great setting for events, but it's an island. We've been through this. You can't really live here, Nicky. Certainly not long-term."

"Oh, but it will be so perfect," said Saffron. "I mean, Wren said the house is perfect, the shape of the house, and now I see it." Thalia sighed and rolled her eyes.

"Sweetie, I admit it's very romantic, and when Wren here has worked her magic on it, I'm sure it'll be a great setting for a photo shoot. But it's going to get very boring very quickly."

"Perhaps you don't understand," said Veronica. "The joy in a house comes not from the building or its location, but from the love its residents have for each other. I assumed that with all the homes you've been in and out of, you'd have realized that."

Thalia's perfect complexion turned red as Veronica bestowed a cool smile on her.

"What...what are you suggesting?" asked Thalia.

"Nothing, my dear. Just that I know such a popular girl like you would be invited to a lot of places, and you'd have the opportunity to observe so many relationships and see what made those houses homes."

Thalia continued to glare. Veronica was in full control of every nuance in her own behavior, as well as everyone else's. Another sign of the difference between an average actor and a great one, Wren realized. Saffron watched wide-eyed, and Cal wrapped a comforting arm around her. Nicky was smart enough to stay out of the conversation.

"Wren has explained the house, and we now know how to make a family here," said Saffron.

Thalia decided to cut her losses. "We're still going out Saturday, Nicky—right?"

"Oh...Yes. Of course."

"Can I talk to you about what to wear?" asked Saffron. "I've never been to a place like that."

"Of course, dear. Happy to help." Half kindness, half condescension. But Saffron didn't seem to notice. Then Thalia turned to Veronica. "Are you going to hit the dance floor?"

"Thank you, but not really my scene," she said.

"Of course," said Thalia. She gave a sidelong glance at Wren, weighed her options, and went for it. "Anyway, from what I hear, you have a boyfriend—someone of an appropriate age."

Wren felt almost dizzy. But if Thalia thought that would upset Veronica, she was wrong. The older woman just came back with a smug smile. "Let's meet again in twenty-five years and see who wants to take you out to dinner."

Cal cut it off then and there. "Uh...Nicky, I think they want you and Veronica back on the set now," he said, glancing at his watch. "A few more hours of filming before we break for dinner."

Cal turned to Saffron. "I have a few things to organize. You can help."

"Oh, sure. Unless you need me, Wren?"

"You go with Cal." Hadley and Wren walked everyone downstairs. At the doorway, Saffron turned to Wren.

"Thank you," she said gravely. "I liked learning all that. It made me really think about the house and its people. I know we'll figure out the rest."

"Yes, Wren. Thanks," said Nicky. "I appreciate it. We both do. You've made me love this house even more, and your enthusiasm just grabs me. I'm thinking buying this house was the smartest thing I did and hiring you to fix it—well, that's a close second." He gave Saffron a squeeze. Veronica gave

Wren a wink—and they were gone.

"That was a nice compliment. But what the hell is going on here?" asked Wren after a few moments.

"Veronica is making a play for Nicky, but whether she really wants him or just likes yanking Thalia's chain—I don't know," said Hadley. "The thing is, Thalia is in a terrible position. She looked so unsure of herself, this renowned model jealous of a woman a quarter-century older than her. But she comes here early instead of meeting Nicky in the city for dinner to keep an eye on him."

"And Nicky? He's just...standing there." Hadley laughed.

"Oh yeah, that's a man for you. Some, like Nicky, are clueless. Others just find it easier to pretend they're clueless. Men like that. It's one of the reasons I'm glad I'm a lesbian." They both laughed.

"How did Thalia find out about Veronica and my father?"

"You can't keep things like that a secret, especially when it involves someone as famous as Veronica. If Thalia has found out, you can bet others have. Is this going to embarrass your father?"

"Nothing has ever embarrassed my father. And I am sure that if anyone in the office finds out, they'll have the good sense not to ask him about it."

"Hushed whispers in cubicles," said Hadley. " Meanwhile, let's not forget Saffron. Don't ask me to explain that. Even someone as oblivious as Nicky can't miss the Saffron-and-Cal show. Maybe Nicky just likes someone young like her sometimes, and she's happy enough with that, and Cal takes up the slack."

Wren shook her head. "Frankly, I think it's something else. This odd daddy-daughter thing they have...." Wren sighed. "'Set me as a seal upon thine heart, As a seal upon thine arm: For love is strong as death; Jealousy is cruel as the grave.' The Song of Solomon. There is something here. You see things I don't always understand. Both Veronica and Thalia look down on Saffron, but they don't seem jealous of her. Or am I wrong?"

"You're right. For some reason, they don't consider her a threat. I don't know—film people are very odd. I just don't get it."

"Ockham's Razor," said Wren.

"You lost me," said Hadley.

"William of Ockham was a medieval philosopher who developed a principle now called Ockham's Razor, which basically says the simplest solution is usually the right one. I don't have all the answers, but I think that's what we have to use here."

Hadley kissed her. "Is it any wonder I love you?"

Chapter Eleven

Right before they planned to leave, Wren looked at herself in the emerald-green jumper Hadley had chosen for her. It went all the way up to her neck, but left her back and shoulders bare. Hadley came behind her in a short crimson dress.

"You're trying to figure out how you look," said Hadley.

"Yes."

"Don't worry—you're beautiful. If I do say so myself, I chose perfectly for you."

"I accept that. But why can't I see it? I see it in houses, even in people. I know shape and color. But not for myself. Why is that?"

"As an armchair psychologist, I'll say it's because you have confidence in your work but not in yourself."

Wren turned her eyes on Hadley and remembered the first time she met her: jealous of how lovely and confident she was. Again, Hadley knew what she was thinking.

"I'm not as cool as you imagine. I haven't been to a club like this since getting sober. I once set up a private party there before we met, but after scoping it out, I left it to my staff to run things so I wouldn't be tempted. I'm only risking it because you're with me."

"Fair enough. If I feel overwhelmed by the scene and you start craving a drink, we'll come back here, make some cocoa and play Parcheesi."

They caught a cab to Steele Primus on the West Side, near the river, where the line was already wrapped around the block. It was the only sign of life there, among the dark office buildings and shuttered coffee shops. A solid brick warehouse, Wren saw, built around 1900, designed to last for centuries. The streetlight showed in letters, carved over the archway, that it had belonged to "Aubrey Bros. & Co." She imagined workmen in heavy shirts and flat caps lining up in a cold dawn to the sound of a metal steam whistle.

Wren wondered about the Aubreys. What had happened to them? She was probably the only one who gave them a thought. Instead, everyone looked at the anachronistic neon sign—the same color as Hadley's dress. A throwback to Depression-era style, it spelled out "Steele Primus" with a blinking arrow pointing to the entrance. It was a handsome design—she'd give them that.

"Back to the past again?" asked Hadley.

"Sorry," said Wren. *I can't help it. It's where I feel comfortable.*

"I don't mind. But what do you think about tonight's crowd?"

"I would say...peacocks. No—parrots. Like a flock of beautiful tropical birds."

"Birds of a feather," said Hadley, linking her arm with Wren's.

"So, do we wait on that line?"

"Of course not! We're VIPs."

They went to the head of the line, and Wren saw everyone look at them skeptically: *are these women arrogant, or do they really know someone?*

Unlike the guests, the man at the door wore a black tee shirt, black jeans, and black boots with dark wraparound shades.

"We're here with Nicky Tallon," said Hadley. He checked his list.

"All right. He's got a private room on the third level."

Lost in examining the design, Wren was almost able to ignore the house band's pummeling beat from the floor. Above it, stainless-steel catwalks, stairs, and platforms crisscrossed the high-vaulted interior. Whoever did this knew what they were doing, Wren concluded, beautiful in itself and practical for socializing, dancing, and drinking.

"It's something, isn't it?" said Hadley. "I've seen a lot of places, but this is in its own class."

Wren almost stumbled several times as they walked up the stairs, she was so absorbed by the people. They were all so beautiful, with the lights showing their colors to full effect and glinting off the steel.

"What do you see, Little Bird? It's all new to you, isn't it?" They were now high enough above the band so they could talk.

"Not really. People don't change. People gather in expensive venues in expensive clothes to attract desirable partners. That ritual was old before this warehouse was even built."

Hadley gave her a wry look. "I love it when you get all professorial on me. But before this evening is over, we're hitting that dance floor, and I promise you'll see some things that are new."

They found the private room with another black-clad guard, who had been clearly alerted by his colleague downstairs and waved them in.

About two dozen people already filled the room. Dom Perignon bottles lined a bar staffed by a man wearing a teal tuxedo but no shirt and a woman in a dress that Wren found a marvel of engineering.

"So glad you came!" shouted Saffron from across the room. She ran to them or did the best imitation of running she could in her tightly fitted dress, an amazing concoction of coral sequins. Quite a change from her usual outfits.

"It's going to be fun. We're all going dancing downstairs in a bit," said Saffron. "Meanwhile, they have all kinds of things to eat and drink here."

Cal appeared at Saffron's elbow, dressed in a blazer over a tee shirt that matched her dress. He had a little plate of food for her and a champagne flute. She kissed him on the cheek.

"You are SO sweet." He beamed.

"Wren, Hadley—good to see you. Nicky was looking forward to seeing you here."

"Us in particular?" asked Hadley.

"Yes. This is really more Thalia's crowd. Nicky, as you know, is more into the folk scene."

"It's what we really like," said Saffron. "He's just so happy. We slip into a folk festival, just the two of us. He likes when I play for him, the real old stuff, the classics. It reminds us of home, and that's important." She looked serious about that. Cal gave her a quick squeeze.

"Anyway, he and Thalia are just talking to some people," he said. "Can I get you ladies anything meanwhile?" He left to get them drinks.

"Nicky likes us, it seems," said Wren making it a half-question.

"Oh yeah, he thinks you two are great, and he loved that talk you gave, Wren. And you two are not, you know, *all over* him, and you both really love the house while a lot of the Hollywood crowd makes fun of him."

"Why?" asked Wren. "I know Thalia finds it boring, and Beebee disapproved, but does everyone feel that way?"

Saffron wrinkled her nose. "I think they think it's too far away, you know, from people. They want Nicky where they can find him all the time."

Wren nodded. "You know, every time I speak with him, I realize that he may not be sophisticated, but he's smart and authentic. I told him we could build a helipad on the island for copters to land. It wouldn't be that hard or expensive. He said no, he said he wanted boats to be the only way to get there. He has a vision of what he wants. That's rare and admirable."

"I know," said Saffron. "That's why I love him." Wren knew then just how right she was about Nicky and Saffron.

Cal came back with champagne for Wren and ginger ale for Hadley.

"These things are so good—what are they called, again?"

"Blinis," said Hadley. "These are fancy ones—with caviar."

"They're originally Russian," said Wren. "Captain Turnbull probably knew them from his Russian trading partners. And I'm not a culinary historian, but I bet in his day, shrimp were available from New York harbor."

"That's so great! Hadley, could you make food like this in our island house? It'll be just you and Wren, and me and Cal and Thalia and Nicky."

"Blinis and jumbo shrimp? That's not hard. You just need money. I can do some great things in the kitchen Wren has planned. Stews in winter. Barbecue in the summer."

Wren could just see Nicky and Thalia in a knot of people at the far end of the room, Thalia was half-hidden by Nicky, but Wren could see her face, stunning in its animation. She was beautiful—but more, there was something lavish about her, as if she were part of the design of the place. As

Wren had noted, buildings put their stamp on people and vice-versa.

Nicky, meanwhile, looked half-bored and half-confused.

Saffron followed Wren's eyes.

"I know. I wish Nicky would come here, and then we'll all go downstairs."

"Are those business associates or friends?" asked Wren.

"At this level, there's a thin line between the two," said Hadley.

Cal laughed. "You got that right! They're people Thalia told me to add to the list. They're influencers of one kind or another. People who know everyone. They can do Nicky a lot of good." Wren didn't know a lot about Hollywood, but she did know Nicky was forty. Even with his looks, he couldn't do those youthful roles forever. He'd need something to take him to the next stage.

Unless he wanted to chuck it all and retire to an island for the rest of his life. He'd have the money—Zach Landau, his wily advisor, would've taken care of that.

It seemed that Thalia decided it was time to move on and led Nicky away. As they crossed the room, Wren saw Thalia was wearing the same dress as Saffron. Hadley squeezed Wren's hand and raised an eyebrow. *How the hell had that happened?*

Wren's knowledge of ladies' fashions only went as far as the Gilded Age, but even she could tell what a mistake the pairing was. Although the two women were both fair-skinned and blond-haired, the similarities ended there. The dress was a perfect fit for Thalia's long, lean frame, and she knew how to walk while wearing it. It was not an ideal dress for Saffron to start with, but when she stood next to Thalia, she looked almost ridiculous. Even though Saffron was pretty, she was half a foot shorter than Thalia and too thick around the waist to carry that off.

As Saffron gave Thalia the obligatory hug, Hadley whispered to Wren. "Thalia did this to humiliate Saffron. And it's working."

Maybe it was working from Thalia's viewpoint, but Saffron looked delighted.

"Look at us, practically twins," said Saffron with a giggle.

"Yes, my ladies look lovely," said Nicky. He looked fondly from one to the other. And Cal gazed with near worship at the transformed Saffron.

A man with a big camera slipped into their group. "Sorry, Nicky. Just a couple of shots."

He sighed. "All right. But fast."

"Me too!" said Saffron. "I want a picture of me in my new dress."

The photographer led them across the room to an empty spot.

"Cal, you're going to behave tonight with Saffron, okay," said Thalia. He turned a little red. The boss's girlfriend was not someone he could tell to go to hell.

"No need to worry," he said, forcing a smile. "And Saffron is an adult."

That was debatable, thought Wren.

Thalia laughed. "I'm not worried about that. I meant don't embarrass yourself by spending the evening pawing her. I'm sure you're incapable of seducing her. She's not the sharpest knife in the drawer, but I think even she knows she can do better than you. Still, there are some pretty waitresses here who might find a fellow servant attractive."

Cal looked furious as he stared at Thalia with her patronizing smile.

"I'll see if they want a drink before they head downstairs," he said and stepped away.

"He needs a talking to," said Thalia. "They *both* need a talking to." She turned to Wren and Hadley. "Look, I know you think I'm awful. I probably am. Think of it as tough love. They chose this world, and they have to learn to live in it. You don't know what kind of mess they're going to get themselves into if they don't behave, and Cal will thank me later for keeping him on the straight and narrow. Anyway, in my defense, Saffron copying my clothes was not my idea. I wouldn't humiliate another woman that way. She insisted. What can you do?"

Wren and Hadley didn't know what to say, so they stayed in uncomfortable silence until Saffron came back.

"Let's dance," said Saffron, and she grabbed Cal by the hand. Thalia just looked at them and shook her head.

Hadley caught Thalia's eye.

"By the way, I saw who you were talking to earlier. You have some impressive friends," she said. Thalia gave her a brilliant smile. "And you'd like them to become your friends too? Let's talk, sweetheart." It made sense. Those influencers could be important new clients for Hadley.

Thalia reached out for Hadley, and the two women headed out, arms around each other. As they left, Thalia looked over her shoulder at Wren. "Don't worry. I promise not to seduce your girlfriend," she said.

"And I promise not to seduce your boyfriend," said Wren. Thalia burst out laughing.

"Oh, Wren, you are *too much!* Nicky, watch yourself around this one." Hadley gave Wren a quick thumb's up, and they were off. Wren was left with Nicky.

"Looks like you're stuck with me," said Nicky.

"There are millions of women who would love being stuck with you," she said. Nicky laughed.

"Oh yeah. But you're not one of them. I don't mean it like that, you know, it's because you're in love with Hadley, anyone can see that. I know the jokes they make. Maybe I'm not the smartest person in the room, but I can see that what you two have is real." She didn't know what to say. *Oh yeah, and I was one of those who thought you were dim.* "Anyway, you're smart, and you've probably guessed this isn't my scene. I don't think it's yours, either." He made no move to follow the rest of the party.

"You like folk music, I understand," said Wren, trying to mirror the easy way her father connected with clients.

"Oh yeah, that's what really gets me excited—me and Saffron. I just hear those tunes...." He grinned and shook his head.

"I'm not a musician myself. But I can tell Saffron is very talented. We like her playing and singing. I envy you getting to hear her so much."

"Thank you, Wren. Thank you very much. It is...very nice." He seemed almost embarrassed. "Anyway, come on, we'll dance downstairs, and you can be in all the gossip columns tomorrow."

It was already past Wren's usual bedtime, so she wasn't thinking as clearly as usual, and the champagne had quickly gone to her head. Which meant she was in a pliable frame of mind for the dance floor. Her beautiful, extroverted mother had encouraged Wren to at least try a middle school dance, and that had been her last attempt at anything more modern than the foxtrot.

At least she had better company now on the floor: a movie star, a supermodel, and best of all, Hadley, who glowed in her cherry-red dress.

She spared a look for Saffron and Cal. The dress made no difference—she looked like a little girl at a party with cake and lemonade. And Cal...he was in love. Nicky knew about her and Hadley. He must've figured it out about Cal and Saffron. He didn't look like he cared, but maybe he was a better actor than Wren had given him credit for.

Wren danced with no sense of time. More people joined them, and Wren soon lost track of everyone except Hadley. The musical noise, with its demanding beat, bothered her at first but then numbed her. Maybe that was the point. Self-consciousness disappeared, and she only saw all the colorful people and the lights reflecting off bracelets and rings and necklaces...

It took a while to realize she was getting tired.

A number ended, and Hadley leaned over. "I need something cold," she said. "And quiet." As more of Thalia's people joined them, the rest of their party disappeared into the crowd. Wren, by this point, was ready for something cold and quiet too. They climbed through the jungle gym back to the private room. Only a few people were still there, some of the film set who were finding the Veuve Clicquot and nova lox more appetizing than the dance floor. Wren didn't blame them.

Hadley got a ginger ale and Wren more champagne, and they sat at a table in a corner.

"Everyone was trying to get into Nicky's golden circle," said Hadley. "But it was really just about Saffron and Thalia."

"I'm thinking we may have this wrong. That the three of them are not... what's the word I'm looking for...*relating* to each other the way we think."

Hadley's eyes got wide. "Oh, Little Bird, are you saying that Saffron and Thalia are the real couple here, after all, like Lieutenant Howard said? Could be, but again, my highly tuned gaydar isn't picking that up."

Wren laughed. "No. I don't think that's it, either. I can't get my mind around them, though. Something is binding them together. And Veronica seems pretty tight with Nicky, although she didn't come tonight. Events like this wouldn't show her at her best. Anyway, I have a feeling that these relationships aren't really...sordid."

"Sordid! What a great word. Maybe you're right."

"Okay, I'm an old-fashioned girl. You've always known that about me."

"Yes, but you continue to surprise me. Tonight, I found out you're more of a disco queen than I imagined," said Hadley.

"You must love me very much to say that."

"I do," said Hadley. "But still, you looked good out there. You actually seemed happy we came."

"It's a new experience, and there's something to be said for those. But how about you? This is something of a step into the past for you?"

Hadley sighed, and looked a little sad, a rare expression for her. "It may not have been the best idea. There are...I'm having a little trouble separating the dancing from the rest of the evenings."

"And here I am, drinking champagne in front of you. I'm sorry—"

"No, I never drank champagne. My choice was an exciting mix of Absolut vodka and cocaine, and it was amazing, Little Bird. I was the Empress of the Universe, and my realm was more beautiful than anything even you could imagine. Until it wasn't. Until I woke face down on the floor of the club restroom or in a stranger's bed, and I dragged myself through the next day until I could do it again, until it was almost too late. But it's hard. It's hard to be here and not go there just one more time. If it weren't for you..." She looked a little shyly at Wren. "Let's go home."

"Yes. Let's go home."

They picked up their bags, and each grabbed a blini for the road.

"Thalia was coked up," said Hadley.

"Really? Did you see her actually do it?"

"No. I didn't have to. Believe me, after all this time, I know the signs. And so were most of her friends. But not Nicky or Saffron."

Wren was mulling over that as they left the room. She suddenly wanted to be outside again. The dance floor was still going strong, and the "parrots" were swaying, drinking, and conducting romances at the various levels, as the waving lights caught them and moved on.

Wren's eye missed no detail, and she caught something odd across the room. On one of the levels, a figure was flat out, and people were beginning to gather around. Every time the lights hit the form, she caught flashes off the coral sequins on a body that wasn't moving.

Chapter Twelve

At least they still had the room, and all the private guests who hadn't already left were there, either sitting alone or quietly talking in small groups. The attorney/manager Zachery Landau showed up. Even in the middle of the night, he was immaculate in a jacket and tie. He barely acknowledged Wren and Hadley and just accompanied his client to the office where Lt. Howard was questioning everyone.

Someone had brought coffee in, and there was still plenty of food, but Wren couldn't bring herself to even look at it. She had made herself as comfortable as possible on a black leather loveseat, with Hadley half sleeping on her shoulder.

Wren had first felt a little guilty, as if she could've done something to prevent it, but even Nicky, with his wealth and the NYPD with its resources, couldn't stop this. She had read some Nero Wolfe detective books. She so envied him: imagine creating a perfect brownstone devoted to one's own comfort and then never leaving it because it was, in fact, perfect! In one story, Wolfe said he never took jobs guaranteeing anyone's safety because if someone wanted to kill someone else badly enough, they would succeed no matter what precautions were taken. And that's what happened here.

Or so it seemed.

Eventually, a uniformed officer brought back Nicky, Saffron, and Zachery. Nicky and Zachery headed to a table in the far corner, but Saffron threw herself at Wren. Her face was blotchy with tears and a runny nose, her makeup was smeared, and she looked more than ever like a little child. Wren looked over her shoulder to Nicky, who flashed her a look of gratitude, then turned back to Zachery. *For God's sake, I was hired as an architect, not a nanny.*

She looked for Cal, but he was either being questioned himself or running an errand for Nicky.

Hadley fetched a cup of heavily sugared chamomile tea. "Have this, sweetie." Wren got a tissue from her bag and cleaned her up a bit while she drank.

"Th—, th—, thank you," she said.

"Cal and I stepped away to rest, and he was going to get me a drink, and then I saw Thalia on the landing. I ran—but it was too late..." and a fresh round of crying.

"Did you see her fall?" asked Wren. Saffron shook her head.

"No, I just saw her body—broken." And more wails. Hadley coaxed her to finish the tea, and then Saffron tucked her head into Wren's neck. "She was my best friend. We were going to live together in the house, all of us."

Yes, I know, thought Wren. *I know.*

Saffron suddenly looked thoughtful. "Wren—could we bury Thalia on the island? It would be like she was there with us."

"We'll have to see. But even if not, we can arrange for some sort of memorial marker."

"Oh, like maybe for Captain Turnbull too, like we're all part of the family."

Wren was saved from answering by Cal's arrival, getting what was no doubt a much-desired chance to comfort her.

"It's okay; let's go to Nicky now. Mr. Landau is going to talk to us again." She gave a final sniff and nodded, and walked across the room.

"Nicky wanted me to tell you how much he appreciates the two of you helping," he said. And then he followed Saffron to Zachery's table.

"I wonder if Nicky really thanked us. Or if Cal just added that. A really good assistant would know to do that. And I think Cal is really good," said Hadley.

"He's obsessed with Saffron."

"Little Bird, that's the way men are. He could have a Ph.D. in physics from Harvard, and he'd still be goofy over that girl. I'm still trying to figure it out, though. You know, Saffron is probably only about twenty, and Thalia was maybe twenty-five. And yet it was like mother and daughter."

"Yeah. She said Thalia was a friend, but the mourning seemed maternal. And what is Nicky in all of this?"

"He seems like a pretty simple guy. I've seen some of his movies, and with all due respect, he's not a good enough actor to be faking that."

"But Veronica Selwyn could fake anything," said Wren.

"Are you accusing her of something? My love, you may not be seeing her clearly. And she wasn't even here tonight."

"Probably another evening with my father," Wren muttered. "And who knows? She could've sneaked in."

Hadley just kissed her.

A uniformed officer entered the room. "Ms. Vanderwerf? Ms. Fontaine? The lieutenant would like to see you."

They followed him along the now-empty catwalks downstairs to a hidden door off the dance floor.

It was the management room, a striking contrast to the intensely designed club, as plain and functional as an accounting office. The only difference was a wall of monitors where cameras scanned the club.

"Let's get the basics out of the way. Again, you two are my outsiders, the ones I can hopefully rely on. No one seems to have seen anything. Have you?"

"No," said Wren. "We were on the dance floor, but quickly lost track of the rest of the party and then went back to the private room."

The lieutenant sighed and pointed to the monitors. "Everything here is taped. Here—let me load it again." A police technician sitting behind her pressed a few buttons to call up images of Thalia's last moments. "It's a funny corner there—people looked out at the band or DJ and dance floor, but wide enough for someone to get pushed. But we can't see who."

"It's brilliant," said Wren before thinking. *Did I say that out loud?*

The lieutenant blinked. "Excuse me?"

"Whoever designed this place is a genius."

"I thought you specialized in houses."

"I do. I know virtually nothing about clubs. But I know what the purpose of this place is. Every building has a purpose—a home, an office building, a dormitory, a garage. This place is for dancing, and meeting, and…hooking up. This design, with the platforms and stairs and landings, makes all of that easy, and that bright No. 7 finish, on the stainless steel, with the flashing lights—the imagery of all those well-dressed people. Design and structure, working in perfect harmony. I'd love to meet whoever did this place."

She stopped, realizing Hadley and the lieutenant were staring at her.

"Wow," said Howard. "Just…wow. Thanks for the lesson. But if we could get back to what happened—"

"But that's it. That platform is extra wide. Everyone would be by the railing looking down. Thalia was behind them, easy to push down the double-wide stairs."

The lieutenant nodded. "Okay. I see what you're saying. But why was that platform extra wide?"

"I can't tell you that," said Wren. "Maybe for…romantic liaisons?" She heard herself sounding like a spinster librarian.

"Oooh, I like that," said Howard, grinning.

"Or a semi-private place for coke," offered Hadley.

"Excuse me…" said the lieutenant.

"Candy, Florida snow, white girl—you know, cocaine —"

"Yes, I know what coke is. As apparently do you." She fixed an eye on Hadley, who shrugged.

"I was another person," she said.

"Uh-huh. Anyway, Wren—they'd design a special place for that?" Now, Wren shrugged.

"I told you this is not my field of expertise. But whoever designed this probably knew a whole lot more about how these places are used than I do."

"So whoever killed Thalia by pushing her down the stairs was very clever. Or very lucky."

"Or very unlucky," said Wren. "Was someone trying to kill Thalia? Or Saffron? Beebee Jenkins was killed with the same coffee Saffron likes. The cocktail of the same kind Saffron was drinking poisoned the dishwasher at the dinner. And Saffron and Thalia dressed alike. Someone could keep getting it wrong."

"Is this more architecture insight?" asked Howard.

"Architects are concerned with patterns," said Wren.

"The two women are hardly built alike."

"But the same coloring and clothes. And with the lights flashing off the No. 7 finish—"

"Yeah, you said that. What is No. 7 finish?"

"Everything here is stainless steel, and there are about half a dozen ways to finish it. No. 7 is glossy, but you can go even further—"

"Thank you, I get it," said Howard. "Blinded by the light. Pushing the wrong woman down the stairs. We'll be checking for fentanyl, but you were all warned, so the murderer—and that's assuming this is all part of the same crime—had to turn to something else. Christ. All right—one more thing. They keep telling me they're all friends—Nicky, Cal, Thalia, and Saffron, even if Cal is an employee. What kind of Hollywood thing is this—Hadley, I'm guessing this is your area of expertise."

"Sorry, all I can tell you is that there's a lot of gossip on the set. So if anyone knows more details, they're keeping it to themselves."

"It's a family," said Wren. "People do that, sometimes. They form a family without blood ties or marriage licenses. People have been doing that for centuries all over. Adoption in ancient Rome—"

"Oh, an architect AND a historian," said the lieutenant. Wren stopped. It was like being in middle school all over again. "Let's get a little deeper here. None of the film people are going to tell me, so do you have any idea of what's going on behind closed doors?"

"We never know what's going on behind anyone's closed doors," said Wren. Once again, Howard just stared. Hadley reached over and squeezed Wren's hand.

"Okay then. Let's leave that alone. I agree this could be about trying to kill Saffron," said Howard. "But you're so into patterns, Ms. Architect. Maybe someone is trying their own murder, piggybacking on the Saffron attempts, in the hope it will be hidden. It could be a lot more complicated." She sighed. "All right then. Thanks for your time. You can go."

Wren was never as grateful to be outside again, even if the neighborhood in the gray pre-dawn looked scruffy. Cops were hanging around, subject to the curious glances of the few people who had to go to or from work that early on a Sunday. She felt a little ridiculous in her party clothes, never imagining she'd be one of *those* people coming home with the sun after a night of partying.

"Little Bird...how much champagne did you have?"

"A lot, I think. It was extraordinary, and I had...a lot. It was that obvious?" She smiled shyly.

"You went on quite a tear with the lieutenant."

"I'm sorry—"

"Don't apologize. You were amazing."

"I learned a long time ago not to talk so much. At least I thought I had."

"I wish you would unlearn it. And we both know you don't need three hundred dollar bottles of Veuve Clicquot to get there. Now, I don't think these nice men in blue will give us a ride, so let's hope we can get an Uber home."

It would be a fifteen-minute wait, and they watched the Manhattan sky get lighter.

"Did you really mean it when you said it was about Saffron? That it was three unlucky screw-ups to kill her?" asked Hadley.

"I said I saw a pattern," said Wren. "But Lieutenant Howard had a very good point about someone hiding the killing of Thalia as if it were part of the Saffron attempt. Saffron was the one thing in common each time, but it's not out of line to think that we're dealing with more than one clever killer, as much as I hate to think that. But Howard will learn a lot more than we do."

"I'm sorry about Thalia. I didn't know her well, and she wasn't the warmest person, but Saffron seemed to like her."

"Thalia told us the copycat dress was Saffron's idea, not hers. I'd like to think that Thalia let Saffron dress like her because it made her happy, even if it wasn't right for her." Wren smiled. "Maybe Thalia was just Thalia because she was never allowed to eat."

"You may be right," said Hadley.

What she really needed, actually, was to stop drawing conclusions on no sleep and a champagne-fogged brain. She and Hadley would sleep and recover, and then it would be back to work.

Wren knew Saffron would be all over her now, fragile as ever and seriously broken, even while someone tried to kill her for no obvious reason. But it started the day they looked at the home. It seemed silly—Nicky and his entourage could not have had any connection to Turnbull House before Nicky decided to live his dreams there. Still, as Wren had said before, a great house would put its stamp on people, and that would happen then as now. A look at Captain Turnbull's mystery would give Saffron a purpose and let Wren and Hadley keep an eye on her. More and more, she could see a single thread that led through two hundred years of the house's history.

Chapter Thirteen

Thalia didn't get a burial on the island. She had family in Ohio, and after the medical examiner was done with her, Nicky took care of sending her body back home. Howard and her people spoke to everyone again and again, but in the end, the verdict was accidental death. In the press of bodies, with the flashing lights, no one had seen anything. But for the gossip bloggers, it became open season on Nicky, his friends, and the whole production.

Wren scrolled through a few of them, then shook her head and got back to work. That was just Hollywood. Her feelings were for Saffron, who seemed crushed. Whether delighted or upset, Saffron had always been irrepressible, but over the next few days, she seemed listless.

Hadley carried plates to where Wren was working in the oval room.

"I was just coming down," said Wren. "But thank you, that was very sweet."

"I thought you might like a little quiet, away from them all. Bobby and his crew love it, though, rubbing shoulders with the actors."

"Saffron still sulking?"

"Yes, our little elf is still down in the dumps."

"Do you think it's because she's lost her de facto big sister? Or has it dawned on her that maybe she was the killer's intended target?"

"I've been watching her, get a friendly word in when I can. She is upset, but I wouldn't say frightened. I don't see her making those connections."

"I see Cal is still courting her."

Hadley laughed. "'Courting!' What a Jane Austen word, Little Bird."

"Yes," said Wren, laughing. "It's this house. People don't *date* in houses like this. They *court*. Anyway, I watched them yesterday. There is something about them, something almost old-fashioned. He brings her the special juice she likes or flowers. It's silly, but also rather sweet. I think it's her, too. I'm guessing there was a piano here once, and one or both of the ladies played. That makes me think of Saffron's mandolin. She seems childlike, but that music is anything but. It's adult. Anyway, I have something for her. Bobby and I engaged an exhumations company—Thanatos Consultants. We've used them before, although not under such…unusual circumstances. They're coming today."

"You found the locations, you clever girl!"

"I think so. Thanatos has ground-penetrating radar, so we can be pretty sure before they start digging."

"Thanatos…that means 'death,' doesn't it?" asked Hadley.

"It does. He was a minor Greek god. His mother was Nyx, the night. Thanatos wasn't always bloodthirsty. He was sometimes seen as an almost kindly god, peacefully accompanying the dead to the afterlife. When this house was built, classical myths were popular. I'd like to think of Mrs. and Miss Turnbull—briefly Mrs. Llewelyn—getting quietly escorted to a better world." She shook her head. "It's the house. It's making me fanciful."

"But you keep saying how perfect this house is," said Hadley.

"Yes. Perfect and orderly. And there's something orderly about what is going on here, I think. But it's the house, really. Think about horror movies. They traditionally take place in gothic houses—so elaborate, so lavish. Out-of-control happenings in those over-the-top houses. Maybe it's silly—but an orderly house needs to have orderly murders. Houses put their stamps on people."

"On the Turnbulls?" asked Hadley.

"And on Saffron. And probably on Nicky, too."

In silent amusement, Hadley watched Wren look around the room, could see the gears turning inside her head.

* * *

Despite the company name, the staff of Thanatos seemed like a cheerful bunch, excited about the unusual task.

"So Wren, we're going back a while this time!" said a young man in a work shirt and jeans. "Our last job with you was that one on the Long Island estate, with the great-great-grandchildren in attendance. At least we knew where everyone was then."

"I'm putting you through your paces today. And I see you're dressed for the occasion," said Wren.

"Ha! I convinced Dad to let me ditch the suit for jeans and a tee, since there was no surviving family to impress."

Nicky, Veronica, and the rest of the cast were busy filming, and Hadley was supervising the food service, but Saffron showed up the moment the launch docked and was watching wide-eyed as the Thanatos team set up a lawnmower-like object. Cal stood next to her, holding her hand.

"Saffron, this is Dave Taylor. Dave, Saffron is representing Nicky Tallon."

"Pleasure to meet you, Saffron. We're going on an archaeological dig," said Dave.

"So…this thing finds bodies?" she asked, looking at the gadget.

"GPR—ground-penetrating radar. It sends signals into the ground that bounce back, letting us know there's something there. It has lots of uses, but today we're going to use it to find bodies. Wren told me you're looking for two to three bodies."

"Two women who lived here, and another man who was married to one of them and then murdered."

"Sounds like quite a story. So Wren, show us where we can start. Also, assuming we do find someone, you've made the necessary arrangements?"

"Yes. Dr. Erik Leopold, a friend from the medical examiner's office. He's excited about this too and will be here later today—I'm optimistic."

"Cool. Lead on!"

Wren tried to fight down doubt that she had picked the wrong spot, that she hadn't gone overboard in concluding on thin evidence that three people were buried on the island. But no…she was going to walk into this full of confidence just like her father would…

Her father. She still didn't want to go there.

Wren led them to a field just above the house. Bobby and two of his men were already there, setting up the mini-digger.

"We cleared the biggest shrubs and mowed to give you a clean field. A little out of our usual line of work, but variety is the spice of life, as mom used to say."

"Okay on the digger, but only if it's a deep grave. The end is going to have to be by hand," said Dave.

"Bobby and his men have a light touch," said Wren. She suddenly realized how excited she was about making a connection with the family who built this house. "Let's get to it. Let's find out what really happened here."

Dave turned on the machine. "Not to be a wet blanket, but this can take a couple of hours. I promise to call everyone before we dig up anything."

"I'll be at the house," said Wren. Bobby told Dave to give him a shout when he needed their help.

"Cal and I will stay," said Saffron. "I want to be here the second you find them."

Wren didn't think that Cal was as excited about it as she was, but the prospect of two hours with Saffron was enough for him.

Wren lost herself in the vague and strange connection between the Turnbulls and Nicky and his...family.

"Woolgathering?" She hadn't even heard anyone enter. Erik Leopold was smiling at her.

"It's the house. It's always the house," she said, laughing. "Good to see you again. Thanks for coming today."

"I wouldn't miss this for anything." He clapped his hands and rubbed them together. "Another historical mystery courtesy of Wren Fontaine. Have they found any bodies yet?"

"Not yet. But I'm hopeful. Where they're searching is the only logical place on the island. Meanwhile, if you want a tour while we're waiting—"

The tour would have to wait. Saffron came charging into the home.

"They found them! All three—"

But Wren cut her off with a wave of her hand. "No details. This is Dr.

Erik Leopold, who will examine them, and he doesn't want any backstory so he can see the bodies without any preconceived notions."

"Oh! Well, I want to hear what you say. You need to come *now*—Dave has already called Bobby." Bobby had been working at the other end of the house. "But I wanted to tell you myself—it's so exciting!"

Wren and Erik had to practically run to keep pace with Saffron.

"So you're a doctor who works with dead people?" Saffron asked.

"Yes, I'm a *forensic pathologist*. I try to figure out how people died."

"That's so great you could come. How do you know Wren?"

Erik smiled and gave a sidelong glance at Wren. "Do we tell her?" he asked.

"She already knows," Wren said. "Erik belongs to the same club Lavinia, and I do, where we celebrate past centuries."

"I think that is so cool."

Bobby was overseeing his men, digging a hole with the mini-digger. Thanatos was working with him, because of the difficulties of bringing over their own machines to the island.

"Something new for you?" asked Wren.

"There's always something new on a Fontaine project," Bobby said. "Anyway, it's kind of neat. I work on these old projects with you but don't usually think about the original owners. But with this place…I'm as caught up as you. Don't tell your father." They both laughed.

Dave stepped over to them. "Three bodies, close together," he said. Wren introduced him to Erik.

"Glad to meet you. I know you spend a lot of time on criminal cases, but even if there's one here, there's no one around to arrest," said Dave.

"I'm not a cop. In my line of work, it's the puzzle that's the thing," said Erik.

"And even if it's too late for an arrest, it's never too late for justice," said Wren. It came out heavier than she hoped for, and she suddenly felt everyone looking at her. She felt her face flush.

"You work with buildings. You take a long view," said Erik, rescuing her.

A few minutes later, Dave stopped the mini-digger, and they turned to shovels.

"Okay—we have something!" said one of the diggers.

"All right—steady boys," said Erik, and he and Dave scrambled into the pit to look at the bone sticking out of the dirt.

"They're just like *that*," said Saffron. "Not even in a coffin?"

"They've been in the ground for nearly two centuries," said Wren. "The simple wooden coffins they used then would've rotted a long time ago. In fact, even the bones should've dissolved after a decade or two. However, certain soils will preserve bones for centuries, and Dave and I agreed there was a good chance that's what happened here."

Dave and Erik were meticulous, gradually bringing the skeletons out of the dirt. Wren knew she should get back to work and return when they were done, but it was too fascinating to turn away.

The word had gone out, and everyone was gathering. Hadley sidled up to Wren and gestured to Nicky and Veronica, arm-in-arm. People would laugh at the age difference, which wasn't fair. It was less than the difference between Thalia and Nicky, but as everyone would say, the wrong direction. But they were a handsome couple. Visually, her more sophisticated look worked better with Nicky's classic face.

"Looks like your father has some competition, Little Bird," said Hadley with a giggle.

"I don't know what's worse—the thought of my father getting his heart broken or having to spend every Thanksgiving with Veronica as my stepmother."

Hadley giggled again.

Eventually, Erik and Dave had three skeletons laid out. Erik opened his leather case and removed a tape measure, calipers, and other tools.

"So what happens now?" whispered Saffron, mesmerized by what was going on.

"Dr. Leopold is a bit of a detective. He can tell all kinds of things by looking at bones."

Eventually, Erik looked up and seemed surprised at the audience—but not displeased. Wren knew he loved the attention.

"Okay! Ladies and gentlemen, mesdames and messieurs. I'm not a wizard. It takes some time to study these skeletons to make firm conclusions. But—" he paused for effect. "There are a few things I can give you now." He clambered out of the hole, and everyone gathered around. Saffron and Nicky especially looked very intent.

"Two of the skeletons were close together, and both are women."

"How can you tell?" asked Saffron.

"That's easy. Grown women have wider hips than men, for childbearing. One of them had at least one child—childbirth leaves pelvic scars. For now, I can tell you these women were likely fairly old. I see signs of arthritis in both of them. I'll need to look more at the teeth. Figuring out how they died is a little more complex. The woman with the child had a broken arm bone at some point—there's no way to tell how it happened for certain, but I'll look into that later. We need to keep in mind that pregnant women are more likely to fall as their body changes. There's certainly no sign of violent death in either of the women. Now the other body—that's a different story."

"That must be Jack," whispered Saffron.

"He was buried at a distance from the women. A man of middle years, who probably walked with a limp—he broke his leg at one point, and it healed badly. I can tell he was a big man—about six-foot-three and broad-shouldered. Not as old as the women when they died. And I don't think he died in his bed. He has a serious skull injury—not showing any sign of healing, so this wound was at time of death. I'll know more after a more complete examination."

"I— I don't understand," said Saffron. "It wasn't supposed to be the Captain who was murdered and buried here. It was supposed to be Jack."

"Who is Jack?"

"He was young, and he didn't have a limp," she said.

"Then this isn't Jack."

"But the song…I don't understand…." Cal put his arm around Saffron, but she suddenly ran and threw herself at Nicky.

"What the hell?" said Hadley. "When things get really bad, she goes back to the original boyfriend?" Nicky comforted her, but Veronica didn't look

130

upset or jealous. Instead, she was amused.

Wren let Nicky's entourage wander through her mind like chess pieces: Nicky and Thalia. Cal and Saffron. Veronica. How did they fit together? It was no easier than figuring out the Turnbulls.

"Abigail pulled a fast one on the coroner," Wren said. "She dressed the dead Captain in Jack's simple clothes so he could pass for Jack. Bedlow noted that the clothes didn't fit. Burying the Captain in his own clothes would've been a giveaway—they'd be too good for a servant. I wish I could've met Abigail," she said.

"Why her?" asked Hadley.

"She was the linchpin here. I think this is really her story. Maybe after Lavinia does more research, we'll know for sure."

"Okay. But why has our little elf gone back to Nicky? People like this have strange relationships."

"I know I'm obsessed, but someone—Abigail—was playing a game then. And someone is playing a game now. Never mind Abigail. I'm beginning to get a sense of Saffron."

"It's more my milieu, but even I can't figure this one out."

"Ockham's Razor," said Wren.

Chapter Fourteen

W ren thanked Dave and Erik for all their work. "You're geniuses," she said.

"This was a fun one, I have to admit," said Dave. I rarely get to work on remains this old. Anyway, glad we could help. If you want to reinter them here, of course, give us a call."

"I think we will," said Wren. "I can't see them anywhere else."

Erik hung back for a moment. "You know, I'm used to that level of emotion from the NYPD cases I work on, but not from supposed crimes that occurred during the Madison administration. What's up with your friend Saffron?"

"She's rather emotional. This is not what she expected."

"I can see that. You know, I was flown to England to consult when they found King Richard III's body in 2012. Even after half a millennium, people got emotional. Anyway, I'll roll up my sleeves and get right on this. Nicky Tallon is footing my bill and told me you're the chief contact point. You'll hear from me soon. Give my regards to Lavinia."

"He's right," said Wren to Hadley. "I am more comfortable in the past and with houses. But as my father keeps reminding me, every now and then, I have to work in the twenty-first century. You know, I could make a case that what's happening here is none of my business, but the safety on this job site is my business, and at the end of the day, there's some sort of connection here."

"What do you have up your sleeve, Little Bird?"

"Logic and order—just like this house. Do you think they're done filming for the day?"

"The light is going. I'm guessing so."

"Okay. Let's meet again in the Oval Room. You and me. Nicky, Saffron, Cal, and Veronica. I know at least one mystery we can end right now."

* * *

"Why am I not nervous?" asked Wren. Her eyes wandered around the oval room. Maybe the shape itself soothed her. Curved rooms were difficult to design—the proportions had to be flawless. But when they worked, the sense of natural shape provided a primordial calm. *Were we back in the womb?*

"Why should you be nervous?" asked Hadley.

"Because this is about people, and people make me nervous."

"It's not, Little Bird. It's about construction. It's about the way families are assembled, and you're super good at that, like the way houses are assembled. It's the *why* you always have trouble with."

"I think," said Wren slowly. "That as we know the *hows* we'll know the *whys*. I know how this house was built, such a perfectly ordered building for what seems to be a disordered family. And yet...there may be a sense of order here as well. It must've stamped its order on the family, if I can find it."

"'On the family?" asked Hadley. "Which family—the Turnbulls? Or Nicky and his entourage?"

Wren gave Hadley a kiss on the cheek as everyone filed in. They took seats in the varied furniture left in the room over the years. Nothing was original after all this time, mostly odd pieces from the 1930s to 1950s when it was last used. Saffron sat on a couch, flanked by Nicky and Cal. She had brought her mandolin. At least Cal had the grace not to touch Saffron so close to Nicky. Veronica sat down in a heavily frayed, easy chair. But she leaned back in it as if it were the best full-grain leather. She had a bottle of diet iced tea dangling from her right hand and a smile just this side of self-satisfied. Was she really that cool? Or was she acting? For someone as good as Veronica, it was a thin line.

"So—do we know more about the Turnbulls yet?" asked Saffron.

"Not yet. This is more about what's happening today." *She took a deep breath. Her father had to do this all the time, build a personal connection with clients, smooth things over when spouses fought over a project when they asked for something impossible. Keeping the whole thing on track could be a matter of psychology. As it was here.*

Her father. She looked at Veronica, watching her with that same smile. Let's not go there.

She turned to Hadley, who winked at her. "You have this, Little Bird."

"My business is this house, so you can make a case that your personal lives are not my concern. But the deaths around this project affect me and my ability to work here. Nicky—" She focused on him. He watched her for a moment, then looked down. No, he wasn't anywhere near being in the same class as Veronica. She had him, and he knew it. "I'm working with you and Saffron. I was led to believe she was your…partner. But that's not the case, is it? She's your daughter."

Nicky sighed and slowly nodded. Cal looked worried. Veronica arched an eyebrow and kept smiling. Hadley flashed Wren a thumbs up.

And Saffron giggled. "I knew she'd figure it out. Wren is just the *smartest*. I told you, didn't I? I *told* you she would figure it out."

"I'm not sure…" started Nicky. "I mean, I didn't know you needed to know that." If he had been more self-assured, he could've managed annoyance or even anger, but it just came out as lame.

"If I'm restoring a house for a family, I need to know about that family," said Wren. "The more honest you are with me, the better I am able to give you what you want."

Veronica was still smiling. *Wren imagined her thinking: you learned that from your father.*

"You're right," said Nicky. "I'm sorry. Zach—you know, my lawyer—said it was bound to come out, but the studio and the PR people wanted to keep it quiet as long as possible."

"Who knows?" asked Wren.

"Cal and Thalia have known early on," said Nicky. That showed why Thalia wasn't at all jealous and why Cal had no problem pursuing Saffron.

Of course, trying to date Nicky Tallon's daughter had its own problems. "I told Veronica more recently. And Zach said I had to tell the police, but they said they'd keep it quiet if possible."

"Everyone was bound to find out sooner or later," said Veronica. "I'm sure we can count on Wren and Hadley to be discreet, but this was beginning to look a little odd." Of course. Wren saw that Veronica was the only one who had the skill to manage such deception.

Saffron rested her head on her father's shoulder and closed her eyes.

"You might as well know the whole story. I was not...Saffron's mother and I were not long-term," he said, then quickly added. "I'm not excusing myself. I'm just saying. I didn't know she was pregnant when I left for L.A. Everyone said I could get some modeling work there. I never saw her again. She had Saffron, but it was not the best situation...anyway, she died when Saffron was one. She went from one relative to another, ignored and abused, eventually, the state took her, and she ended up in some godawful...I'm sorry...I just can't..."

He shook his head. Saffron looked up and decided to finish the story herself.

"Yes, it was absolutely terrible. But I don't like to think about it. I did have a picture of Nicky from my mom. It's like the Johnny Cash song, A Boy Named Sue: 'Well, I knew that snake was my own sweet dad, from a worn out picture that my mother had.' I didn't see a lot of movies or TV when I was little, but then I saw him in a movie, and I realized my father is Nicky Tallon." She beamed at Nicky.

"It's not my real name, you see," said Nicky.

"How did you get to Nicky? Women are probably always trying to meet him with one crazy story or another," said Hadley.

"Oh! I saw that right away. So I went to a lawyer. I had my mother's birth certificate and driver's license. We're from the same small town in Idaho. I think that at first, they were going to give me some money to go away, but I never had a family, not a real one. So eventually, we met with Zach, and he had me take a DNA test that proved I was Nicky's daughter."

I bet he did, thought Wren. "So when was this?"

"About two years ago," said Nicky. "That's when we started talking about a home. L.A. never felt like home to me. Or to us."

"Yes, I wanted a real home where we could be a family." She looked adoringly at Nicky.

"It was my mistake," said Nicky. "I never had much of a family either. This is going to be a new chance for us in this house that Wren is fixing up for us. A real house. Some land for ourselves."

Wren glanced at the group. The assistant wore a perfect mix of love and sympathy as he gazed at his beloved. Veronica was harder to interpret: Was that a playful smile? Hadley was looking at her, too—she would read her better.

Is this a new family? Mommy Veronica, Daddy Nicky, Daughter Saffron, and...son-in-law Cal? Well, why not? The actors were still in their costumes—they rather looked the part. And there were many stranger family situations out there.

"I'm glad it's all out now," said Nicky. Saffron smiled back at him. "Also, I want to tell everyone that Zach will be coming here to look things over, and he wants everyone to be assured he's arranging for extra security."

"Okay, but it's still my worksite. And I need to know what's going on here going forward," said Wren.

"Of course," said Nicky. "Anyway, I don't know what any of this is all about. The police don't know yet who killed Beebee. Or what happened at the restaurant. Or exactly what happened with Thalia. I can't imagine what it has to do with Saffron and her being my daughter." He stood. "We're done filming for the day. I want to go back to the hotel and have dinner. Come on, guys. I want to get out of this costume." He headed out the door. Cal took Saffron's hand and followed her father out. Veronica made no move to leave. She hadn't said anything, but Wren could see she had caught every syllable, every facial expression.

"You don't want to go back and change out of your costume, too?" asked Wren.

"I should. But I rather like these clothes. There's a simple elegance that makes them a lot more flattering than those monstrous Victorian get-ups I had to wear once. I hope the Regency makes a comeback. But the costume mistress is going to get anxious. Seriously, I hung back to say I'd like to talk to you two but didn't want to say so in front of everyone else. Just come to my trailer in half an hour or so, and we'll talk. I may not hear you knocking if I'm changing, so just walk right in. I can help you sort out some of this. See you ladies later."

Hadley and Wren sat alone in the oval room.

"What the hell," said Hadley eventually. "I'm trying to think what this changes. If anything. And how did you know, clever girl? This is Ockham's Razor, right?"

"Everyone was saying that they seemed like father and daughter, but they were overthinking it, as if Nicky has some sort of weird…fixation. It really was father and daughter." She smiled wryly. "I'm just a simple girl and see things simply—as I said, '*Mon innocence est ma forteresse.*' My innocence is my strength."

Hadley laughed. "Oh yes, you got it right. Now that you've uncovered this, it makes sense. The L.A. crowd likes to see Nicky as not very smart, but that's not it at all. In fact, he's down-to-earth and authentic. He related to Saffron as her father only because he was her father."

Girls and their fathers. Would she ever be able to look Veronica in the eye again?

Hadley finished a few tasks at the catering tent while Wren wrapped up things with Bobby for the day, and then they walked to the set together. At great trouble and expense, the film company had transported trailers on barges for the actors.

"It's a big deal who gets what on a film set," said Hadley. "As you can see, only Nicky and Veronica got private trailers. They're like little houses, really, on high-profile movies like this. You could actually live in one for a while, although in this case, they can go back to the hotel for the night. What? I know that look, Little Bird."

"These trailers, sleek, modern, and temporary. Right next to this house, enormous and classic, designed to last forever. And yet, they're all homes."

"I thought you'd look down on something as plebian as a trailer," said Hadley.

"Cottage or castle, each home is built for a purpose. I'm curious to see the inside. I wonder what it's like, living in a little home like that, even briefly. People put their stamp on homes—"

"—and homes put their stamps on people. How do you think these homes affected them?"

They knocked on Veronica's trailer. There was no answer, but she had said they could just walk in. Smooth jazz played quietly. Wren looked around—she had been right. Cunningly designed and surprisingly comfortable.

"I'd like to talk to whoever designed this," said Wren, but Hadley was already walking into the living room.

"Whoops," she heard her say. "So sorry—you did say we could just enter."

And then Veronica's musical laughter. "No apologies necessary. Just one of those things."

Wren stepped into the room with them. Veronica was on the couch, smoothing out her clothes, but looking completely cool. It was Nicky who looked awkward. He clumsily began buttoning his shirt.

"I have to...see you later," he said. He slipped by them, and they heard him exit the trailer.

"He's so sweet," said Veronica. "All that money and fame, and he's still just a farm boy. I rather admire that, actually."

"Sorry if we interrupted," said Wren. Veronica waved it away.

"Never mind. I'm just waiting for him to get up the courage to ask me to the prom. Okay, I know what you're thinking. Why me, when he could have someone like Thalia. A piece of advice from my mother: A beautiful woman fascinates a man, but a sympathetic one always gets him. Anyway, I like you ladies, and I don't want anything to interfere with his house project."

"Because you're hoping to live in it someday?" asked Wren. That startled Veronica for a moment, and Wren felt a little thrill of satisfaction at that.

"Ooh, good one. You're understated but sharp. I had that coming. It might be nice at that. But seriously, I like old houses too, and I'd hate to see this work interrupted. Look, I just wanted to give you some inside information. It can be hard if you're not one of us to figure us out. We can be like a family on a set. A dysfunctional family—" she laughed "—but a family nonetheless.

Look, I care for Nicky and Saffron. I want them kept safe. I think you two do as well, and that's why I'm talking to you." She looked at them closely to see if they understood her, believed her. Wren and Hadley nodded.

"Okay then. I had a feeling something was off with Nicky and Saffron. You create relationships on a stage, in front of cameras, and you begin to see what works and what doesn't. They didn't work—not as lovers. So I asked Nicky point-blank, and he told me. I wasn't upset. Saffron can be rather sweet and appreciated my taking her in hand."

"What about Thalia? Were you jealous of her?" asked Wren.

"Please. She wasn't going to last. Nicky isn't stupid, just simple, but Thalia was stupid. Actually, greedy *and* stupid, a terrible combination. I've known dozens of girls like her. God knows whom she upset, who killed her."

"But that's just it," said Wren. "Did someone want to kill Thalia? Or did they mean to kill Saffron? The police seem to be proceeding as if it's a murder. Or was it simply an accident?"

"Please. They hardly look alike," said Veronica.

"You weren't at Steele Primus," said Hadley. "They wore the same outfit, Saffron copying her father's glamorous girlfriend. And it was dark in there. Believe me, I know those places. You can't recognize anyone."

Veronica nodded. "I didn't know that, about the clothing. And I tend to avoid places like that. So maybe someone does indeed want to kill Saffron."

Wren jumped in. "She was drinking the same coffee as Beebee. The poisoned cocktail in the restaurant may have been meant for Saffron. And Saffron may have been the one who was meant to be pushed down the stairs."

"You're a detective, Wren?" asked Veronica.

"In a way. I assemble buildings. Each item in a home works together. And every item here is working together."

Veronica nodded. "You're quite a character yourself, Wren. When you're talking about architecture, it's like you're a different person."

Wren felt the heat rising to her face. "Did you just insult me?" Veronica laid a hand on her knee.

"Not at all. I like you. More than that, I admire you. You're a woman of passion. You know what you want."

"I know…right?" said Hadley. She and Veronica laughed, and Wren smiled. *Working with people…it was a learning process.*

"Wren, my dear, I know nothing about houses. But I know something about scripts. And a script where someone tries to kill a woman three times and keeps screwing up is a hell of a dark comedy. Our assassin is very clumsy or very unlucky."

"Or maybe," said Hadley. "Someone is watching out for her. What about Cal? He seems to worship her. Maybe he's protecting her without evening knowing who wants to kill her. Or he knows but can't prove it. I've watched him. I think he really does love her."

"Dear Cal," said Veronica. "He's always there, and like any good assistant, you don't really notice him until you need him. Yeah, I think you may be right. But another quote of my mother's: When a man worships the ground a woman walks on, it's because he knows her father owns the land. Being Nicky's son-in-law—but maybe I'm just cynical. I tend to agree; he really does care for her. And she seems to like him. Anyway, let's hope the police get somewhere. For now, the best we can do is keep an eye on Saffron."

"I suppose," said Wren.

"Meanwhile, you have the Turnbulls to unravel. That was quite a show this afternoon."

"That's going to be even harder," said Wren.

Veronica shook her head. "Families."

Chapter Fifteen

Hadley had brought home some leftovers from the set and reheated them for dinner that night.

"I want you to know," said Wren, hearing the formality in her own tone. "I heard back from Doris. Next Friday morning. She has some great places in lower Manhattan, cool neighborhoods, and convenient. I can't believe I'm going to live somewhere cool."

"Little Bird, you've always been cool. You were just so cool you didn't realize it."

* * *

The next day, Wren looked for any signs of change on the worksite. Actors wandered around the building when they weren't needed, and Hadley mixed among them during the shooting, but there were no signs that Saffron's parentage had become public. On the other hand, these were actors, and even the least of them were good at dissembling. *And even if they weren't, uncovering them would not be among my skills*, thought Wren.

She found Bobby. He was the most grounded person she knew, and talking with him would clear her head.

Nicky wanted everything in the house—the most modern heating, air conditioning, and lighting—and Wren was determined to give it to him without changing the beauty and character of the house.

"Design is your area," said Bobby. "Building is mine. And I'll tell you that this place was well-built. Not every old house is, but this one was. The best materials, top workmanship. You can easily tell the changes that were made over the years since it was built. They're second-rate. But the original construction—our Captain Turnbull made sure it was the best."

"How do you know it wasn't the architect, Mr. McComb, who insisted on the best?" she said with a smile. Bobby laughed.

"Good question! We have architects like your father, of course, who want to approve every nail."

"He lets his clients know up front that he isn't going to let them get away with anything but the best. Something that passes building codes won't necessarily pass his."

"Right," said Bobby. "But not all architects are like your father. I don't know about McComb, but I've seen plenty for whom just looking good is enough. So I'm guessing the Captain wanted something perfect. He must've been a tough character—the sea was no place for weaklings back then. He trusted his life to a well-built ship and trusted his family to a well-built home. My crew and I are doing our best to live up to it."

Wren laughed. "Bobby. I came to you because I was having fantasies about this place and the family who lived here, and I find you're just as captivated as I am. I saw you looking at those staircase newels. We're so fortunate they survived—so simple and yet so…perfect. Those moldings, again, a perfect simplicity. There is something very restful about them." She was aware Bobby was looking at her with a mix of amusement and admiration. "And don't get me started on the curves, the gentle arches over each doorway, the half-circles that top each window, and of course, the oval room." She took a breath. "I'm not religious, but seeing this house makes me feel that all is right with the world."

Bobby nodded. "Yeah, you're right. A house this old, a family so far removed from us—and yet, somehow so modern." He shook his head. "The movie people—that's another story. They come around when they have a break and peer in. But they look at it differently. Okay, maybe I'm being crazy now. I see how you look at a house and how your father looks at a house. The Fontaines see residences for people. The film people see a set." He shrugged, a little embarrassed. "Or so it seems to me."

"I think you're right. I wonder about Nicky, what he sees."

"Your father wonders about clients all the time. Why should you be any different?"

But not like this, thought Wren.

Bobby gave her a fatherly pat on her shoulder and got back to work. Wren headed down to the field by the water, where they had paused for lunch. Hadley was overseeing the food service, those large eyes taking in every morsel. Wren realized with some amusement that her girlfriend treated food the same way she and Bobby treated houses.

"You're the architect, the caterer's partner, right?" asked a teenaged girl, an extra in costume.

"Uh...yes," said Wren.

"She's a great cook. Everyone says so. I guess she cooks for you? You're lucky."

"I guess I am," said Wren, wondering why beautiful teenaged girls still had the ability to disconcert her.

The girl lowered her voice. "And she's so cute, too!"

The girl went off with her friends, leaving Wren shaking her head. Hadley made her way to Wren with two plates, and they found seats together at a small table.

"Talking to actresses? You looked alarmed."

"They're so much...poised," said Wren. I don't relate, as they say. I feel more in touch with the Turnbulls."

"Pat yourself on the back. You're the one who understood who Saffron was while the rest of us had put together all kinds of lurid scenarios."

"Like Freud said, sometimes a cigar is just a cigar."

"Mind if I join you, ladies?" It was Nicky's lawyer, Zachery Landau. He wasn't in his usual suit, but in a blue blazer over a polo shirt, with a perfectly folded pocket square.

"If you don't mind the nerd table," said Hadley.

"I'm an attorney with an estate practice," said Zachery. "The nerd table suits me fine."

"I thought you'd be wanting to rub shoulders with the glamorous actors," said Wren.

"Actors. That's right. I charge a mint for every minute I have to spend with them. Dear God. Anyway, I came out here to have a look at the set for myself. I've made some… arrangements to keep everyone safe, and I want to personally make sure they're in place. And also, I wanted to talk to you two."

"Ooh, I can guess about what," said Hadley.

"Yes, I found out Wren uncovered the secret. I'm impressed but not surprised. I knew it would come out, but the PR people wanted to hide it. I'm not going to ask you to sign any sort of papers, but as I represent Nicky—indeed, the Tallon family, I should say—I am asking you on their behalf to be discreet."

"Architects are used to discretion," said Wren.

"And chefs. I won't even tell you who puts ketchup on their eggs," said Hadley.

Zachery smiled. "Thanks—I appreciate it. The papers will get hold of it eventually, but for now, the fewer, the better. Actually, I'm glad you know. You two are interesting. With this crowd—" he waved his arm "—yet separate from them. Nicky rather likes you both. And Saffron absolutely adores you."

"She's a funny creature," said Hadley.

"Well put," said Zachery. "Did she tell you about her past? I won't break a confidence, but if she told you it was grim, she wasn't lying. We had to extricate her from a terrible situation. She didn't have much of a childhood. Nicky offered any counseling she wanted, but she said she was fine now that she was with family."

"I see she didn't want a clothes allowance either," said Hadley. "How much do orange high-tops cost?"

"You got that right," said Zachery. "We gave her a credit card, but she barely uses it. I know—all bills come through my office. My profession makes me cynical, so I expected a spending spree, a sports car, and couturier clothes, but all she seems to want is…Nicky."

"She wants this house," said Wren.

"That makes sense," said Zachery. "Her living conditions were horrendous for years."

"That's not it," said Wren. "I didn't say she wants a house, or even a nice house. She wants *this* house. This magnificent oddity."

Zachery raised an eyebrow. "I see what you're saying—she has an obsession with it. But you called it an 'oddity.' Are you saying it was a mistake to let him buy it?"

"Are *you* saying that 'oddity' is pejorative? This is a *magnificent* oddity," said Wren. "Here's what I think. Nicky likes the *idea* of this house, the old place on the private island. But I've watched Saffron watch this house, seen her eyes as I talked about it, and she really understands it. She has a connection with it. She truly loves it."

Zach seemed surprised at that, which pleased Wren more than she expected.

"You can tell that, just from looks?"

"My father and I know what it looks like when someone falls in love with a house," said Wren.

"What about you? What house have you fallen in love with?"

"I'm an oddity, too. I'm constant with people"—a quick glance at Hadley, who winked at her—"but I'm always in love with the latest house I'm working on."

Zachery laughed and stroked his chin. "I like that. It's useful to me. You try to understand houses. And even though my business is law and finance, I try to understand people. You've made me understand people better."

Wren toasted him with her lemonade. "So you're trying to keep your people safe. I want to keep this house, this worksite, safe. I wonder…." She hesitated. *No, go for it.* "Beebee Jenkins. Some sort of studio functionary who was killed the day we first looked at the house. Right before he died, he was arguing with Nicky about this house. I don't know how it all works—could he have somehow stopped Nicky? Or made it difficult for him?"

"Fair question," said Zach. "Beebee was somewhat low on the food chain. And no one could stop Nicky from doing anything he wanted. It wasn't just that Nicky is rich. Every one of his movies makes a fortune. That makes him powerful. They were nervous that he would hide himself away here. They want him where they can get at him. But I had told Nicky that. I advised him that they could scream, but if he wanted the house, he certainly could afford it, and no one could stop him. He wanted to make a home for Saffron. He wanted to be able to promise her that. So he did."

"Okay—you're telling me that, and I accept that," said Wren, "because I don't know anything about Hollywood. But who else doesn't? Who else might've killed him—assuming it was about the house?"

"I hate maligning the dead, but perhaps Thalia?" asked Hadley.

"Oh God, Thalia," said Zachery. "Women like her come with the territory. Is 'gold digger' still a politically correct term? You know how many wealthy older men I've had to protect from the Thalias of this world? And visa-versa."

"You don't want to think that Thalia really loved him, do you?" asked Wren with a smile.

"Do you?"

"I wouldn't know. I'm very bad at things like that, actually. Hadley is much better than I am."

"Ha! Let's just say she was very fond of him," said Hadley. "I know plenty of women who would take him if he was flat broke."

"Fair enough," said Zachery.

"But regardless of what she felt about Nicky," said Wren. "Would she want to kill Beebee? Was he harassing her? I have a feeling she knew how to take care of herself. She wouldn't have killed him over that."

"Or even if Nicky didn't believe Beebee could stop him, think of Cal," said Hadley. "He's devoted to Nicky and adores Saffron."

"I think he'd kill Beebee if he thought Beebee was threatening Nicky's dream of providing a house for himself and his daughter," said Wren. "He knew the importance of the house."

"And he did know everyone's drink orders—it would be easy for him," said Hadley.

"I could see that," said Zachery. "But I know Cal—he takes care of Nicky's life, so we work closely together. I don't see him going off the rails like that."

"But back to Thalia," said Hadley. "I don't see her killing for the house.

146

She didn't even seem to like it."

"It's true she didn't want to live here. Would Thalia have gone out of her mind with boredom here? Probably. And she knew that. But she loved the idea of being chatelaine—"

"I'm sorry—" said Zachery.

"Chatelaine. A special hook on a belt on which women would wear the keys of a house, and later, it came to mean the mistress of a great house. I sound like a professor giving a lecture—I'm sorry."

"You do. But don't apologize for that. You're saying Thalia would like the *idea* of being mistress of this house more than the reality. Have a few parties here in the summer, and that's it. Get herself interviewed with this place in the background. Is that right?"

"Exactly," said Wren.

"Rather like Nicky. You said he also liked the *idea* of this place."

"I wonder about that. But then, I do that with a lot of my clients. I work on very special houses, and I'm not sure if they all get the realities of residing in a living piece of art." Wren shrugged. "A relationship with a home is very personal."

"But then Thalia died, too," said Zachery. "Presumably murdered." He gave Wren a small smile and raised his eyebrow, daring her to have a theory.

"Beebee was killed to make sure Nicky had the house. Perhaps Thalia was killed to make sure he wouldn't have to share it with her."

"You mean dear Veronica?" asked Zachery.

"Oh, she could do it," said Hadley. "Do you think that she wanted Nicky that badly?"

"Not Nicky. This house," said Wren. "Does Veronica love Nicky? I don't know. But I think she's among those who appreciate this house."

Zachery laughed. "I love it, Wren! We toss around theories, and for you, it's never about love or hate but desire for this house."

Once again, she fought a blush. "It's the way I view things." She heard the defensiveness in her voice.

"No—don't apologize. I am very grateful for your insights. I see houses as just items on a balance sheet. But you see them differently, and that helps me."

"Helps you…how?" asked Wren.

"Same as you. Keep everyone safe. Look, we're not even sure of who was supposed to be killed. I'm sorry, but I'm a lawyer, and we have to look at things a dozen different ways. I know the police are considering the two deaths and one attempted poisoning as attempts on Saffron's life."

"It's the house again," said Wren. "I can't imagine anyone hating Saffron."

"Because you don't suffer from jealousy," said Hadley. "If someone was jealous of her position with Nicky."

"Jealous of her position as mistress of Turnbull House?" asked Zachery. "Back to the house? No, I'm not laughing at you. It started with the house." He stood. "Thanks to both of you. This lawyer has received an education. Oh, and one more thing." Zachery reached into his jacket pocket, pulled out an envelope, and handed it to Wren. "I work with a service that makes sure every single mention of my clients gets clipped and forwarded to my office. As you can imagine, we keep them pretty busy. A popular website that delights in Hollywood gossip had this. We printed it out for you. Pleasure spending time with both of you—and now I have to catch the next launch back."

Wren absently slapped the envelope against her palm and stared across the bay.

"Aren't you going to open it?" asked Hadley. "Maybe you're now being listed as 'architect to the stars.'"

"Do you think I'm crazy for thinking it's always about the house?" asked Wren.

Wren knew Hadley wouldn't just dismiss the question as silly. She would give it thought, and they sat in silence for a minute.

"You're the one who figured out who Saffron really was, Little Bird. You always say you don't know people, but you do. You just see them in a different context from the rest of the world."

Wren laughed. "I see them in the context of their homes."

"Why not? Nicky and Saffron, wanting a family home. You knew that. We don't know what's happening here yet, but if you say it's about the house,

I'm inclined to trust your intuition. Now, what's in the envelope?"

Wren pulled out a piece of paper. "Oh, God. My nightmare continues. 'Veronica Selwyn In Love Triangle. The veteran actress is still turning heads at age fifty. Her most recent conquest seems to be famous architect Ezra Fontaine, sixty. They've been seen together several times. But it's hard to pin down Veronica—married and divorced four times—and she has also been seen cozying up to new co-star Nicky Tallon. He may be ten years younger, but Veronica can be hard to resist. And here's the fun part: her boyfriend architect is renovating a classic mansion for Nicky! Will the two men get into a fight over her? We can't wait!'"

"Wow," said Hadley. "Just...wow." Then she started to snicker. "I'm sorry... so sorry. I can't help it." Guffaws poured out of her. "I can't stop imagining your father and Nicky getting into a fistfight."

Wren fought hard—but a moment later, she burst out laughing too.

Chapter Sixteen

E rik had said it was no problem meeting in the early evening and was prepared to share his findings on the bodies—Wren could only hope the skeletons would not lead to a fresh round of tears from Saffron.

So on the day he was ready, they caught a launch to Manhattan.

"Do you want to come too?" Saffron asked Nicky. He was leaning against the side of the launch, the breeze ruffling his perfect hair as Veronica cuddled against his shoulder.

"I'm guessing that Saffron is going to get a stepmother soon," whispered Hadley.

"Better her than me," said Wren.

Nicky glanced down at Veronica for a second. There was no mistaking the look in her eye: night on the town on Nicky's arm or a pathology lab.

"Thanks, sweetie, but Ronnie and I have…a studio thing." He looked embarrassed, but then turned to Cal. "But you go with Saffron. I won't need you tonight." His face lit up, and he grabbed Saffron's hand. "Keep an eye on her," said Nicky.

Saffron's limo waited for them right by the pier. The chauffeur looked around as they got into the car; the bulge of a gun was clear under his jacket. Nicky wasn't taking any chances with his daughter. The chauffeur drove them uptown, and Saffron looked eagerly out the window at the city. *It's still new and exciting to this country girl,* Wren realized.

The chauffeur saw them into the university building, where Erik greeted them.

"Just follow me. We're going to meet the freshly reassembled members of the Turnbull family. I'm going to give you my 'full-scale presentation,'" he said and waved away Wren's thanks as they walked down the hall. "You know I love talking. It's a funny thing, really. I was told in med school I had a good bedside manner. And then I go into pathology. Go figure." He led them into the examination room. Wren was pleased to see Saffron was not upset—just looked at the sheet-covered skeletons with wonder. With a showman's flourish, Erik pulled off the sheets: Brown-tinged skeletons on their backs.

"These are the Turnbulls?" asked Saffron.

"As far as we can tell," said Erik. "Skeletons don't come with name tags. As we say, in the science biz, they're *consistent* with being the Turnbulls."

Saffron didn't let go of Cal's hand but led him along as she wandered around the tables.

"This one is Verity Turnbull, the sister?" she asked.

"Yes. Good guess?" asked Erik.

"I don't know…she just seemed to be Verity," she said.

"This woman didn't have a child. Her bones show no sign of injury, although some arthritis. She was elderly when she died. Now, turn around—that woman appears to be Katya Turnbull—also elderly. She did have a child at some point. Also, certain skull shapes are consistent with certain ethnic backgrounds. You can never be completely sure, but her skull shape is indicative of being Russian. It's not a slam-dunk, but it seems likely. Now I do want to show you something…gather around kids."

They stood by Katya's skeleton. "As I said earlier, her arm was broken at some point, and it was many years before she died, because it healed nicely."

"Oh! Then it was true—her husband broke her arm," said Saffron. "I can't believe any man…" She looked down at her feet, and when she looked up again, her eyes were filled with tears. Cal put his arm around her and squeezed.

Erik, however, gave a triumphant smile. "Hold your tears a minute. I'm not done. Time for an anatomy lesson. This is where detective work comes in." He produced a telescoping pointer from his jacket pocket and extended it. "This is Mrs. Turnbull's forearm, which runs from the elbow to the wrist. Forearms have two bones—see where I'm pointing: The ulna is on the pinky side, and the radius is on the thumb side. I'm going to greatly simplify things here, but here's how it works in broad strokes. Wren—if I may?" Erik grabbed her right wrist and raised her arm, so her forearm was blocking her face. "I am very angry at you. You're in the kitchen. I pick up a nearby rolling pin and come at you. You block your face as I swing. I'm going to break your ulna, your outside bone. Thank you, Wren."

"Is that what happened to Katya?" asked Saffron, her eyes wide.

"In a word, no. Both ulnar bones are as perfect as the day she was born. But look at this…" He picked up his pointer. "Look closely. This is her radius, the inside bone. This is where it snapped and eventually healed. And it did so pretty well, considering the state of orthopedic medicine at the time. The thing is, it's much less likely that she was deliberately injured. Radial breaks are much more common in garden-variety falls. Did she fall while pregnant? Quite possibly. It can be awkward walking in your third trimester. The bottom line? I can't be one hundred percent sure, even with modern bodies, and lord knows all the ways there were to hurt yourself back then. But if I were testifying today, I'd say on the stand, I'd seen scores of broken arms over my career. The ulna are very often signs of battery. And the radial are almost always a fall. Whatever you may have heard, I am as certain as possible no one ever deliberately broke any bones in this woman's body."

"Oh!" said Saffron. "I'm glad, of course, no one hurt her, but we had heard a story that her husband had attacked her."

Erik shrugged. "Not every sign of abuse shows up in a bone. If we had a body to work on, I could probably tell you a lot more. But if someone told you the Captain had broken her bone, they were mistaken. Or lying. Anyway"—and he grinned—"I know a forensic psychiatrist. We'll see what she can tell you about how people thought two hundred years ago. Now, on to the third skeleton."

It was obvious, even at a quick glance, that the third skeleton was much larger than the first two.

"As I initially estimated, this man was six foot three. He was broad-chested—big all over. And getting back to broken bones, he had a limp, a broken leg that healed imperfectly. He'd probably get around okay, but it would be noticeable. He was not elderly, probably died in his middle years."

"So, it's the Captain," said Saffron.

"It would seem so. And now, we're going to look at his skull. It was smashed at the back. It's my belief it was the wound that killed him. It was something blunt and heavy, like a crowbar, which no doubt would've been easily accessible in a tool shed on the island. From the angle, it was probably someone reasonably close to him in height."

"So maybe Jack?" asked Wren.

"Do we know how tall Jack was? I can't reconstruct it exactly. All I can give you are ranges and probabilities, and that's after making some assumptions. My educated guess is that someone, five foot ten at the shortest, came behind him with something heavy and metal and killed him with one blow. All I can tell you is that unless one of the women sneaked up behind him on stilts, that leaves out the two ladies in there. They're both around five foot two."

"According to the Bedlow account, Jack was almost as tall as the Captain," said Wren. "But there's clearly a conspiracy here. Abigail lied to Bedlow—we know that much. The Captain didn't kill anyone and run away. He was killed. So let's say Jack wasn't killed. But if he really did marry the Captain's sister, Verity, why wasn't he buried with her? We can't even know if they really married. The three bodies—one of them murdered—is all we really know."

"Sorry I can't tell you anymore," said Erik.

"Don't apologize! This has been amazing," said Wren. "We know much more about the Turnbulls now. Isn't that right, Saffron?"

Saffron was tucked into Cal's shoulder, with a Madonna-like sadness on her pretty face.

"That beautiful house," she said. "That beautiful, beautiful house. What happened? Who lived there? Was it those women all by themselves? Why did Abigail lie? If Jack killed the Captain—what happened to him? Did he just run away and never see Verity again? And if the Captain didn't really hurt Katya, why did Jack kill him?"

"You sound like the detectives I work with," said Erik. "Anyway, they'd tell you not to assume. What if Katya had told the others the Captain had attacked her? Lawyers are always looking for a loophole. I can only show you what happened. What people said? Not my area."

"Oh, but Wren can figure it out. Right? We can make the house *right* again, okay?" She flew from Cal to Wren, who met Hadley's eye over the girl's head. Hadley gave her a wry smile.

"I guess we'll have to," said Wren. "Now, I think the good doctor would like to get home to dinner."

"If you don't mind. Monthly meeting with fellow pathologists. You should watch the lot of us carving a duck."

With more thanks for his quick and complete work, the four of them left. The chauffeur was waiting for them downstairs.

"Do you two have dinner plans?" asked Hadley. "I imagine the film dinner will run late. They always do, so Nicky won't be back for a while."

"I guess we'll just have something in the hotel," said Cal.

Wren looked at Hadley, smiled, and then spoke. "Maybe the four of us can find something a little more entertaining. Hotel restaurants are always dull."

"Absolutely! I know just the place," said Hadley. "The most stupendous Middle Eastern place—Salah's—fantastic Mediterranean food. Plate after plate of food, fresh pita bread, and their special blend of coffee. The owner knows me—we've worked together. Just let me call."

Saffron and Cal looked a little startled but said nothing as Hadley called. "Table for four...we'll be there in just a few minutes. Thanks!" She clicked off. "This'll be great. Baba ghanoush, tabooli, falafel, hummus, souvlaki."

Wren looked at the couple. Cal had been on the L.A. scene long enough to know what Hadley was talking about, but Saffron had no idea. Just as well. The girl could use something new.

Hadley gave the address to the chauffeur, uptown on Columbus.

"Wren—your friend Professor Lavinia said there was 'violence in love' at the house. She said we might figure it out later. Does that mean that someone was hurting Katya Turnbull? The Captain?"

"Like Erik said, we can't know," said Wren. "We weren't there. We can't go back in time. All we know is that no one broke Katya's arm. Was her husband cruel to her? Did he hurt her in other ways?"

"Who lied and why?" asked Hadley. "What did Jack and Abigail do? As servants, were they in it together? I keep thinking about how Jack married Verity, except that didn't seem to happen—or did it?"

"Something else we don't know," Wren said. Saffron frowned. "But I have some ideas. Let's have some food, and we can go over it."

Salah's was crowded as usual, with midtown business executives, well-heeled West Side matrons, and young bohemian types from uptown. Salah himself, round and beaming, came from behind the counter and gave Hadley a kiss on each cheek.

"So good to see you, my dear, you and your friends. We have a nice table in a corner where you can talk."

He personally showed them to the table and gave instructions to the waiter in Arabic.

"That's nice, to have so many friends," said Saffron. "We have lots of friends in California, but they're not like real friends, you know, just people who come in and out." Cal put his arm around her.

"It'll be okay. You'll see. We'll make a life and make friends. Look—Wren and Hadley are friends, and we'll make more friends. We'll have a real place in the house, right?" The neatly delivered sentence showed why he was such a good assistant for Nicky, smoothing the way for his boss. Now, he looked to Wren and Hadley for confirmation.

"Absolutely," said Wren. "I'm making the house perfect for you. Cal—if I understand you correctly, Nicky's California house is less a residence than a headquarters for the business that is Nicky. Is that correct?"

Cal looked with surprise at Wren. She had only thought of him as Nicky's shadow or Saffron's ardent suitor, but he must have something on the ball to manage such a job. She remembered how he had told off Beebee. He certainly had a nice sense of his position.

"Yes," he eventually said. "That's a very accurate description. I didn't realize you knew how things worked in L.A."

"I know nothing about how things work in L.A. But I know about homes and the way people use them, react to them, and think about them," said Wren. "You and Nicky—and I'm guessing you too, Cal—want a house just for family and friends. True friends; the people you trust."

"You do understand," said Saffron brightly. Cal seemed pleased by Saffron's cheeriness and gave her a kiss. Wren was amused, watching a man as sharp and shrewd as Cal turned inside out by a girl just out of her teens. *Am I that way with Hadley? And so what if I am?*

Hadley ordered for the table, and meanwhile, the waiters served everyone iced tea.

"I'm glad we're talking about homes," said Wren, looking to see if she had Saffron and Cal's attention. "Because although times change, patterns don't. Saffron—you say how important it is that we understand the house, so you can be comfortable there. I understand that. So let's keep the house in mind as we try to figure out what happened. We know the Captain was murdered. The most likely suspect is Jack."

"If the Captain was cruel to his wife, even if he didn't hurt her physically, and Jack was in love with Verity, he'd have a motive. In fact, he'd have several motives," said Hadley. "Solidify his place in the household, especially if the Captain didn't want a mere servant to marry his sister. And he'd save Katya from abuse. They'd all have a reason to keep quiet about it."

"That makes sense," said Wren. "But we're still left with what happened to Jack. Let's say we're right—Jack killed the Captain, and they lied to Coroner Bedlow."

"Why lie?" asked Saffron.

"People would care less about an important and wealthy man like the Captain killing a mere servant," said Wren. "But a servant killing his employer would be worth lying about. Especially if the motives came out—a forbidden marriage, an unhappy marriage, and access to the Captain's fortune. It would have been so easy to pretend he boarded a boat for the East and eventually put out word he died abroad. You couldn't easily check those things back then."

"But if Jack really loved Verity, where did he go?" said Saffron. "If he killed for her and then couldn't be with her?"

"We keep coming back to that," said Wren. "Especially since he might not even have had to run away. He was an unimportant man. If his work was on the island, he may never have gone into Manhattan or elsewhere on the mainland. The provisioning would not even be his responsibility. Wait a year, change his name. The whole crime would be forgotten. Probably only the island residents knew what he looked like. No reason to disappear. If he wanted to marry Verity, they could quietly do so upstate or out in New Jersey. So where is he?"

"If he stayed, why didn't we find him?" asked Hadley.

"I can't answer that one. But there's one person we keep forgetting. Abigail. She doesn't immediately appear to be part of the problem—like the secret spouses, Verity and Jack, or the abused wife, Katya. And yet, she's there. And, like I said at Lavinia's, she was probably a woman of some intelligence and character."

Saffron frowned. "But didn't we think that Abigail might've been jealous because she loved Jack, but Jack loved Verity?"

"Marrying into the Turnbulls would mean a softer life than marrying a fellow servant," said Hadley. "Money can be a powerful force in love."

Saffron frowned over that, but Wren watched Cal. He seemed very solicitous of Saffron, but was he also thinking of the money, the career advantages, to marrying the boss's daughter? He wasn't even thirty and must've had a lot on the ball to get his position. He no doubt didn't want to spend his whole life as Nicky's shadow.

Or am I wrong? He seems to really care for her, and even though she was sweet, being her partner was not without its challenges. And I think they look at each other the way Hadley looks at me. As far as I can tell. And the Turnbulls? If I couldn't figure out the modern couples, how can I figure out the Turnbulls....

"You're right about the money. But it's more than that. It's also about the house"— Hadley grinned—"I know, I always come back to that. But you see the house and what it does to us. It probably did the same thing to the Turnbulls. And whatever we want to think about the love triangle there, we don't know what happened to Jack, and that's the big unknown.

Think about it: if Jack had killed the Captain and run away, why wouldn't the women just turn him in? Why go through the elaborate charade?"

"I think," said Cal, slowly, "that although this is interesting, we really want to look to the future, to making a home for ourselves." He wrapped his arm around Saffron, and she smiled.

"Don't forget that there are modern crimes as well," said Wren. "All of this is centered on your new home."

"Oh, that's nothing," said Cal, waving it away. "I mean, no disrespect to the dead, but you wouldn't believe the weird and crazy messages we get, the things posted about Nicky on social media. Who knows what this is all about? They'll probably find out it's some crazy stalker."

The food arrived, and Saffron looked at it, not knowing where to start.

"This is falafel, a chickpea mash that's deep fried. You have it with this tahini sauce made from sesame seeds and lemon juice. Ooh…and this is Bulgur, a grain salad I'm sure you haven't had before. Do you like eggplant? This is baba ganoush…."

Saffron showed a genuine curiosity in all of it and seemed to enjoy everything. Cal needed no coaxing and helped himself to all of it with a practiced hand.

"This is fabulous!" said Saffron. "Hadley—could you make this?"

"Much of it, yes, but not as good as Salah. I've brought him along to help me with some clients who love this—here, have the stuffed grape leaves."

"Cal—you seem already familiar with it," said Wren. He smiled wryly.

"Yes—I haven't met a cuisine I dislike, but Nicky…let's just say he has a simpler palate."

Hadley laughed. "That's just temporary. The pair of you will get him to open up."

Cal smiled, but Saffron seemed to take that seriously.

"Is that someone's job?" she asked. "In a house like ours, who's in charge of the food? What gets bought and cooked, and served? Like when the Turnbulls lived here?"

Cal seemed unhappy going back to the Turnbulls. Was he afraid his girlfriend was becoming obsessed? Or was he just not that interested?

Wren remembered what her father had advised about talking to clients: "Read the room."

"Back then, the mistress would set the menu with the cook. Keep in mind that at that time, you were limited to what was available. New York was a big city, but there were no railroads yet to transport food. Abigail may have been in charge. There were likely more servants, young girls who worked under her and lived in an outbuilding—but we don't know. They weren't important enough to mention. But I'm guessing she'd be calling the shots."

"Not Miss Verity, if they went to buy produce together?"

"It could be funny," said Wren. "She was the Captain's sister, but Katya was his *wife*. The wife was in charge. It would be assumed that Verity would become the head of her own household when she got married."

"Okay…I see that. But if she had married Jack and stayed there, then both of them would run the house?"

"That could be problematic," said Wren. "I don't know how close the women were, but there could've been friction with both of them trying to run it. There's a word that's hardly used anymore—although it has come up before with this house. Chatelaine. An old word for a special type of hook a woman wore on a girdle around her dress to hold keys. They were often made of fine materials and were elaborately decorated. Great ladies wore them, and eventually, the word came to mean the mistress of a great house herself. Understand that a house like this needs a great lady, a *chatelaine*."

"Chat-a-lane," said Saffron, testing out the unfamiliar word.

"Nicky has people in California. There's no reason you can't have people here," said Cal. "You can choose. You want more middle eastern food, we can have more middle eastern food—right, Hadley?"

"Absolutely," she said. "There's nothing you can't get here."

"Will you come and cook for us?" asked Saffron.

"I'd love to. Wren is building a super kitchen for you guys."

She nodded again, then turned back to Cal, who was enjoying another round of warm pita bread with hummus.

"Cal—will Veronica be moving in with us? Will she be marrying Nicky and becoming my stepmother?"

That gave him pause. *I bet you're wishing we stuck to the nineteenth century now,* thought Wren. But Cal had clearly honed his diplomatic talents working for Nicky. He gave Saffron a patronizing pat on the shoulder.

"Come on. You know how many female friends Nicky has had over the years. They're just friendly because they're working on the picture together."

"But they seemed—"

"I know. But she's a decade older than he is, and she's been a good and supportive friend to him while he's been getting over Thalia's death. Anyway..." he glanced at Wren. "Anyway, it's moot. Veronica has other plans. Everyone knows she's been going out with Wren's father."

Chapter Seventeen

Saffron didn't seem to know what to do with that while Wren flamed—there was no controlling it. Hadley reached under the table and squeezed her hand.

"I'm sorry, Wren, but since it's been in the papers…" said Cal. Papers that Saffron hadn't seen, apparently.

"Wow!" she eventually managed to say. "Veronica is dating your father *and* Nicky? Just…wow." She screwed up her face in thought. "What's your father like?" Wren was left speechless.

Hadley jumped in. "Ezra Fontaine is smart and amusing, like his daughter. He is debonair."

Saffron processed that.

"They met at the house of a mutual friend, and my father loved her performance in *The Glass Menagerie*. They had dinner. That's it. Everything else is some gossip columnist's imagination," Wren finally said.

But Saffron looked like she was taking it to heart. Wren watched the neurons sparking behind those wide eyes.

"Veronica is very smart. And I'm sure if he's your father, Wren, he is also very smart, so I can see why they'd want to talk to each other. They probably have a lot in common, and after all, she is ten years older than Nicky. People want to be with the right people." She focused on Wren, a solemn look on her face. "Just like they want to be in the right house. Veronica is so…sophisticated. Even more than Thalia. I know she likes the house, but I'm not sure she'd like to spend her whole life there."

The silence hung there for a moment.

"The right house…yes," said Wren, quickly moving to change the subject. "Speaking of which, the right house needs the right furniture. Have you given some thought to what you might like? Because I have some suggestions on what would work well with the house, a period look without being too fussy or old-fashioned…."

Eventually, they finished eating, and Cal looked at his watch. "We should be getting back to the hotel. We can drop the two of you off anywhere."

"We appreciate that, but we're going to have a little more coffee before we grab a cab," said Hadley.

"I'm glad we could spend this time together. I hope the house is coming together for you now?" said Wren. It was a question, not a statement.

"It is, Wren! I know what's happening now," said Saffron. "It's still important that we find out what happened to the Turnbulls, to Jack and Abigail, but I know now it will be. The house just needs a family to love it again—it needs a *chatelaine*, right?" She gave both women kisses. Cal shook their hands. "Thank you both for everything you've done. We appreciate it, and I know Nicky does too. See you on the set."

After Saffron and Nicky left, Wren and Hadley sat in silence for a minute.

"Thank you," said Wren, eventually.

"For what?"

"For not coming to my rescue and letting me shut down the discussion about my father. I'm glad you let me do that. I mean it."

"I knew you could handle it. Anyway, I think we gave her something to think about."

"A lot. She seemed to gain a connection to the Turnbulls, even if Cal was trying to discourage her. I can't say I entirely blame him. She is obsessed—but then again, so am I! Anyway, I didn't want to get Saffron's hopes up, but I bet Lavinia can help us take the next steps. For now, I'm thinking about today. About Veronica and Thalia."

"And your father," said Hadley with a wry grin.

"Look, I'm not good with this kind of thing at the best of times, and when it involves my father's love life, I really can't look at things clearly. That gossip site said they've been seen together several times. It's ongoing."

"I don't suppose it would be right to sit Veronica down and ask about what her intentions are," said Hadley. It was a statement of fact more than a question.

"Oh, she was honest. She made it perfectly clear that my father is just a diversion—even I could tell that. And as bedazzled as my father is with her, I imagine he knows how unhappy he'd be with her long-term. I feel like I'm stuck in one of those M.C. Escher prints, with the geometric figures that look so real but are logically impossible. What about Saffron?"

"What a fascinating place it must be behind those large eyes of hers," said Hadley. "You may have Escher drawings in your head, Little Bird, but our dear Saffron has a continuous loop of anime running through her brain. Something changed this evening, though."

"I agree. She has a sense of the house. I think she's still emotionally invested in finding out what happened to the Turnbulls, but…she's made peace with the house, in a way. I think she understands it's *her* home. *Chatelaine.* I used it earlier with Zachery Landau, the lawyer. I think it's occurring to Saffron that as Nicky's dearest, it will be hers. She will be chatelaine."

"Okay then, she'll be the boss, Nicky will make movies, and Cal will actually keep things running behind the scenes, as he always does," said Hadley. "Sounds good to me."

But Wren shook her head. "No. I don't think so. Control of the house, then and now. Not just who is living there, but who is running it. They couldn't stop Nicky from buying it, but someone is worried about who will be running it. We're overcomplicating things—let's get back to Ockham's razor. This means we assume that one person, or group, is trying to kill Saffron and, between incompetence or bad luck, isn't succeeding. They saw she had a connection to the house. Maybe if she's out of the way, Nicky won't want it anymore…or someone can take her place. I started thinking about Cal."

"I've worked with lots of Cals," said Hadley. "They're low-key but shrewd. So Saffron is a stepping stone to running the show. He means to kill Beebee, whom he hates and was being difficult, and means to kill Thalia, who had too much influence over both Nicky and Saffron."

"In that case, Cal will want to kill Veronica next," said Wren. "Unless they're in this together. They're both smart. Veronica will partner with Nicky and run the show while Cal gets to be 'Mr. Inside,' taking care of everything behind the scenes while setting himself up as Saffron's one-and-only. With Thalia, there was a good chance Nicky would have a child with her, confusing the inheritance. But not with Veronica. Or am I overthinking this?"

"You're the queen of overthinking. My love, in that scenario, Veronica is just hanging with your father to mess with you."

"It's possible," said Wren, realizing how ludicrous that sounded even as she spoke.

"Yeah, it's possible. But it's more likely she's dating your father because he's a silver fox."

Wren buried her face in her hands. "Thank you," she said. "Thank you very much."

"I'm sorry, Little Bird. But we're overinvolved here. I know it's about the house, but it's also about people, and people can behave in very strange ways." She grinned and lowered her voice. "Especially straight people."

That got Wren to laugh. "You're right. But I'm still worried about Saffron. Two murders, one attempted murder, and she's just beginning to realize her role and how important she is. When all is said and done, she remains a likely target. Well, the film shooting isn't going to last forever, and the police are no doubt throwing all their resources at it. Anyway, I'm going to call Veronica."

Hadley raised an eyebrow. "To grill her?"

"To make friends with someone who is important to my father," said Wren. "Even if it is temporary." She pulled out her phone and called the Millennium, which connected her with Veronica's room.

"Wren! Good to hear from you. How can I help you?"

"If it isn't too late in the evening, I'd like to come over and talk. I didn't behave very well, and I wanted to talk to you." Veronica responded with a musical laugh.

"Oh dear, if anyone should apologize, it's me. I wasn't very understanding.

164

I assume that you aren't going to ask me if my intentions are honorable." More laughter. "I guess the ship has sailed on that."

"No," said Wren. "And I'm not going to ask if we're facing a shotgun wedding."

"I love that! I forget how witty you quiet girls can be, but then your father is witty too, so I shouldn't be surprised. I'm looking forward to seeing you."

"That sounded okay," said Hadley.

"Yes. I'll come by afterward...and that reminds me. We have an appointment on Friday morning with my Realtor friend Doris. She said she'll have no trouble finding what we want in our budget."

Hadley grabbed Wren's hand. "We're going to be so happy. Are you going to research our new home's history?" Wren shook her head.

"Maybe I'm growing. But I'm thinking more and more that people will leave the stamp on the house rather than the other way around."

* * *

Veronica didn't have crowds mobbing her the way Nicky did, but she was nevertheless a star and merited a luxury suite. She opened the door when Wren buzzed. It was late, and Wren thought she might be in a bathrobe, but she was wearing a simple but obviously expensive dress.

"I'm glad you called and came over," she said. "But before we go any further, I want to tell your that your father is here—I didn't say anything on the phone because I wanted you to come, and he agreed."

"That's okay," said Wren after a minute. "Thank you."

Around the corner was a small dining area by a window. Her father was sitting by the remains of a dinner and stood as she entered.

"We bought more wine than we could finish. Please, have a glass," he said, and she did while looking around the room.

"It's not badly designed, but I'm not thrilled with the proportions," she said.

"What a surprise. You haven't been pleased with the proportions of any residence built since the McKinley administration." His eyes went to an

165

amused Veronica. "We'll discuss hotel design at another time. So, you and Hadley were dining in the city?"

"With Saffron and Cal," she said. They all took seats.

"It's very nice of you to take her under your wing," said Veronica.

"I don't mind. She's a bit eccentric but really rather sweet. It's Cal who has her under his wing."

"For what it's worth, I think they're genuinely fond of each other. Of course, I may not be the best relationship expert." She and her father laughed.

"Speaking of which," said Wren. "I wanted to tell you both how sorry I was if I caused any awkwardness. We're all grown-ups. I need to remember that."

"Thank you," said Ezra. "And I'm sorry, Wren, if I made life awkward for you on the job site. There's been some teasing, I imagine?"

"Among the actors, yes," said Veronica.

"And Nicky's lawyer, Zach Landau, gave me a clipping from a gossip site noting that you were bouncing back and forth between Nicky and my father."

"A rather unexpected position for me, rivaling Nicky Tallon for a lady's hand," said Ezra.

"Oh, dear. Business as usual for me," said Veronica. "You and your late wife, your daughter, and Hadley. The Fontaines have had more luck in love than I've had. To be fair, a lot of it was my own fault. Anyway, I'm glad we can all be friends."

"Me too," said Wren, realizing she meant it. *See, I can be a grown-up. And now that I'm here, I should talk with Veronica before I lose my nerve.* "And if we are friends, perhaps you can give me some insights into your friends on the set. I'm afraid that my skill in understanding how houses are put together is not matched by my skill in seeing how people are put together."

"I can see that, my dear. Especially when they're people in our sphere. But you don't strike me as someone idly curious about celebrities. This is important to you in some way."

"It's Saffron," said Wren. "I believe someone has been trying to kill her."

"Surely that's something for the police," said Ezra.

"Father, I'm staying out of your personal life. My friendship with Saffron is part of *my* personal life."

"Ooh, she got you there," said Veronica.

"It's not your father who's asking you about this, Wren. It's your boss, Miss Fontaine."

"When it's about the house, it's a matter for an architect," said Wren. "And as Nicky Tallon's daughter, she's a de facto client of the firm. You may be the boss, but she's the *client*."

"Okay," he said, with bad grace. "So how does this affect this house? You haven't exactly been keeping me up to date on your progress."

"Fair enough," said Wren. "Saffron has an obsession with the house. Some people seem to have an obsession with Nicky not having it. Two murders and one attempted murder. And it connects to what happened to the Turnbull family in ways I don't yet understand. It's connected with the house."

Ezra folded his arms across his chest and leaned back. "Wren—I have to say this sounds like a stretch. A big stretch. Where did this even come from?"

"From you," said Wren. "The first lesson you gave me was understanding the personality of a house and how people relate to it. I was twelve. This was right before you tried to get me to master the concept of the cantilever."

Ezra rolled his eyes and sighed. "Wren...for heaven's sake."

"Come on, Ezra," said Veronica. "I've seen enough of your girl here to know she's onto something, and I don't want to see anything happen to the house. I'll be honest...I didn't spend a lot of time mourning Beebee or Thalia, but I'd hate to see something happen to that pixie."

Ezra spread his arms grandly. "Very well. You have the floor, Miss Fontaine."

"Okay...Nicky." Veronica raised an eyebrow. "Is he who he seems to be? That is, he seems to want the house, but is there anything else?" She saw Veronica look closely at her to see if there was any secondary meaning behind the question.

"Briefly, what you see is what you get. I don't think he could fake that. He wants that house. It's not that he's more honest than everyone, but if he were playing games, you'd know it. But for what it's worth, I think, good actor or not, he's one of the few truly genuine people I've met in this business."

"Okay, he likes the house. Is that for him, do you think, or for Saffron?"

"Now, that's a good question. As I said, I know he's excited about the house. He didn't seem to like California. And I can tell you every time he spoke about the house, he spoke about it regarding Saffron, how they would be so happy, about how she would finally have a real home—near a big city where they could have fun, but be apart when they wanted to be. So it's certainly tied in with Saffron."

"She—and the house—gave him a purpose," said Wren.

"Nicely said. He was very indulgent of her. Anything she wanted."

"But she didn't want much," said Wren. "Not fancy clothes, jewelry, a sports car. All she apparently asked for was a house. *That* house. Right?"

"Nicky told me she asked for a house, a real place, where they could settle down, not that glorified movie set they have in L.A. But I'm not telling you anything you don't know. She wanted a house and fell in love with that one. It was really her obsession. Nicky was happy to get her that house. It made him feel like he was doing something. Being a movie star didn't give him a sense of accomplishment, but keeping Saffron happy...I think he's genuinely fond of her. Not like a daughter—it's much too late for that. But like a...favorite pet." She drank some wine. "God, I'm a bitch."

Ezra touched her shoulder and gave her a reassuring look.

"And he had Zachery Landau manage things for him."

"Ha! Isn't that right. Now, that's a man you want to keep an eye on. He's always three moves ahead of everyone else. Thinks the worst of everyone, but I guess he has to in his line of work."

"Do you know if he was in favor of the house?"

She gave Wren a wry look. "The house? No problem with that. Real estate always keeps its value." She turned to Ezra. "What's your favorite movie line?"

"'Land is the only thing that matters,' Gone with the Wind," he said.

"I'm betting Zach has opinions about whom he was going to share it with," said Wren.

"Is that an oblique way of asking if Zach was worried about Thalia installing herself in that house? Or me?"

Veronica was amused, but her father was unreadable as always. I always knew what my mother was thinking, but never my father. Did she ever know what he was thinking? Wren bet an extraordinary actress like Veronica could. That may have been part of her attraction. Didn't she love Hadley for how well Hadley could read her?

In the end, Wren treated that question as rhetorical.

"There's a word that keeps coming up," she said. "Chatelaine."

Ezra glanced at his girlfriend to see if she knew it.

"Mistress of a great house," Veronica said. "The Turnbull house deserves a true mistress. Saffron isn't up to it, unfortunately, but we're just talking about a two-person household service provided through an agency Zach hires."

"Not two—three," said Wren. "There's Cal. We forget about him. Servants get forgotten. But he'll be there."

"Good point. We do forget about people like Cal. I think he really loves Saffron and is devoted to Nicky. Is it sexist to call a man a chatelaine?"

"Hardly," said Wren, earning a chuckle from Veronica. "Perhaps he didn't want to fight Thalia for the role?" *Or you, either, Veronica. Did Cal slip that "love triangle" piece into the paper to upset Nicky, spiking Veronica's plans to set herself up in the house?*

Veronica smiled and shook her head. "You keep coming back to the house. Wren, I really like you and think you're very smart, but maybe you're a little too close to this house. Zach would've made sure no one could get ahold of it—it was locked down for Nicky and Saffron. Anyone could understand that. Beebee. Thalia. That's all window dressing. We're all difficult, vain, and selfish. But rational. And any rational person knew that house was Nicky and Saffron's." Veronica leaned over and placed a hand on her cheek. Wren saw the perfectly manicured fingers, felt the perfectly smooth palm. "It's people, Wren. The house is magnificent, but it's people who are making this a tragedy."

"In the nineteenth century," said Wren, "someone committed murder at that house. Someone killed *for* that house. I've almost figured out why, and when I do, I'll know why people are dying today. We leave our imprint on houses. And they leave their imprint on us."

Veronica leaned back and studied Wren—then looked at Ezra. "What's your take on this?" she asked him. *Are you going to side with your daughter or your lover?*

Ezra steepled his hands as he slipped into his professorial mode. "It occurs to me that you two are opposites in this. Veronica, your passion is acting, where characters are real and the sets are in the background. Wren, your passion is the home, where the buildings are real, and the people are in the background." He filled his wine glass again. "Cheers."

Veronica leaned over and kissed him on the cheek.

"He's really quite a dear," she said to Wren.

"I ought to be getting home," Wren said. "I'm glad we could talk."

"Don't misunderstand me," said Veronica. "Saffron may be in danger, physically and emotionally. You and Hadley are her only disinterested friends, and I'm glad she has you looking out for her."

"Not you?" asked Wren.

"Wren, I think you're smart enough to know that as much as I like Saffron, I'm not disinterested. Good night, my dear."

"I'm just going to see her into a cab," said Ezra. Wren was about to protest that she could take care of herself, but then realized that he wanted to talk to her in private.

"I'd appreciate that. Thank you."

"I'll be right back," he said to Veronica.

They had the elevator to themselves.

"Going back to Brooklyn?" he asked.

"No. To Hadley's."

"Okay. You said 'home,' so I was confused." He had a faint smile.

"You're right. We're getting our own place soon. We're looking at properties this week."

"I'm not surprised. I wanted to tell you that I understand that. I like Hadley a lot."

The elevator hit the lobby.

"You're staying in the house," she said, halfway between a question and the statement. She felt silly but had to know.

Her father laughed. "Wren. All those years spent making it perfect, and you think that now that you're going, I'm going to drop it for a bland apartment somewhere? I'm like Nicky Tallon now, only maintaining a house for my daughter?"

"All right. It was silly."

"No. It was loving. You love that house and want it to remain. And you love me and want me to be happy. Me too, Wren. Get yourselves a nice place to build your lives together." He kissed her on the cheek. "Goodnight."

Chapter Eighteen

As much as Wren was enjoying working on the house, she was glad for Friday. She was emotionally drained from all the verbal fencing. *That's me all over. I put in a twelve-hour day on a house and feel fine. One hour with another person, and I'm completely drained.*

It was too exhausting figuring out Veronica. Friend? It seemed so. Nemesis? Quite possibly. Her father's lover? Oh, yeah. Was Veronica lying about anything? She had the ability to be a world-class liar. She had won an *award* for lying—wasn't that what a Tony was? Veronica's words chased themselves around her head, but at least she was sure that moving in with Hadley was the right way forward. They had made lists of what they wanted, created a budget, and were all set.

"This is going to be *great*," said Hadley. "Your Doris sounded terrific. I'm sure she'll find us something great."

"I'm sure she will, too," said Wren. "Let's just make sure we choose something right for us."

"Oh, of course. It's just a first step, though, until we can buy someplace and make it ours. Our own little townhouse where we can build a reputation as the crazy ladies who do a stupendous job decorating for Halloween, and I give out my homemade macaroons."

"It's a plan. But I have to have arched windows. That's a deal-breaker."

They met Doris outside the first apartment. Doris was her usual elegant self in a pants suit, her gray hair perfectly coiffed, and a bag coordinated with her outfit.

She greeted both of them with kisses. "My dear ladies. I've got some great,

172

and I mean, great, opportunities for you. Your only problem will be making a decision among them. I've held them back from others." She turned to Hadley. "I don't know if Wren told you, but I've been doing business with Ezra for about a hundred years, and I just love, love, love him. Any chance to do a favor for the Fontaines...say, you're one of *the* Vanderwerfs, right? You're all Upper East Side people. Rentals, co-ops, townhouses, I'm the lady to see." She gave Hadley a bunch of cards. "Hand them out at the next family dinner. Onward and upward."

Doris knew her clients. She had a list of one-bedroom apartments in old buildings. Hadley gushed over the lively neighborhood as Wren turned a professional eye on the fixtures, walls, ceilings, and floors.

They were all acceptable in size, condition, and cost.

"I'm saving the best for last," said Doris. "I have something really special." They walked briskly past the offbeat restaurants and quirky stores to a handsomely restored building. Wren looked at it—she wondered who had done it. Someone who cared.

The hall was clean and freshly painted. Doris opened the apartment door and let them in. Wren rapped on the walls and gently jumped on the varnished wooded floors. She cast her eyes on the window frames and ran a finger around them. Hadley nodded approvingly at the kitchen, and then they walked into the bedroom. Wren whipped a tape measure out of her bag.

"You don't trust the landlord's data," said Doris. "You are your father's daughter."

Wren felt Hadley's curious look as she walked around the room, looking at each angle. It was solid, she could tell. She was indeed Ezra Fontaine's daughter. But more than that, she considered the shape of the rooms, the feeling. Whether by luck or planning, it worked. Maybe Hadley didn't realize it, not yet, but Doris did. She had worked with the Fontaines long enough. Wren felt the sense of the place, a sense of peace. A sense of harmony with the apartment, the building, the neighborhood. Doris was right.

"We'll take it," said Wren. Hadley laughed. "I'm sorry...I was being presumptuous. We need to talk it over."

"No, Wren. We don't, not when you're being so decisive."

"I'm always decisive about buildings."

"You're being decisive about *us*. You know this is the right place for *us*."

"It has harmony," said Wren with a smile.

"I knew there was a reason to fall for an architect," said Hadley. "Yes, Doris. Where do we sign?"

We're going to be chatelaines. It isn't a grand house, but it's ours.

"Excellent! I knew, right? I really knew. Done and done. And it's ready for a quick move." She lowered her voice. "Which I know is especially important for you, Wren."

"We're ready to move quickly, but it's not urgent—what made you think that?"

"It's okay. I know Ezra is very private, and I don't want to interfere, but I couldn't help hearing…there's going to be another resident in that smashing Brooklyn townhouse…right?"

Wren's first instinct was embarrassment…but no. At the end of the day, it was just too funny. And the apartment had put her in a good mood. She rested her hand on Doris's shoulder.

"Doris—You know me. You know my father. You knew my mother. How many women do you really think could share a house with Ezra Fontaine?"

As Doris considered that excellent question and Hadley snickered, Wren's phone rang.

"Hi, Wren, it's Zach. Are Saffron and Cal with you and Hadley? I know you two are off today, so I thought they might be with you."

"No…we didn't have any plans. Hadley and I are off for personal reasons. You can't find them?"

"Nicky's all worked up. Cal was supposed to be around and didn't call, didn't leave a message, and he can't reach either one of them. Saffron is Saffron, but Cal is usually reliable. "

"Sorry," said Wren. "They're young and in love."

"Yeah, well, Cal is about to be young and in love and unemployed. Nicky is very unhappy. I know Cal didn't expect Nicky to need him during the filming, but he had some time while they set up a shot, so Nicky wanted to reach Cal to arrange a special dinner this weekend. Unless…Christ, you don't think something has happened to them? They're supposed to stay with the limo driver. I'll call the agency—"

But no. Wren suddenly knew where they were, and it made her feel good to be able to read people. *But is this about people? Or the house?*

"Don't bother," said Wren. "We're in Manhattan. We'll find them. She wants to be the chatelaine. Just like me."

"Excuse me?"

"Don't worry. I think I know where they are." She clicked off.

"Saffron and Cal are missing. Nicky and Zach are worried. We're going to find them. I think I know where they are. We may be too late to control the damage, but perhaps we can mitigate it. Doris, business calls, but consider this a done deal. I can't thank you enough." They left the beaming Doris to lock up.

On the sidewalk, Hadley threw her arms around Wren and gave her a big kiss.

"We're going to be so happy here. I can tell. You don't even mind your dad having a famous girlfriend." Wren laughed.

"You're right. And we're going to have a celebratory dinner. But first, we have a job. Can we get a cab? Actually, this time of day it's faster to walk. I still can't believe I got roped into playing nursemaid to my client's wayward daughter—I'm an architect, but…."

"What are you talking about?"

"Off to Louis J. Lefkowitz State Office Building, which is actually owned by the city now."

"Okay…"

"I've always had a fondness for it. It was built in 1930—a very solid example of Art Deco."

"And you have a craving for Art Deco."

"I could take it or leave it. All right, I'm off track. That's what you get for cohabitating with an architect. It's what's inside the building. Cal and Saffron."

"Why are they running away for city business…oh my God…you don't mean...."

"I do mean. And I suppose it's my fault, all the talk about who is going to run the household, who was important...."

It was a warm day, so they were a little sweaty as they walked up the steps.

"We could be too late...but I'm guessing they didn't want an early appointment," said Wren. Once inside, they followed the signs—and there were Cal and Saffron sitting on a bench. He was wearing another one of his colorful jackets, and as a concession to the formality of the occasion, she wore a mid-length skirt and matching blouse with espadrilles on her feet. It added a few years to her. She was idly staring at the scene, but Cal was no doubt looking for someone looking for them—and saw Wren and Hadley first.

"Wren...Hadley...what...?" He looked a little uncomfortable and was glancing over their shoulders to see if anyone else was coming.

Saffron, however, was thrilled, jumping up and racing to them, giving them both hugs.

"We didn't tell anyone, but you figured it out! You can be here for us. You can be our witnesses. We were just going to see if there was anyone around. We're on in fifteen minutes."

"How did you find us?" asked Cal.

"Educated guess," said Wren. "All the talk about being mistress of a great house. I put two and two together. You don't have to get married to run a house. You can be a single chatelaine."

"Oh, I know that," said Saffron. "But it just seemed right, you know?" She cast a fond look at her fiancé.

Cal jumped in: "I want you to know I did not push Saffron into this. I've wanted this for some time, but I didn't pressure her."

"I believe that," said Wren. "But Nicky is rather unhappy with both his daughter and his employee."

"I'm sorry about that," said Cal. "He hardly ever needs me in the middle of a shoot. I thought we'd just pass it on to him as a fait accompli."

"How do you think he's going to react?" asked Hadley.

"Nicky has known about our feelings for some time. I think he'll be happy," said Cal. Now, it was his turn to look down fondly at Saffron. "I'm going to take care of her now."

Was that it? Was Nicky just plain tired of taking care of Saffron, even in their short relationship? He never asked to be a father. There was no doubt Cal was willing to step up. He may have been a little silly over the girl, but he was dependable, responsible. He wouldn't have lasted this long in his position if he weren't. It could be a relief for Nicky just to write the checks and make it Cal's job to keep her from going off the rails. To keep her safe.

"You're both sure of this?" asked Wren. "Marriage is a very big deal."

"You're right," said Hadley. "But I think these two are ready."

A woman called their names.

"We're up," said Cal. "Would you two be our witnesses?"

"We'd be honored," said Wren. The woman told them New York required only one witness, but when Saffron said she wanted both, the woman gave them a "knock yourself out" look and ushered them in. It didn't take very long, and a few minutes later, they were on the street in front of that Art Deco masterpiece.

"I'm going to text everyone that you're both okay. And now you need a wedding breakfast," said Wren.

Saffron wrinkled her nose. "It's a little late for breakfast," she said.

"By old tradition, the first meal after a wedding is called a breakfast, even if it's in the afternoon. But first, you need to call your father/father-in-law/boss and hope he isn't too upset."

Chapter Nineteen

Fortunately for the new couple, Nicky had been more worried than angry—and Cal knew how to handle him. Wren could only hear half the phone conversation, but she could tell how smoothly Cal managed Nicky.

"I am so sorry, Nicky...didn't want to worry you...Saffron just stole my heart—can you blame me? We're coming over right now...."

They realized they didn't have time for a meal, but Hadley picked up a white frosted cake at a bakery and called her staff on the island before they caught the launch. Saffron was chattering on about a honeymoon trip. She wanted to go to Hawaii. "We'll sit under palm trees and drink those fancy drinks." Wren thought it rather sweet, how authentic her dreams were. She pulled Hadley aside to the other side of the boat to leave Saffron to prattle on to her new husband.

"We have to talk to him now," said Wren. "This is...not a coincidence. Everything is too tightly timed. And also..." She looked away, feeling she couldn't finish the sentence.

"Also, what?" asked Hadley.

"You'll laugh at me," said Wren.

"For God's sake, we're moving in together. You think I will laugh at you?"

"Abigail. This island's superior servant, who took charge with Coroner Bedlow. And Cal. A superior servant. It goes round and round."

Hadley just nodded. "That's the thing about us, it seems. If anyone else had said that, I would've laughed. But not you. Tell me about Abigail."

"I just got a text from Lavinia—she said she found something and wants to meet. I keep thinking about Abigail and Cal. By the nature of their jobs, they're reactive personalities. That's what good servants do. This marriage was Cal's idea, but Saffron finally went along because she wanted to be Chatelaine. And Abigail..." she smiled. "We'll see what Lavinia has found. But I see this house, and I also think of Abigail and Jack—the people who ran it." They were approaching the pier, and a group of laughing women were waving to them—Saffron waved back. Wren shook her head, as if to get rid of her fancies. She had a house to work on. "Are you with me? We grab him now once we're on dry land."

Hadley saluted.

Saffron reveled in the attention she got, the chorus of well-wishers welcoming the new bride to her home. Nicky came down, a lopsided smile on his face, followed by Veronica. She met Wren's eye, and her smile was sardonic.

The new couple found themselves in the center of kisses, hugs, and back slaps. One of Hadley's assistants joined them; Hadley gave her the cake and had a few words with her. Cal looked very pleased with himself. Why not? He had a beautiful and sweet wife and a wealthy father-in-law. He started to join the crowd making its way to the set when he felt arms link to his on both sides.

"We need you a minute," said Wren. "You can join them shortly."

"But I think Nicky—"

"You have a lifetime with Nicky and a lifetime with Saffron," said Hadley. "But before you go any further, you need some lessons in how to be a spouse."

"Seriously...?" said Cal, trying to make light of it.

"Yes," said Wren. "Seriously."

They led Cal into the house, up to an empty bedroom, where a few old office chairs remained, forgotten when the last government residents moved out and locked the doors behind them.

"Take a seat," said Hadley. Looking halfway between amused and nervous, he did. Wren and Hadley sat opposite him.

"Quite a move, marrying the daughter of the boss. The daughter of the very rich boss," said Wren.

Cal spread open his hands. "Yes, I know how it looks. But I genuinely love her. And I flatter myself she loves me. I'll make her a good husband, I swear."

"Will she make you a good wife?" asked Wren. That seemed to stump him, and she was amused at that. That loopy behavior could be charming in a young woman but would become increasingly annoying as she hit her thirties.

"I said I loved her," said Cal.

"I accept that. But I asked if you thought she'd make a good wife. She'll be the mistress of this house. That's a lot of responsibility."

"I have some experience," Cal said with a wry smile. "Anyway, one call to Zach, and we'll have a houseful of servants."

"But Saffron will be chatelaine. She'll be the lady of this house. That's very important here. That means something, especially to her."

Cal nodded. "You've got a point. You gave her those ideas. She looks up to both of you."

Wren nodded. "What about Thalia and Veronica? What did they want? I don't think Thalia wanted to run this house. Oh, maybe throw some parties here, but I never saw her taking care of it, ruling over it. You have to love this place to stay here through a New York winter."

"Thalia...look, I can't talk about that," he said. "Nicky pays for my discretion."

"Don't go there," said Hadley. "You're a married man. She's your top priority now, not Nicky, and we need to ensure her safety. I've been around plenty of women like Thalia and Veronica. I doubt if you're going to tell me anything I haven't heard before."

Cal grimaced. "You're right. Although, I don't think I need to tell you anything about Thalia you didn't figure out yourself."

"Probably," said Wren. "But now she's dead. Maybe they were trying to kill Saffron—but maybe she really was supposed to die. Saffron seemed to genuinely like her, but I don't think the feeling was necessarily mutual. I think Thalia would've been happy for Nicky to buy Saffron her own place, far away."

"Come on, Wren," he said with a smile. "Thalia was the cool girl. Saffron worshiped her. You remember what it was like at school—the cool girls." He laughed. "You—Hadley. You were a cool girl."

"All right—guilty as charged," said Hadley. "But none of us are in high school anymore. Are you saying that's the way Saffron looked at Thalia?"

"Look, she had a miserable childhood. I'm not a shrink, but Saffron has some things to catch up on. Some things she missed."

"Do you think Thalia liked that? Or was annoyed by it?" asked Wren.

"I think she was amused, at least at first. She didn't mind Saffron dressing like her."

"Thalia told me it was Saffron's idea to do that. Are you sure that's how it played out?" asked Wren.

"Oh...I don't remember exactly. I think Saffron asked for some help, and maybe Thalia thought it was funny Saffron wanted to imitate her."

"Models generally don't like anyone copying them," said Hadley.

"Unless she thought at the end of the day people would be laughing at Saffron," said Wren. "Not that it worked. Saffron seemed delighted."

"Look—Thalia was hardly a deep thinker. She had a very limited agenda. I know it seems odd, but she had hit her peak as a model. Cash in those looks and become Mrs. Nicky Tallon. She didn't want this house—where's the fun in getting stuck here? Frankly, I don't think she gave much thought to Saffron one way or another. Thalia wanted endless parties. If Saffron wanted to tag along..." he shrugged.

"What about you?" asked Wren. "I don't think you love this house."

"No, I don't. But I love Saffron," said Cal. "Maybe you don't believe it. I mean, it's awfully convenient having an incredibly rich and famous father-in-law. No, Wren, this isn't my ideal residence. I'm one of that rare breed, an L.A. native. But if Saffron is happy here, I will be happy here with her. For what it's worth, even if this house isn't my first choice, I do appreciate its magnificence. If nothing else, you showed me that."

Wren looked at him and tried to figure it out, to see if he was honest about it. For all his sophistication, he was still young.

"And Veronica?" asked Wren.

"I don't mind telling you she scares the hell out of me," said Cal. The women laughed. "Nicky is in complete awe of her. Saffron idolizes her, but it's not like with Thalia. Thalia was an older sister. Veronica is a mother. Are you going to ask if she loves this house?"

"No. I know that already. But does she love Nicky?"

"I don't know. I thought she loved your father?" He thought he was funny, but a second later, he saw the look on Wren's face and realized he had made a mistake. Wren saw the fear in his eyes and at first, was pleased. And then ashamed of herself.

"We're off-topic," she said.

"I run interference for Nicky. That's a key part of my job. All the women throwing themselves at him. But I really don't know her game."

"What about Nicky? Does he love her?"

"Wren...he's my boss. And my father-in-law."

"And my client. Nothing about this house is out of my purview," said Wren. Cal looked away.

"God's honest truth, Nicky never knew what the hell he wanted. That's what he had me and Zachery for."

Wren looked at Hadley, who gave a half smile and shrugged.

"He loves this house," said Wren. "I can tell you that. Just like Saffron does. You mentioned her awful childhood. We know the basics, of course, but how did she live in Idaho?"

"She doesn't like to talk about it," he said. "Bounced between distant relations and a variety of foster homes. Nicky, Zachery, and I went to get her in a trailer park."

"A mobile home," said Wren, more to herself. "So you saw it. What did it look like?"

"Oh...you know, a trailer. Kinda small inside. Saffron slept on a chair that turned into a single bed."

"Was it well-kept?" she asked. She saw the confusion in Cal's eyes.

"It looked like hell. I've heard there were nice trailer parks where people plant flowers, but this wasn't one of them. It was awful. Half the people there looked like they were on drugs. Saffron—she just seemed untouched by it all. You've seen her, talked to her. I don't understand it, how she kept herself together in that nightmare."

Wren nodded. "You were a USC film major, right? That's what someone told me. How did you get your job with Nicky?"

"I got lucky. I was a glorified gofer on a film set two years ago with Nicky. We just hit it off, and I found myself with a new job. And that business manager of his, Zach Landau. He okayed me, thinks I'm good for Nicky. Why are you interested in that?" *How nice*, thought Wren. *USC cost a mint. They gave scholarships, but Wren doubted Cal had to rely on one. He was too polished. Four years of USC didn't do that to him. He had probably never seen a trailer park except on a screen. He was young, but shrewd.*

"Never mind," said Wren, vaguely aware that she was saying something aloud that she could've kept silent. "A mobile home? From an architectural perspective, they're not necessarily something to look down on. Properly made and situated...but I suppose Saffron's was overcrowded, if she was sleeping on a pullout."

"I guess, but I didn't do a Census. I can tell you it was awful."

"Did she seem..." Wren waved her hand, looking for the right word. "Beaten down? Depressed? Abused?"

Cal looked at Wren hard, and she forced herself not to flinch. She didn't even want to risk a glance at Hadley.

"She knew we were coming," said Cal, finally. "She was excited about it. I don't know what she was like before. She wasn't living with...nice people. They were glad to see the back of her, but they still hit up Nicky for cash. It was dark there. Are you saying someone came back from Idaho to stalk her here?"

"Perhaps," said Wren. "But when you said it was 'dark,' were you speaking metaphorically, or was the house really dark? Or both?"

He was getting angry now. Even Wren could sense that. And that was something. A man in his position could only get angry on Nicky's behalf, never on his own. She saw him clench his hands.

"I realize you have a home to fix here. And I realize you've become friends with *my wife*. She had a rough time of it. But it's okay now. She has me to look after her. I *will* look after her. Nothing bad is going to happen to her again. I don't know who has killed anyone or why, but this film shoot will wrap soon, and we won't have to worry about it anymore. It'll be me, Saffron, and Nicky on this island. I will take care of her forever, and I will see that nothing happens to her."

He stood. "So, did I pass? Am I going to be a suitable husband?" It often happened that Wren didn't get her father's sarcasm, but she got Cal's.

"Thank you for indulging us," said Wren. "We'll be along to the celebration shortly." Cal looked uncertain for a few moments.

"Just one more thing," said Cal. "We're a little worried about Saffron getting too worked up about the crimes, so we're trying to play down her amateur detective aspects."

"For old Turnbull crimes or the new ones?"

"Both, actually. It's just a matter of keeping her on an even keel, as they say. Anyway, thanks for being our witnesses." He left, and they sat in silence.

"What the hell, Wren," said Hadley after a while. "From mobile home to overly protective husband while the ink is still wet on their license."

"Yes—all that talk about mobile homes. I keep coming back to homes, but I can't be sure if it's because homes are important or because that's what I truly understand."

"I'm going to correct you, Little Bird. You do understand people, but it's in the context of homes. That's an important difference."

Wren smiled. "Thank you. That makes me feel less crazy."

"So you think that somehow this relates to Saffron's background? Maybe someone is very unhappy this poor girl, kicked from pillar to post as an old nanny of mine would say, suddenly gets this place. And they've come back to stop her. Do you think someone has inserted themselves here? Let's not forget Nicky is also from Idaho, local boy made good. Jealousy—the green-eyed monster."

"Unless Lieutenant Howard is an idiot, and I don't think she is, I bet she's been all over the Idaho connection," said Wren. "How many people do they have to check? The whole state has fewer people than Brooklyn. But you know, there was one question Cal didn't really answer. He said he'd be a good husband to Saffron. And I believe him. But he was unclear about whether she'd be a good wife to him."

"Ha! People never really know that. People can know if they love each other, but whether they're *good* for each other, that's something else."

Wren nodded. "That…is very interesting. I never thought of that." Her parents were good for each other. But her father and Veronica?

Wren felt shy but had to ask anyway. "I think you have been very good for me." And she left the reverse statement hanging.

"You've made me a better person," said Hadley.

Chapter Twenty

Wren thought Hadley looked shy too, which was unusual for her. They sat in silence for a few moments. Then Hadley stood. "We could hardly run out and reprovision ourselves here, but I gave my people some instructions to put together something festive, and we have the cake."

Hadley's staff had indeed put together some festive treats from what they had and were cutting the cake. Saffron was in the center of a group of women, looking both confused and happy. Eventually, she retrieved her mandolin and started playing songs for her appreciative audience. She was kept busy enough not to notice her husband had been spirited away.

In fact, the men had waylaid Cal for a few minutes of backslapping, and they were laughing at something, which Wren was sure was vulgar. They seemed to tone it down when Nicky, who had been enjoying his cake, joined them.

Wren's phone buzzed. "It's a text from Lavinia. She found something interesting, and can we join her tonight."

"We can tell her about our new apartment. Should we bring Saffron and Cal?"

"I don't think so. Let the happy couple celebrate. It's their wedding night, after all. I think Cal had a point about Saffron becoming obsessed with this house. Maybe her marriage will get her to focus on the future. She was already moving there; no need to pull her back. What do you think is going through Nicky's mind right now?"

The crowd was reshuffling. Veronica had gently led Saffron away, and

Nicky had thrown his arm around his new son-in-law.

"He's thinking about how this makes his daughter happy. And about how Cal will be around to take care of both of them."

"That sounds right. As for Veronica…"

"I can't even guess," said Hadley.

"Let's pretend we're in the nineteenth century. Veronica is dressed for it. After a meal, the ladies retire together."

Veronica seemed happy to see them.

"Ladies! Saffron told me that you two tracked them down and saved the day by serving as witnesses. Clever girls."

"We're all going to live here!" said Saffron. "Me and Cal and Nicky and Veronica—she really loves this house. Also, she likes theater more than movies, and it's so easy to get to the New York theaters from here. Nicky will travel when he has to for movies, and I will be *chatelaine*," she said, enunciating each syllable perfectly.

Veronica smiled slowly. "We'll take it day by day, dear. Wren is still working on this house. Now, why don't you go talk to your father and new husband. And best wishes again." Saffron gave Veronica a hug and skipped over to her family.

"Giving her advice on how to be a good wife?" asked Wren. Veronica laughed.

"For God's sake, I've been divorced four times. I may not be marriage material but I'm not stupid. No, advice on honeymoon locations. I have to say, even though I had terrible marriages, I had great honeymoons. Did she tell you Hawaii? Overrated."

"Are you planning to live here?" asked Wren. She felt her heart pound.

"Do you mean here as opposed to Brooklyn?" Veronica asked coolly.

Wren was prepared. She forced her voice to be steady. "Hadley and I are moving into our own apartment in lower Manhattan. I have no interest in what happens in Brooklyn. But if you are going to be living here, I'd be happy to discuss furnishings. I do that along with the architectural work, and I have a feeling that you'll be of more help than the other residents."

Veronica nodded. "I somehow think that California Modern isn't going to work here. It's not fair, I know, but I see this place and think about my grandparents' furniture from Newark."

"I don't know what your grandparents' furniture looked like, but considering the time, the location, and the milieu, I'm inclined to agree with you. I guess I'll just have to work with the new chatelaine."

Veronica laughed. "You should have an easy time with her. She'll happily go along with whatever you suggest, and Nicky will write the checks, happy you're keeping her happy. Cal too. He'll be a good husband for her, providing love and guidance. I'm thinking our little Saffron is doing better out of the gate than I did in four tries."

"That's the funny thing," said Wren. "I'm hardly a relationship expert either, but I keep wondering about the other way around. Will Saffron be a good wife to Cal?"

"Oooh, I like that. I like that a lot. Figuring out what a man wants from a wife? That's a very hard one. She's a sweet girl. I wonder if she'll always be like that. That childlike view of the world can get wearying."

"She had a very hard childhood," said Wren. "I'm not a shrink, but I can see how that might've made her who she is. Some people become bitter and angry. But it's like she just built a shield around herself. Perhaps...." Wren gave it some thought. "Perhaps in her own mind she was able to find some solace in whatever home she grew up in, and that's why the idea of a home is important to her."

"This has to do with the house?" asked Veronica.

"Yes, it does. Cal and Nicky found her in a trailer." Wren took a breath. "We make jokes about this house, as if it's nothing more than a set for whatever costume drama you're filming, and 'chatelaine' is just a crossword puzzle clue. But to people like me, it's an almost sacred responsibility. And a sacred honor. I know you think I'm on the wrong track, trying to tie it to the house, but Saffron is married now. She seems to think this is a big step—which, of course, it is. But to Saffron, this makes her a chatelaine. I'm afraid that's my fault—I indicated that wives had a special status to run a house. Things are different from when you and I spoke with my father. Everything makes sense to her now. You and Nicky will live here with her, and she and Cal will run things as a married couple."

"Ha! Well, she can have her dreams. Meanwhile, if I were you, I'd look at Cal. He's cemented his position. Not just a disposable servant but a member of the family. He's set for life."

"We've concluded he really loves her," said Hadley.

"I'm sure he does. But it makes it a lot easier if Daddy is rich and famous," said Veronica. "Okay, we're in a new place now. It's not just a fling; they're married. I'm an actress. I'm in the motivation business. Cal hated Beebee—they fought right before Beebee died. Thalia was too unsure of herself to have anyone else close to Nicky hanging around, like Cal and Saffron. Maybe Cal thought Beebee and Thalia would block his marriage. Remember, Saffron was still new to Nicky. Her arrival changed everything. Cal falling in love would change it further. They wanted Nicky to themselves. Cal knew that and got rid of them."

"Cal doesn't want us to involve his new wife in our... discussions on crimes, both old and new," said Wren.

"He's a sharp man, our Cal. He wants to keep Saffron from going off the rails. I wish him luck. As I said, he's good at manipulation. This marriage thing surprised me, actually. Keep an eye on him."

"Do you believe he's capable of murder?" asked Wren.

Veronica laughed. "Believe? You know what I believe? I believe I need to get in as many roles as possible, until that inevitable day when my agent calls me for a remake of 'Driving Miss Daisy.' Listen, ladies, it's not that I don't love playing detective with you, but this costume weighs a ton. Love to both of you." She gave them each a kiss on the cheek and headed to her trailer.

"She's a real piece of work," said Hadley.

"Kind of makes me rethink my father," said Wren, shaking her head. "Still, I'm sticking with my theory that it's about the house. That's when this started happening. And I'm thinking about Abigail. There's more that's going on there. Something else we're not seeing." She brooded for a few minutes, felt everything slip away as people ran round and round her head. Then she looked up and saw Hadley look at her—and laughed.

"Oh God, I can't believe you put up with me!" said Wren. "Here I am, being that strange and gloomy high school girl. Do forgive me. I want whatever celebratory snacks you've prepared for the happy couple, and then we're going to Lavinia's."

"Little Bird, I hate to break it to you, but if you ranked the craziness of people I've known, you're not even in the top ten. You'll have to settle for just being my favorite."

"I can live with that!" Wren felt her heart go back to normal, and she looked around at the cast and crew, still celebrating Cal and Saffron, and sharing jokes with a pleased-looking Nicky. *What made me think I could figure out these people?* She looked up at the house. Now that was clear. Grand and yet cool, confident in its own elegant simplicity. The house was proud and completely unapologetic, knowing its proportions were enough. She understood that, but wished the house could speak to her more clearly.

Wren shook her head. She was looking forward to visiting Lavinia—maybe they'd find the final piece—even if it was two hundred years ago.

She was looking at the house when Hadley broke into her thoughts.

"Uh, Wren...something is happening." She saw a woman in costume and a man with a bag running among the actors and racing into a trailer while people watched.

"That man—he's the medic for the set."

"And that trailer is Veronica's," said Wren. She felt her mouth go dry. It was impossible on this set—they couldn't hire an army, but if someone really wanted to commit murder...

People were starting to gather. The set security guard set himself outside the trailer to keep everyone back, even Nicky, Cal, and Saffron.

"What happened?" Wren asked.

"Veronica and I were in her trailer talking," said Saffron, "just wedding stuff. Then she told me she wanted to change, and I should go and find Cal."

"So she was fine when you left?" asked Wren.

"Yes. We were just sitting there...with coffee."

Coffee. Someone had poisoned the coffee.

"I found her," said a voice behind Wren. It was an extra, one Wren had seen leading the medic to the trailer. "I asked her for some career advice because I admired her so much, and she told me to come by her trailer, and she looked like she was so sick. I ran to get the medic."

"Did anyone call the police?"

"I did," said the guard. "Lieutenant Howard is on her way."

They waited in silence. Wren closed her eyes and reached for Hadley's hand. Did she get it wrong? Could this still be about Saffron—the fourth attempt on her life? It seemed insane. Or was this just about people close to Nicky? Or just to introduce panic on the set?

Or—

The medic stepped out. "It was a close call, but I recognized the signs—opioid overdose, possibly fentanyl. I was able to give her Naloxone just in time. She'll be okay, but we will want to get her to a hospital."

"You were prepared," said Wren.

He smiled. "Mr. Landau arranged for staff here who had special experience recognizing an opioid overdose and treating it. *Good for you, Zach! One cool-headed medic was worth more than a dozen armed guards.* "Are you Wren? Ms. Selwyn can receive visitors, but she said only Wren and Hadley. You can have a few minutes before we put her on a launch and take her to the hospital."

Wren glanced at Nicky to see if he seemed insulted at being excluded, but all she saw was concern.

The medic remained outside while Wren and Hadley stepped in. Veronica was pale and looked a little dazed, but she smiled at them.

"Take a seat, ladies. We don't have long."

"How are you doing?" asked Wren.

"I'd like to say I've been worse, but that would be a lie. This is the worst. But never mind. Saffron and I were drinking coffee earlier—I told her to bring some, and we'd talk. I reached for hers. It was disgusting."

"Fentanyl, if that's what it was, has no smell or taste," said Hadley.

"I knew you'd know that," said Veronica. She laughed and winced. "But she over-sugars everything. That's what was disgusting. I never put sugar in coffee. It was the coffee, I'm sure." Wren saw two coffee cups on the little table. The cups were from the tables Hadley's staff had set up. But who knew what path Saffron had traveled from the tables to the trailer. Maybe the killer was desperate. If Saffron's preference for lots of sugar was known, the killer may have had a chance to slip it into Saffron's coffee. She was easily distractable.

"Anyway, I drank some, began feeling weird, and if that extra hadn't come in I might've died. I wanted to tell you two in case something goes wrong before I can talk to the police. Also, you two...know things. Watch out for her, would you?"

The medic came in with another man. "Ms. Selwyn? We're going to put you on a stretcher."

"Okay. 'All right, Mr. DeMille, I'm ready for my close-up.'"

Wren and Hadley couldn't help but laugh.

"Good reaction, ladies! I can finally say the old saying is true, 'Dying is easy. Comedy is hard.'"

Wren and Hadley stepped outside. The medics knew their business and smoothly removed Veronica. "We're getting you onto the launch," one of them said, "and there's an ambulance waiting for us at the Manhattan side."

Bobby had shown up too, and Wren quickly told him what happened.

"Jesus. I was afraid it was you. Your father would hand my head to me if you broke a fingernail. Can we do anything?"

"Actually, yes," said Wren. "Send me one of your men you won't need for a half hour or so."

"Sure, boss." He pulled out his phone to call his foreman.

Wren turned to the guard. "No one goes inside this trailer until the police arrive. One of Mr. Fiore's workers will remain with you, so there's no... misunderstanding." A guard might feel he could be overruled by someone on the set, but Bobby's workers answered only to Bobby.

The guard clearly had little idea of who Wren was, however.

"But miss—"

"But what?" said Wren. "I am the architect. This entire island is my worksite, and I am the ultimate authority here by state law and custom. Is that clear?"

"Yes, miss," he said.

"Saffron—Cal, Nicky, and everyone on the set will be busy until the police get here. You are coming with me to the house until the police arrive. You'll be safe among the work crew." She just nodded, and Wren, Hadley, and Saffron headed up to the house.

"Wow," said Hadley, eventually, "just…wow."

"Didn't think I had that in me?" asked Wren.

"I knew you did," said Hadley. "I'm just glad it finally came out."

Wren threw an arm around Saffron. "Don't worry, sweetie. Veronica will be fine."

"What's happening?" asked Saffron. It came out as a whisper. "I just want a home. That's all."

Chapter Twenty-One

Eventually, a grim Lieutenant Howard let everyone go, although she did thank Wren for securing the crime scene.

"I'm glad someone had a cool head," she said.

The police said only Saffron's cup was poisoned, and they hadn't been able to trace its path—almost anyone could've poisoned it. Saffron had indeed stopped several times, bringing the drinks to the trailer.

Veronica was recovering well in the hospital. Wren called her father to tell him.

"This is…entirely unacceptable," he said. "I am not risking you for this. Or Bobby and his people."

"The movie people won't be around much longer. And I don't think Hadley and I, or Bobby and his people, are in danger. There is something about this very much tied to the movie community, and I'm an outsider. Despite the fact that this seems like a series of errors, there is something precise and coldblooded about this."

"A feeling?" asked her dubious father.

"I see houses assembled, and now I'm seeing a…plot, I guess you'd call it. I don't think it's a series of errors. That would be too much. I don't know more, but I think something is being planned here. I just don't know what."

"Just be careful. Anyway, I'll leave the office in the next few minutes and bring some flowers for Veronica."

"I don't know, father. Glamorous actresses don't like being seen without their hair styled and make-up on."

"Wren—I've seen Veronica without her hair styled and make-up on."

"Of course. Thanks for the reminder. Anyway, give her my love." She clicked off.

"Visiting his girlfriend in the hospital? That's sweet," said Hadley.

"Hmm," said Wren.

"Lost in thought?" asked Hadley.

"Yes. A really horrible thought. A thought that makes me deeply ashamed, and you're the only one I can admit it to." They waited alone by the launch, but Wren looked around to make sure no one else could hear. "What if, to deflect suspicion, or another reason we can only guess at, Veronica poisoned herself and timed it so she'd be saved by the visiting extra she had promised to help?"

"Christ! That is a horrible thought, which comes from your very conflicted feelings about her." She paused. "But it just might be true. Still, she'd have to time it pretty fine. That was a hell of a risk."

"Not if she poisoned a cup she didn't drink from. Do you think she could've faked a poisoning? She's an incredible actress."

"Wow. Now there's a thought. You know, Naloxone has no effect if you haven't taken any opiates, so no risk there. Don't ask me how I know that. That would be the performance of a lifetime...but to what end?"

"I don't know," said Wren. "I could be wrong. Someone may have really wanted to kill Saffron. Or someone may have really wanted to kill Veronica."

After arriving in Manhattan, they grabbed a cab to Columbia.

"Come on in, ladies," said Lavinia. "Angela sends her regrets, emergency surgery. The perils of being married to a doctor. But I've got some very interesting things to share with you.

"It's already been an interesting day," said Wren, and they gave Lavinia a summary of the latest poisoning.

"Dear lord. I'm glad everyone is okay now, but how frightening. My mother always told me never to mix with theater folk, and I can see why. I'm glad I've only been drafted to help you with the old murders."

"Speaking of sharing, I have something for you," said Hadley. "If I do say so, I've outdone myself on the set today. Some fantastic leftovers for you. My own personal take on tamales...."

A moment in the microwave and Lavinia was almost purring. "My God. Don't let this one go, Wren."

"I'm not," said Wren. "We finally did it. We got our own place—a lovely lower Manhattan one-bedroom."

"I'm so glad for you two! I'm not a hugger, as you well know, but I'll make an exception for this. I'm sure you'll get along well. I've known dear Ezra for years, and if Wren has been able to live with him for her whole life, she'll be able to live with someone as easygoing as you, Hadley."

Then she gave Wren a tight smile, and Wren braced herself for what was coming.

"So, my dear, your impending move wouldn't have anything to with your father's romance?"

Hadley giggled as Wren sighed. "I can't believe you read those rags."

"Come on, my dear. You know academics are the worst gossips in the world. Your father is an adjunct here, and how often do Columbia professors get to date Hollywood stars?"

"I'd ask if my father was embarrassed, but he's never been embarrassed in his entire life."

"I know nothing about Veronica Selwyn or actors generally. But I know your father, and I don't see him marrying again. He and your mother were two puzzle pieces that fit only each other, but I'm not telling you anything you don't know."

"Thank you," said Wren quietly.

"The problem is that Veronica is part of our puzzle," said Hadley. "We just told you an actress was poisoned. That actress was Veronica. Ezra is on his way there now with flowers."

"Of course. This is getting tangled."

"The thing is," continued Hadley, "that Veronica is not very clear about her relationships. She's smart and such a good actress, there's no telling what is going on behind those lovely eyes."

"Well, good luck to everyone here. We can only hope that, like in a Shakespearean comedy, everyone ends up where they should be. Anyway, let's turn our attention to the past. We have some interesting discoveries here. Your little friend Saffron wasn't interested in coming?"

"She has been busy," said Wren. "With everything else, I almost forgot: She got married today—to Nicky's assistant. Hadley and I got to be their witnesses. If you've been following the news, you've found out she's Nicky's 'love child,' as they used to say."

"Oh my. Haven't heard that term in decades. Well, a hearty mazel tov to the young couple. All I'll say now is that this is all going to be very interesting when you hear what I have to tell you." She found her laptop under a pile of books. "We're going back to the dawn of the U.S. Census. There were also property deeds and other items. I work with some genius librarians and archivists. It wasn't terribly difficult."

"You just manage to make it look easy," said Wren.

"I'm always afraid of spoiling you. Okay...to begin with, the records show what we know so far, with the Captain, his wife, his sister, and the two senior servants, Jack and Abigail. We know when the Captain disappeared, and we know who stayed on the island forever—Erik sent me a copy of the report, of course. The Captain never left, but we couldn't find Jack and Abigail. Until now." She turned around her laptop. Like most professors, she was part showman.

"A marriage license, issued in the City of Brooklyn, between Jack Llewelyn and Abigail Bloodworth, dated just a couple of weeks after Coroner Bedlow's investigation."

"Oh!" said Hadley. "But don't you mean between Jack and Verity Turnbull?"

"My dear, as Wren will tell you, I don't say anything I don't mean."

Wren laughed. "I'll attest to that."

"Okay—but I don't understand. I thought we had concluded—" Hadley stopped and laughed. "I'll just shut up now."

"Doubt is the beginning of wisdom," said Lavinia. "So here we have a nicely done example of copperplate handwriting. It's been a long, long time since anyone taught handwriting, I suppose. I miss those days. Anyway, this shows that Jack married Abigail, not Miss Verity. So what do we know now?"

"That Abigail was a liar," said Wren. Lavinia raised an eyebrow. "Coroner Bedlow had no reason to write a false account, and the only one he apparently spoke with was Abigail. She lied about Jack dying. She lied about Miss Verity marrying. She lied about the Captain leaving. The question is, why?"

"She was a sharp one, Miss Abigail," said Hadley. "And the family knew it. She was left to be the spokeswoman for the household. She pulled a fast one on the coroner."

"Yes," said Wren. "They obviously knew she was good at it. But let's think what they got out of it. The Captain was killed, not Jack, probably murdered. Was Jack the killer? He married Abigail—but they tried to keep it quiet, at least from the city authorities, as they married in Brooklyn, outside of Bedlow's sphere of influence. I don't know—five people, three women and two men, and then one of them was murdered, and some of them are lying. Probably all of them." *This is pointless. I can't even figure what modern people are up to. Now, I'm going to draw conclusions on those I never knew, who lived two hundred years ago, based on a few documents.*

She became aware Lavinia and Hadley were looking at her.

"There's one thing connecting the past and the present," said Wren. "Turnbull House."

"I was wondering when we'd get to that," said Lavinia, laughing. "Do you want to enlighten us?"

"Maybe the Captain didn't abuse his wife, but I can see him being a hard man."

"So, they killed him instead of grabbing what they could and running away, to save Katya Turnbull from being beaten to death by her husband," said Lavinia. "They did it to keep the house. Even if Abigail was just a servant, this was her home too. She liked her mistresses—but not her master. Ladies and servants wanted to remain in that house free from fear of the Captain."

Wren shook her head. "Yes, that's true. But it's more than that. The house...the house speaks of order. The house speaks of...serenity... civilization. It's ironic. He built a house to protect himself from the disorder of his life at sea, and it turns out to be his death warrant, because he could not adapt to the house he had built. The others could, but not him."

CHAPTER TWENTY-ONE

Silence hit the room heavily.

"Wren, I hope you're not telling us the house is haunted," said Lavinia.

"I prefer to think that the house has a strong effect on the people who live in it. Then and now. No, the Captain's ghost is not making anyone do anything. But whatever affected people two hundred years ago affected people today. When I know what happened to the Turnbulls, I'll know who is trying to kill Saffron. And why."

"We'll see," said Lavinia crisply. "Meanwhile, I have a few more items for you. First, a baptismal certificate for Katya and the Captain's son, Alexander Turnbull, born seven months after Coroner Bedlow's investigation. It would seem he grew up on the island and took over the family business. That's all we know about him—I couldn't immediately find any definitive records for him, but perhaps more searches might turn up something. Government records only show that the state eventually bought the house and island from 'Turnbull & Company.' It was doubtless after Katya and Verity were dead, or they wouldn't have been buried there." She clicked on the laptop.

"Next, a pair of death certificates for Abigail and Jack Llewelyn. They are buried together, in Queens, where they lived. Maybe you can find their gravestones, even after all this time. So it was clear that this was a true marriage, not some pretense to get away from a charge. Jack died in 1860, aged eighty. Abigail died in 1877, aged eighty-nine. The house and island had long passed out of the family by then."

"But who was in the house then?" asked Wren. "Had Jack and Abigail left, or were they still there?"

"Is that important?" asked Lavinia, and Wren heard the hint of a tease in her voice.

"It's very important. It's essential," said Wren. She heard the tension in her voice.

"Why?"

"Because I am convinced that, in a way I can't understand yet, there is a pattern of behavior between the Turnbulls and the Tallons. Love and hatred and a desire for a home that was as unique then as it is now."

"An instinct, Miss Fontaine?" asked Lavinia.

"Instinct is what we call a feeling based on seeing the same situations, the same patterns, over and over again. I have seen this again and again—a two hundred-year thread that ties Abigail to Saffron."

Lavinia looked a little taken aback.

"I wouldn't tangle with Wren," advised Hadley. "She put the entire film crew under her authority today. I'll give you the details later."

"I can't wait," said Lavinia. "Very well. Let's continue. Census records back then often didn't directly name everyone at an address, but we do have government documents about the sale, and some meticulous anonymous clerk, to whom we owe a debt of gratitude, named each person relocated from the island." Another click. "Mrs. Turnbull died in 1845. Miss Verity, two years later. That's when the sale took place. The clerk on the bill of sale noted several maids and manservants—for outdoor work, no doubt—left. Probably to seek new employment in the city. And Mr. and Mrs. Llewelyn, described as 'housekeeper' and 'house manager,' departing to live in the County of Queens, in a house purchased for them by the estate, according to the final wills of Verity Turnbull and Katya Turnbull. What does that tell you, Wren?"

"That everyone was on good terms. This conspiracy would require all of them to be on the same page, and they stayed together. They stayed together in that house until the Turnbulls, sister and wife, were dead, and the household was dissolved. That's important. The four of them taking their secrets to their graves."

"Okay," said Hadley. "So this is where we are. We're going to guess—and let's keep in mind; it's just a guess—that the Captain was an unsatisfactory husband to his bride. Abigail, the maid, was very close to the women, I'm sure. I know what I'm talking about: My ancestors had ladies' maids back when this was still New Amsterdam." She grinned. "I'm afraid those days are gone. Anyway, Abigail got her boyfriend, Jack, to kill the abusive husband. They put together that song and dance so no one would get in trouble for killing the Captain—a wealthy and influential man. Abigail sold the story to the coroner. So that's what happened, right?"

"Yes," said Wren, and then she became aware of how Hadley and Lavinia were looking at her, and she gave a wry smile. "Okay, okay, you're expecting me to say it's about the house. But I can see killing for that house."

"For the house, my dear?" asked Lavinia. "Not to stop the Captain from abusing his wife?"

"Of course, that's important," said Wren. "Women had no power, and there was little recourse back then. But it wasn't the unhappy wife or even a relation who killed the Captain. It was Jack. He'd be more likely to throw in his lot with a fellow man. He wouldn't have had the same closeness to Mrs. and Miss Turnbull, I'm guessing. And it wouldn't be easy to sneak up on the Captain—a man like him would've learned to protect himself."

"And the house? Where does it come in?" asked Lavinia.

"Now, I'm not being fair," admitted Wren. "I can only guess. We'd like to think Jack was so in thrall to Abigail that he'd kill for her. But maybe that wasn't it. Maybe it was about control of the house. All four were influenced by the power of this house, but none more than Jack, who, with the Captain dead, would be the de facto master, his position assured by the secret that bound them forever. That was the true motive. Jack wanted to be master. And even if the deed was not in his name—he married the servant Abigail, not the family member Verity—he would solidify his position."

"Nicely argued," said Lavinia, which pleased Wren. "Unfortunately, we've reached the end of the road here. There aren't likely to be any more revelations about motives. All we can be sure of is that they were all in a conspiracy."

"I'd like to think the house, with its strength and order, gave the women the courage," said Wren. The other women nodded.

"Yes, the house...oh, just one more thing. Not really relevant to this particular problem, but you may find it useful. I found something in the John McComb archives. No drawings, I'm afraid, but some financial documents, bills of sale. You had told me there were a few pieces of original furniture, and here is a receipt." Another page of copperplate, with numbers, listing furniture.

"Yes, this is interesting. We have a few original pieces left, and if I can match them to this, we can establish certain items as personally designed and built by McComb." Wren squinted. "Could you enlarge it a bit...there... now that's interesting. 'As ordered by A. Bloodworth, housekeeper.' That's interesting. The family really let her run everything, even the furnishings." She frowned, as thoughts chased themselves around her head. *Abigail, more than she appeared. Saffron, also full of surprises. Lovers who seemed to take the lead from their ladies—Jack and Cal. But surely all that was coincidence. Still, they had the house in common...*

"What were they like—Katya and Verity Turnbull, the sisters-in-law?" asked Hadley. "I'm not getting a picture of them."

"Katya was from Russia. Her English may have been poor, probably heavily accented," said Lavinia. "So she may have wanted to avoid dealing with others outside her family."

"And Verity may have been raised under her brother's shadow," continued Hadley, "and then under his thumb, not paired with an eligible bachelor, and stuck on this island with no chance for a husband. I bet she was very unhappy."

"We wanted to think she was engaged to Jack, but he married Abigail in the end, the poorer woman," said Wren. "If he had married Verity and then killed the Captain for the house..."

"But I want to think it was a woman's story. I know, back to the house—who was controlling it? Who was running the show? Katya? Verity? I think it was Abigail, de facto mistress."

"'The Admirable Crichton,'" said Lavinia. "An Edwardian play. An upper-class family is shipwrecked, and since the butler is the only one who knows how to do anything, he becomes, as you said, Wren, the de facto leader for years. And when they're rescued, he awkwardly has to go back to being a servant. Where does that take you?"

"I don't know," said Wren, shaking her head. "Not yet. I may have to sleep on this. I keep thinking of this makeshift nineteenth-century family, making their lives in that magnificent house in its magnificent simplicity, three women, one married, raising Katya's son. And now today, a new makeshift family, in the wake of more death, making a home again in that house. I'm still at a loss. But I still feel the connection—if I see one pattern, I'll see another."

"What we need is some home and hearth shopping," said Hadley. "A new bed, a real bed. I'll have more room in the kitchen. We're going to need decorations for the walls—that's your area of expertise, Wren."

"You're right." She stood. "Lavinia, as always, thank you so much. You and Angela will be our first guests when we move in."

"We'll be honored. But don't forget your father, Wren."

"I suppose he'll come for Hadley's cooking," said Wren.

"He'll come for you," said Lavinia. "I think Ezra may be a little more sentimental than you realize." Then she gave a wicked smile. "Especially if he's losing his girlfriend to Nicky Tallon."

Chapter Twenty-Two

Wren and Hadley stayed up late to scroll through furniture and bedding for their new apartment. They viewed headboards and dining room tables and dressers, and Wren had to remind herself they were furnishing a one-bedroom apartment, not Windsor Castle. She wistfully thought of the Turnbull furniture she had shown Saffron.

"Any chance Nicky would give any of that to us?" asked Hadley.

"I think Saffron has her heart set on it, although she might find furniture like that is better to look at than to actually use. There's a chair that would do nicely. But that linen press—I don't see how we'd even get it into the apartment." She sighed. "We just don't live that way anymore. I don't know if Nicky and Saffron have realized that. I don't see where they're coming from. They're hard enough to figure out, especially Saffron, and let's face it, reading people is not my strong suit."

"You're too hard on yourself," said Hadley.

"You're sweet, and I'm getting better, but it might be time to call in someone who's been working at this more intently than we have, has more knowledge—people spoke with her because they had to and tell her things they wouldn't tell me. Best of all, she's a people expert. Lieutenant Howard."

"Oooh…a partnership with her. This'll be like one of those TV shows where you keep bothering the professional. She tells you to mind your own business and stay out of her way, but you're the one who really knows the answer."

Wren laughed. "That sounds about right. Except I have some things to trade with her. I know the house. I know what it did to the Turnbulls and what it's doing to the Tallons. Also, it's been a while since Beebee's murder. No one's been arrested, so she may be a little nervous. Especially with this fourth attack."

"Good point, Little Bird. She's probably being pressed to bring this to a conclusion, and the East Coast production is wrapping up soon. But on the other hand, it'll be a disaster if she arrests the wrong person. She has to be sure. So maybe she'll be flexible about working with civilians."

Feeling emboldened, Wren pulled Howard's card out of her wallet. "Am I really going to do this?"

"If you think too much about it, you'll think of reasons not to," said Hadley.

Wren punched in the lieutenant's number. She expected voicemail but was surprised into a moment's silence when she heard Howard's voice.

"—Oh, Lieutenant Howard. It's Wren Fontaine. I…I have some information that may be of interest to you."

"About the Veronica attack? The whole thing? Can you tell me?"

"Yes…but it's better if I show you."

"This isn't a dead body, is it?"

No, it's a living house. "Architects are visual. I think it would help if you could come to the island." Wren heard a sigh.

"Tomorrow afternoon. Okay? I have a few things I can ask about anyway and want another look at the trailer—the crime scene people are going over every inch. Thanks." Wren clicked off.

"She's coming?" asked Hadley.

"Yes. I'm thinking you're right—she doesn't know where to go next. I'm going to introduce her to a suspect she doesn't know very well: the house."

* * *

The next day started with business as usual. Shooting would be done soon, and everyone was looking forward to getting away from the claustrophobic island, except for Wren. She'd miss Hadley's daily presence, but otherwise would be happy for weeks more, contemplating those well-proportioned rooms and the grandeur of the curved drawing room. She liked looking at it, but wished she could get further away from it for a wider look than she could get on the island. Perhaps...

Cal and Saffron were completely open now about their romance, holding hands and sharing kisses—not even a pretense of discretion now that they were married. Wren saw Veronica speak with both of them during a break, perhaps admonishing them to stop behaving like high school students and remember that Cal was not just Nicky's son-in-law. He was his employee.

Saffron made her way from the set to where Wren was working on the house.

"We've been thinking about honeymoon places," she said. "I know you said it'll be some time before this place is all done, but I'd be happy right here."

"I see your point," said Wren. "But it's also nice to get away. You appreciate a place more when you've been away."

"Hadley gave us the number for a travel agent who will find a great spot for us, even better than Hawaii." *Good, far away from danger.*

"I'm sure you'll find a great place. And speaking of marriage, I found out some more details from Lavinia about this house."

"Oh! I knew she would. She's so smart, like you. Did you find out everything that happened?"

"Not everything. It was a very long time ago. But Lavinia found a marriage license—"

"So Jack married Verity after all?"

"Actually, Jack married Abigail."

"Wow. Really? So..." She thought about that for a while. "Did they stay there forever?"

"Yes, actually. Jack and Abigail stayed here with Verity and Katya. Katya had a boy named Alexander. After Verity and Katya died, Alexander sold the island and moved away. But Jack and Abigail were given a house in New York and lived there for the rest of their lives, and they're buried there."

Saffron considered that with a gravity that was almost comic on that sweet face.

"So it's okay, then," she said. "Everyone was happy there. I guess it doesn't matter who killed the Captain. They stayed together and were happy."

"It would seem so," said Wren, and then decided to add, "And you and Cal and Nicky can be happy too."

"Good. And I think Veronica, too. I think she'll stay. I'm so glad she's going to get all better. Anyway, Cal and I are going to raise our family here. Maybe I should name the first Alexander or Alexandra, after Katya's baby. Veronica can help." Wren hadn't seen any evidence of Veronica's maternal instincts as a sort of step-grandmother, but that wasn't her problem. "Anyway, it's going to be okay now. I know it. It was okay for them, and it's going to be okay for us. Thanks so much, Wren, for everything." Another hug and kiss on the cheek. "We're going to leave the island soon, but we'll visit and see how things are going."

"Of course," said Wren. She looked closely at that sweet, cheerful face. Everyone said what you saw was what you got with Saffron, but no one could be as simple as she seemed. She was unsophisticated and uneducated, but not stupid. Wren knew that house better than anyone, and she could tell Saffron had a connection with it too. Someone else knew that about Saffron as well. That's why she was in danger.

Everyone also said Wren couldn't read people. Perhaps. Then she smiled to herself. *Perhaps I can read their reactions to this house.*

"You can visit any time," said Wren. She looked down at the film set. The actors were just milling about—no doubt they were just setting something up. All the better. She looked at her watch—she had time before Lieutenant Howard showed up. "But for right now, how would you like to take a boat trip?

I don't think we're looking at it right—that is, the house," said Wren. "You really appreciate it. We need to see the house from the water, as it was meant to be seen, the way the Turnbulls saw it. I have an idea."

Lavinia had told her she would have more perspective on the house if she waited a few days. Perspective was both literal and figurative, she realized. And it was a funny thing about a house on an island. Most houses were on roads. They were made to be seen from the road, or if it was a grand house, set back, from a driveway.

This house was seen from the pier where they docked, not the best view. But at least it was a short walk. Had it been that way two hundred years ago? Wren doubted it. The house had barely changed in two centuries, but Wren bet other things had. It was time to check.

Wren and Saffron walked to the pier, where one of the launch pilots was sitting with his feet up, reading a paper and waiting for his next trip. He was one of her favorites, looking as if he had been cast for his role in his fifties, with a face burned to a leathery color by years of wind and sun.

"You're the architect, right? I'm heading back to Manhattan in an hour," he said.

"Thanks—but I'm just here for a question. What do you know about these waters?"

He laughed. "Everything. I've been piloting boats here since before you were born. What do you want to know?"

"This pier. Of course, it's not the original one, but would you know if there has always been a pier in this spot? "

"Now that's interesting. Why do you ask?"

"It's a poor angle for viewing the house. There was no engineering reason to build it like that—that is, the house. They could've just as easily faced the path from this pier. So I'm wondering why."

He nodded. "If you're coming in with an engine, this is the closest spot to Manhattan, no problem. But because of prevailing winds and currents, it would be very difficult to sail or row here. Your best spot is further along the coast. If I came in on a sailboat with no engine, that's what I'd do. I'd build something there. Better land and better for coming in if you're sailing."

"Could you take us there?" asked Wren. "I don't mean drop us off. I mean, just take this boat and show us that spot, so we can see the house as the original owners would've seen it."

"Now?"

"Yes."

"It has to go on my log, and you'll get charged for it."

"Show me where to sign," said Wren.

The pilot started the boat, and Wren and Saffron boarded.

"Understand I can't be one hundred percent sure," he said, "But I can show you where they likely would've put it. Where I would've put it."

Wren watched as the view of the house changed as they made their way around the island. She could see the grand portico come into view, surrounded by the handsomely framed windows with their black shutters. From this distance, you couldn't see how faded the paint was and how dirty the glass had gotten. It was as if Wren was seeing the house for the first time. On land, she couldn't get back far enough to view it like this.

"This is it," said the Pilot. "This is where I'd put a pier. Less convenient but much safer. They say the guy who built it was a sea captain. He'd know this, and I'm sure he put it here."

Yes, agreed Wren. *Captain Turnbull would know.* Abigail, and the others, would see the house like this. They would see it in its civilized beauty and would know there was order on the island, order in the city.

Order in the world.

"If you sent some divers down, they might find remnants of a jetty," said the Pilot.

"Not necessary."

She looked at Saffron as she saw the house the way it was meant to be seen. Was it McComb who had decided this? Wren thought not. The Captain was the man of the sea. He wanted to see it this way when he sailed home.

"So this is the way they saw it, every time they came?" Saffron eventually asked. "This is how they saw their home?"

Wren nodded. "I can speak with Bobby about getting some marine specialists to build a pier in this spot again."

Saffron gave that a lot of thought. "I don't know if that's important," she said. "We're going to stay here, stay inside and on the island. I want the house perfect, but how we get there is not important. I mean, I'm really glad you brought me here, but we don't have to build a new place to land. Only our friends will visit, and they'll be here to see *us*," said Saffron. Wren looked closely at the girl's set chin. *She understands the importance of this home more than I do, more than the Captain...*

Wren turned to the pilot. "Thank you for the trip. I think we can go back now." Saffron had turned and was looking at the city.

"This is the view from my new room," she said. "I'm going to like that."

Chapter Twenty-Three

"Do you think Nicky and Veronica will want to bring a lot of people to the house?" Saffron asked when they got back.

"Why do you ask?"

"Veronica likes to be with lots of people. She seemed very interested in how the house looked on the outside, the impression it makes when people see it."

"I don't know Veronica well enough to say," said Wren. Seeing that didn't satisfy Saffron, she said. "Veronica is an actor, and actors are concerned with how things look. That doesn't mean she doesn't want to make a home here. Your father is an actor, and he clearly wants to make a home here."

"I get that," said Saffron. " I'm worried because Nicky likes her so much. I mean, he likes her more than Thalia. I wonder if I'll still fit in?" She looked to Wren for reassurance. *That's a very adolescent thing for a married woman to ask. Maybe she needed a reminder.*

"But I thought we decided you're now the chatelaine?" said Wren. "We've joked about it, but it's a serious responsibility. The house must work in a certain way. That's the chatelaine's job. Even if you have a housekeeper and cook and cleaning staff, the chatelaine is in charge. It's more than just being a...homemaker. Nicky will be busy making movies. Cal will need to help him. But you'll be in charge of this house."

"But what if Veronica becomes my stepmother?"

"I don't think Veronica will be interested in managing the house. That doesn't mean you and she can't work together, like Katya and Verity probably worked together."

"I'm thinking of Abigail. I'm thinking she ran things, even if she didn't own the house. She must've been very strong and brave, don't you think?"

"I think you're right," said Wren. The house ended up with four: Abigail and Jack, Katya and Verity. And now it seemed to come down to Cal and Saffron, Nicky and Veronica. No one ever figured out what happened to the Captain. Would they ever figure out who killed Beebee and Thalia?

"Will I be safe now that I'm married?" asked Saffron.

"Nicky is taking good care of his daughter," said Wren. "For now, I'd stay in groups with trusted people." Saffron seemed satisfied with that. *I'm glad to see she hasn't realized I didn't exactly answer her question.*

Saffron went back to the set, and Wren walked to the house. Hadley and Lieutenant Howard were waiting for her.

"Here I am with the architect and the caterer," said Howard. "Outsiders, among the in crowd. No offense." Hadley and Wren laughed. "So, you have something you want to share with me?"

"Let's go inside," said Wren.

Howard raised an eyebrow, but let Wren lead them into the curved great room.

"I didn't really appreciate this the last time I was here," said Howard. "I've never seen a room like this."

"A great architect like McComb knew how our eyes and our minds take in shapes. Only truly great architects know that. You will always feel wonder here because that's the way it's designed." She was aware that Howard was still looking at her. "Anyway, let's sit." The lieutenant took a cracked leather chair and Wren and Hadley a matching couch, equally dilapidated.

"Why did you want to speak with me? And why did it have to be here? Was it a casual word dropped that you heard? Are any attachments forming in recent days? Any falling apart? Or maybe—" and now she grinned. "Is this about the recovering Veronica? Did you want to update me on the love triangle of the year: Veronica Selwyn, Nicky Tallon, and your father?"

Hadley snickered, and Wren rolled her eyes. "Lieutenant, aren't there laws against police brutality? Anyway, my father and I stay out of each other's personal lives."

"I'm sure," said Howard. "And yet, I have to consider my options. I've been thinking about you since you called me. You are indeed connected to this house by more than your job. I'm wondering if you're going to get pushed out of your house by a new stepmother, or will it be Saffron?"

"That's ridiculous," said Hadley. "Wren and I are moving in together anyway. We've already signed a lease. And you probably know that Saffron and Cal are now married."

"I know. Cal is consolidating his position, no doubt. He can't want to spend his whole life as Nicky Tallon's gopher—that struck a chord with you, Ms. Fontaine, I can tell. I'm enough of a detective to know there was a reason you had to talk to me in this house, in this room, right?"

"Yes. It has to do with Jack and Cal, killing for this house all those years ago," said Wren. "For mastery of this house. But I don't think you've met Jack."

"One of the movie people?"

"No. He was a servant who, I believe, killed for control of this house two hundred years ago." Wren smiled. "I'm not a lawyer, but I'm guessing the statute of limitations has run on that?"

"You'd think so, but there's generally no statute of limitations on murder," said Howard. "Anyway, after two hundred years, it's safe to say no one is left to interrogate. But Cal—are you accusing him?"

"I'll be honest," said Wren. "I have zero evidence that Cal has killed anyone. He didn't like Beebee or Thalia, and they were also possibly standing in the way of the house. But I'm an architect, and we work with patterns. People work in patterns, and they like how the patterns in their homes reflect their lives and vice-versa. And that's happening here. I just can't put them together."

She looked closely at the lieutenant. Was she listening? Did she really hear her? Or did she think Wren was wasting her time? Her father was so good at sharing his enthusiasm for a house with clients, even skeptical ones. But even he never had to convince a police detective.

"Wonderful," said Howard. "So Cal is reflecting what this Jack did all those years ago. Would you like to be there when I tell the DA that I'm ready to make an arrest based on something the architect is pretty sure happened a couple of centuries ago?"

"I know," said Wren. "I know it's crazy. But the only way I can understand the houses I work on is by seeing them in the long-term context of the people who lived there. I am not a detective. My idea was to help you see these people—the suspects, I guess—in the context of such a powerful house. And you couldn't do that unless you really saw the house."

"And keep in mind," said Hadley, with a sidelong glance at Wren. "You don't seem close to making an arrest, lieutenant. If you were, you wouldn't have humored Wren by coming. We're not saying Cal has killed people. But maybe you could use some *context*." Wren felt herself flush with Hadley's support as Howard flashed back and forth between them.

"Yes, exactly. I think this is related to the house," said Wren. "I am hoping you will tell me what you know about how these people relate to each other and, ultimately, the house. If you'll excuse a pun, architects are always looking for new perspectives. You want to catch a murderer, and I want to complete my job with no interruptions."

The lieutenant smiled wryly. "Is that all?"

"All right. I have struck up a friendship with Saffron. I don't want to see anything happen to her."

"Oh, okay. You have a point. It's not that we don't have any angles; we have too many. I'm sure I'm not telling you anything new, but we can't find a reason for someone to want to kill Saffron. She has no money for now except what Nicky gives her. No power to change anything. And we would have to assume someone is so incompetent or unlucky they have failed four times to murder her. We're going to stick with the idea that someone really wanted to kill Beebee, to kill Thalia. Even Veronica—she's had a busy past. Look, can I trust you to be discreet? It's not usual to share things like this…but this isn't a usual case."

"Hadley and I work with rich and famous people," said Wren. "If we weren't discreet, we'd be out of work. I know there are things you can't tell me. But if I had some context for some of the people, it may all come together. Joking aside, they are related to this house."

"Well put. Okay. We've been over everyone's background. Hollywood is a mess—I reached out to some colleagues there. Everyone has some secrets. First of all, we wanted to find out where this fentanyl was coming from. We may know that now. Ironically, our first victim, Beebee Jenkins, was known to provide drugs on the side. Less as an income stream than as a way to make himself useful. But how something he may have dealt ended up in his drink is unclear. Still, we're following it up. But that's not even the most interesting thing I found—after all, drugs are rampant in L.A. I hear. It's about the house, as you keep saying, Wren. Was it your impression Nicky found it?"

"Yes—it was his dream, I was told," said Wren.

"A little pressure on Zach Landau got me a different story. It was actually Saffron who found it, scrolling through realty ads—they didn't want to make it look like Nicky was under her thumb, so they passed it off as his choice. He really wanted a big spread in the rural West, but Saffron wanted as far away as possible from there. As it turns out, she had bad memories, as we know. And she was insistent. Zach approved it—it satisfied their need for privacy, plus Zach and the movie people could reach Nicky easily, just outside of New York. It was Beebee who objected, feeling he was getting cut out of the party; he wanted Nicky to remain in his sphere of influence in L.A. Bottom line? Saffron was the intended victim, targeted by someone who knew it was her desire to live here, not Nicky."

"But four failed attempts?" asked Wren.

"Yeah. We're wondering if someone else is piggybacking to kill for another reason, making it look like it's the same motive." Howard sighed. "That's the hard part. I can't tell you everything, but we're spending hundreds of hours digging into everyone's pasts as a result. No big reveals here—just a slog through data."

Wren didn't respond, just kept looking around the room. Then she suddenly felt Hadley and Howard looking at her.

"I'm sorry. Just organizing my thoughts," said Wren. "It doesn't matter about all those other people with their other motives. It doesn't matter Beebee was dealing drugs. And there is no piggybacking, as you say. I'm focused on patterns, and the patterns are clear. Abigail and Saffron. Cal and Jack. Strong-willed women like Katya and Verity and Thalia and Veronica. And this two-hundred-year-old house."

Wren suddenly realized she was saying all that out loud and felt embarrassed. Hadley, she saw, was amused. Howard had apparently concluded Wren had lost her mind. She leaned back in her chair and chuckled, then turned to Hadley. "Is she always like this?"

"Is it any wonder I love her?" said Hadley.

"All right, I know it sounds crazy," said Wren. *I have to bring back Howard. I have to make her see.* "But last night, I started thinking about Buckminster Fuller, the great architect and inventor. He once said when he was working on a problem, he didn't think about its beauty, just the solution, but when he was done, if the solution wasn't beautiful, he knew it was wrong. I can feel this house. I can feel the Turnbulls and the Tallons *responding* to it. What you're saying is wrong. You tell me this was a Hollywood mess, but then there's always something going on in Hollywood. The murders started with this house, at this house, and I know Saffron is in danger because of that."

"Sell me on it," said Howard.

Okay, almost there. "With all you told me about what was happening here, with Nicky and those close to him, makes me see how they work as a de facto family. This helps me as an architect. All those people are stones in the arch but get rid of the keystone, and that's it. Saffron is the keystone. Get rid of Saffron, and the whole thing falls apart. That's why someone wants to kill her."

"Okay, but who wants that," said Howard. "And who has screwed it up *four times?*"

"I don't know," said Wren. "But I will. And meanwhile, I'll tell you one thing about this house you can be sure of. Lots of people admire it, but as I said, Saffron is the only one who loves it. If I've figured out Saffron loves this place enough to essentially force Nicky and Cal to live here, with the blessing of Zach Landau, you can bet at least someone else has noticed too. That was the one important thing you told me—*Saffron* found this house."

Howard nodded, and they sat in silence for a few minutes.

"I have to go," she said. "Thank you for your time. I'd like to say you made this easier, but I'm afraid not. I appreciate your insights, but it's still a slog." She walked to the door. "However, that doesn't mean you haven't been useful."

She left Wren and Hadley sitting alone on the ancient couch. They didn't speak, and eventually, Wren collapsed onto Hadley's shoulder.

"I've never been so tired in my life. Just…people."

"I know. People are the worst," said Hadley.

"Did I just look like a complete idiot?" Wren asked.

"Not at all. You were absolutely brilliant, in fact. The question is whether you convinced the lieutenant. And the jury is still out on that one."

"My father would've convinced her. I've watched him again and again persuade clients when they had ghastly ideas. Look at him—he persuaded Veronica to sleep with him."

"Wren, I know you're an architect, but that doesn't mean you have to build a house for Veronica in your head where she can live forever. She's messed with you, and you can't get rid of her."

Wren sighed. "You're right. Let's look to the past. I think I have everything I need to figure it out. I need to understand what it is about Saffron that makes her such a threat and to whom. And Abigail. There's a connection. Hey—here's an idea. Can we do a sleepover?"

"What?"

"An air mattress and a blanket, and we'll spend tomorrow night in this house, in the master bedroom. It will give me a sense of this house."

"A slumber party! What a great idea. And you're always saying you're not cool or spontaneous. We'll find what secrets Katya and Verity hid."

"Not them," said Wren. "Abigail. Somehow, this is Saffron's and Abigail's story."

Chapter Twenty-Four

The next day went by fast. Wren and Bobby went over walls stained by decades of leaking water and discussed the plumbing requirements. Some of the moldings were beyond repair, but enough of them were left to recreate the whole house. She'd soon be able to go over lighting fixtures with Nicky and Saffron. Would either of them be interested in details like that? Or maybe Veronica? No—as Hadley said, evict her from her head.

"This is going to sound funny, but I'd like to have been there when they built this," said Bobby. "I know about the Victorians, but something this old…I can't even figure out how they did some of the things they did with what they had. And I wouldn't even know where to go to reproduce some of the things they did here. They didn't even have kerosene back then—it was another world, I'm thinking."

"And I'm thinking you're right," said Wren.

There was still a lot of work ahead, but she could begin to see in her mind the house when it was complete. What would Nicky think when it was done? How would it be with Nicky and Veronica, Cal and Saffron, rattling around in it? It was a big house, an isolated house. But then again, it had been for Captain Turnbull and his wife and sister. Was it a refuge for them back then? It may very well be a refuge now, from Hollywood and from Saffron's past. And that was indeed worth something. *What if it could belong to me and Hadley, just the two of us here, inviting friends when we wanted, but day by day, just the two of us, in this masterpiece? When I was a girl, I wanted to live in Manderley all by myself. But not anymore. People made a home, no matter how big or small. Would the next residents understand that?*

Hadley said they were almost done with the filming and there was a celebratory air among the crew. Would Lieutenant Howard be able to just walk away from this as her suspects scattered? It would be months before the house was ready for Nicky.

Maybe tonight, Wren would get a sense of the house, of Abigail and the other residents.

Saffron had been excited when Wren told her that she and Hadley were spending the night. "Oh, that sounds like fun. Can I come too?"

"That's not a good idea. I need to connect to the house. It won't be comfortable. We'll come to your housewarming party when the house is done."

"Okay." And then Saffron lowered her voice. "But aren't you afraid the house is haunted? I don't mean like horror movie ghosts, of course. I mean—the memories, I guess, the personalities of the people who lived before. They could be emotionally scary."

"Every old house is haunted that way," said Wren. "I'm not afraid. That's why I work on them."

* * *

Hadley and Wren watched the crew close up, lock away their equipment, and take the launches back to Manhattan.

"Okay, Little Bird. I've put together a smashing dinner. We'll set up the bedroom, open up the laptop, and choose furniture and rugs and wall hangings for our new apartment."

The sun went down, and they enjoyed Hadley's cold barbecue chicken, sesame noodles, and salad by the lights of the few lamps Bobby had set up in the oval great room. "They didn't even have kerosene yet back then," said Wren. "It was whale oil—with its fishy smell. They were in the dark here most of the time. They'd look across the water to a dark city, just the small family and their servants. We can't imagine what that was like, day after day, night after night. What went through Abigail's mind here? What were they all thinking?"

"You're in luck: I brought my own herbal tea. Guaranteed for pleasant dreams."

At eleven, they slipped under the covers in the corner master bedroom and turned off their battery-operated lamp—the generators keeping the worksite running were now off.

"Good night, my love," said Wren.

"Good night, Little Bird."

Wren soon heard Hadley's gentle breathing. She always fell asleep quickly. Wren just stared into the dark. She could really think in the house now, no noise from the workmen, from the film crew, from Saffron. Just a chance to absorb the house and think about its first residents.

The Captain—no doubt a hard man but ultimately a cipher, killed by his own servant. Jack—what had driven him to the worst of crimes? If Jack had been Verity's or Katya's lover, yes, but he was not and had served the Captain for years. Verity—alone, with no husband, no true responsibilities, no place in the world. Katya—far from her home on this empty island in an arranged marriage. And finally, Abigail—the guardian of the family who managed Coroner Bedlow so adroitly. Abigail, the perfect servant, probably the true chatelaine here, caring for this house so well. They had fine linens, no doubt, stored in that beautiful linen press. Abigail would handle them herself. Linen was expensive, and she wouldn't trust a lesser maid with them. Abigail, wandering from room to room, checking the bedding, farming the cleaning out to her juniors, watching them with a sharp eye, then checking on the cook to make sure dinner was proceeding. Were they running out of anything?

Jack, teasing her, flirting with her. Or did they just come to an agreement soberly, these stolid Anglo-Dutch citizens?

There was no understanding that, so she focused on what she knew. The house. The strong, responsible Abigail, managing this eternal house, making sure all those moldings were dusted and that the house looked perfect, as she came back from the city, seeing it as it was meant to be seen—from the water.

The furniture. So sad it had been scattered more than a century ago. Abigail, moving around carefully, telling Jack to repair every loose hinge that rattled. But that linen press was there, that beautiful linen press, so big. Had Abigail commissioned it from the architect?

It was huge. How many linens did they have? How many quilts?

Suddenly, Wren had to see it. Now. She slipped out of bed and into her sheepskin slippers. She had a flashlight but didn't need it. Wren now knew every inch of that house. With a wry thought, she realized Abigail was probably the last person who knew it this well.

It was enormous, black on black, in the unlit room. A bright city provided some light. Wren opened it up and reached in. Just like Abigail had, putting the precious expensive linens on the highest shelf. But she couldn't. That's what had been bothering her. Why did a bright, organized woman commission a piece of furniture from a great architect like McComb that was too tall for her to easily access?

Wren felt her heart pound. Thoughts rolled one after the other. The puzzle pieces fell into place quickly: Abigail and Jack, and the Captain. Nicky and Saffron and Cal.

Shuffling feet and a flashlight interrupted her.

"Uh, Wren? You're not going to make a habit of midnight furniture inspection once we move in together, are you?"

"It's too big," said Wren.

"It sure is. Were you going to ask Nicky to give it to us? We couldn't even get it through the door."

"Abigail. This was hers, you see. This was hers, so she must've been tall enough to use it."

"Okay...."

"And if she was tall enough to use this enormous piece of furniture...you follow me?"

"Oh God," said Hadley, suddenly getting it. "Erik said the Captain was killed by someone at least five foot ten, so we assumed it was a man. But it wasn't. Abigail was tall. Abigail killed the Captain."

"Yes. The Captain was no doubt a cautious man, his instincts honed from a life at sea. But he wouldn't have thought anything about Abigail approaching him. After all, she was just the housekeeper."

"But why?"

"I was right," said Wren. "It wasn't as much about love or jealousy as it was about this house—and the power it gave her. It was about control then, and it's about control now by someone as clever and resolute as Abigail. It's less about *why* than *who*. Not to Coroner Bedlow, not to Lieutenant Howard, of course, but to me."

"But Saffron...isn't it about her?"

Wren slowly nodded. "Yes. I'm sorry. I have to get out of architect mode. It's about Saffron, of course...." She looked at Hadley. "History is repeating itself."

"This is insane, Little Bird. You do know that. I'm not saying you're wrong. In fact, I can't think of any other way this works. It's...perfect. Like this house, as you say. But as the lieutenant said, how are you going to sell it?"

Wren felt the pulse in Hadley's hand. The sky had begun to turn gray over Manhattan. People would be commuting soon. The film crew and Bobby and his team would be getting up and returning to the island.

"I'm supposed to be working on the house, and I keep getting stuck talking to *people*. And now I'm going to have to talk to Veronica about this...mess. She's the only one who can help us now."

"Wren, I think it would be easier to just turn this whole thing over to Lieutenant Howard. We can convince her. It'll be easier than tackling this directly."

"And if someone else dies meanwhile?"

Hadley surprised her by laughing. "You're a fake. You want me to think it's about the house, but you're putting people first."

"Don't tell my father," said Wren.

"Okay. We'll talk to Veronica. It's going to be a challenge. She's tough and smart. But I'm with you." She squeezed Wren's hand.

The sky continued to get light.

"You know, it really is a beautiful house despite everything," said Hadley. "I really like it. Maybe it's in my DNA, but my family has been here since the seventeenth century, so along the way, we probably lived in something like this. I would hate to think these killings poisoned this place."

"I think…" said Wren, in that slow, thoughtful way that Hadley had learned, signaled a major statement from her girlfriend. "I think that I may have to reconsider my theories. I am not going to say the house caused any tragedies. It was the reactions of the people who lived here or wanted to live here and expected something that couldn't be. Houses stamp themselves on people; that's true. But maybe people can stamp themselves on houses. And if we're lucky, the next people who live here will give it…."

"Good karma?" suggested Hadley.

Wren smiled. "Something like that."

Chapter Twenty-Five

Wren met with her father at his favorite midtown steakhouse. His doctors had warned him about red meat and cholesterol years ago, but Ezra still gave himself the occasional treat.

"The doctor keeps telling me that I'm not getting any younger. I'm so glad he spent four years in medical school to learn that time moves in a linear fashion. Anyway, I'm having the porterhouse."

"Speaking of doctors, how is Veronica?"

"Full recovery. She's been released and, as you can imagine, eager to be done with the filming. Now, this is your meeting, Miss Fontaine. And it's worth a celebration when you actually want to report to me on your project."

Her head was still a little fuzzy from not enough sleep. She had found a room where Bobby and his crew weren't working and grabbed a few hours in the afternoon, so she could have a profitable talk with the senior partner of her firm.

"It's a magnificent house. The fundamentals are all good. Bobby is delighted to go over the initial construction—he says it was put together by a master. A few places that need shoring up—nothing we can't do."

"The budget?"

"Oh, Father, we can shoot for the moon here. Our client has limitless funds." She smiled wryly as her father glared at her.

"It's a good thing you're a good architect, because you're a failure as a comedian."

"Don't worry. We're on track. Actually, Zachery Landau watches every dime. He frowns at each bill but always signs off. But mentioning a lawyer brings me to my next topic."

He raised an eyebrow. "This is about the murders."

"Yes. It's about a studio executive named Beebee and a model named Thalia, and I think it's going to come to a conclusion soon."

"An unpleasant one?"

"I don't think the end of any murder investigation is pleasant," said Wren.

"You always did like word games like that. It drove your mother crazy. You know what I mean. What you're saying is that this isn't going to be some deranged outsider who thought he was getting instructions from space aliens, but someone close to our client."

"Yes," she said.

"The police told you."

"No. Lavinia and I uncovered a murder among the Turnbulls, and it all adds up."

"Your professor is one of the most brilliant people I know, even if she does think I'm stuffy. So I'll give you the benefit of the doubt."

"I want you to know that it's going to involve Veronica Selwyn."

Her father took a moment to intently contemplate his creamed spinach while Wren watched him closely. She wondered if he was going to ask her if Veronica was going to be arrested for murder and, if so, how she'd respond, but he didn't.

"It was casual," he finally said.

"I didn't ask."

"But I want you to know anyway. I hope you're not moving out because you were afraid Veronica was moving in. That was never in the cards. Both of us knew that."

"Oh God!" said Wren, louder than she meant to. People actually looked from other tables. "There should be limits even to your arrogance. You think every decision everyone makes revolves around you. I'm leaving for no other reason than Hadley, and I want to make a life for ourselves together."

Her father didn't turn a hair. Of course. "And I wish both of you every happiness." He added more sour cream to his baked potato. "It will be rather empty in the house, but I'd be happy to host visits."

"Good. Because I want to discuss the Brooklyn house."

"New topic now? We're done with Veronica and the police?"

"No, same topic," said Wren. *Okay, this is your father, your senior partner, don't look weak.* "I am always trying to be a better architect. And that means, in my case, learning how to deal better with people. There is going to be fallout affecting our client, and your inamorata Veronica."

"Yes, Wren, I have friends who have helpfully emailed me the gossip pages. Apparently, I'm trending on Twitter."

"Good for you," said Wren. "And yes. It's going to affect everyone. I want to keep the project on track no matter what, and that means managing people, which is not my strong suit, as you keep pointing out. It means managing how people are relating to that extraordinary home. And how families react to homes generally. And how you, me, and Mom related in our Brooklyn house. I guess what I'm saying is, I know that house was practically falling apart when you bought it, and you made it what it is. But Mom made it a home." She eyed her father closely. "Is that insulting?"

He laughed. "Perhaps. But it's also true. I can't point here and there and say, 'this was me' and 'this was your mother.' But she did make it home for all of us."

"But she's been gone for over a decade. And yet I still feel her there. Again, it's a people thing, but I feel it nonetheless."

"In this case, you're right. I do too. And that, dear daughter, is the power of architecture. Not just the building but all the appointments, the furniture, the people who live in it. It's as true in our house as it was in any other."

"All right," said Wren. "But I want to take it a step further. Is there something about our house that was conducive to making it a residence, even before you and Mom made it our home."

"Wren, architects have been doing that for centuries, for millennia. You know that. What are you really asking?"

She felt nervous. Would her father think her insane? Lieutenant Howard already thought she was. "I am asking if there was something inherent in our house that made it easy to make it a home. And if it's possible that there was something in the Turnbull house that makes it conducive to...well, to death."

Her father paused—but he didn't laugh.

"So this is where this has been leading," he said. "Did the Turnbull house turn Veronica into a killer? Could our Brooklyn house have turned her into a loving wife and stepmother? Interesting." He was a master of sarcasm, but she heard none now. "Remember the house I designed in Connecticut for Conrad Agnew, that tech fund manager?"

"The one the Times called a 'true modernist masterpiece.' Of course, I remember."

"Anyway, I wasn't the least bit surprised when he and his wife divorced two years after moving in. Bitter fight over alimony, child support. I think the wife got the house in the end. I could've told them that house wasn't a suitable family environment."

"Ah. So you deliberately designed a home to promote divorce."

"Thank you, Wren. I'll put you in charge of the firm's marketing initiatives. No, I didn't deliberately do that. I was asked to create what was essentially a stage for a man with a monstrous ego and boundless greed. And I did that. I did that perfectly. If he had wanted a nurturing environment, I would've created that. I'm an architect, not a psychologist."

"Aha! So you set up your wife and baby daughter in a sweet Brooklyn townhouse instead of a 'modernist masterpiece' because it was more nurturing for a family?"

"I loved your mother very much. I knew I could turn that townhouse into a perfect environment for your mother, to make her happy. And I was right. The house was indeed a perfect environment for us. Coffee?"

At least today, that was all she was going to get on her mother. But she had heard what she needed to know about both Brooklyn and Turnbull House. She watched her father add some cream, no sugar, into his coffee and precisely stir it.

"So Wren, you seem to think that there is something in Turnbull House that, let's say, promoted these crimes. Houses are neither virtuous nor evil. They are well designed and constructed or not. It's when people look for something the home can't give them that we run into problems. As for

Turnbull House, I can't say. You know that home, and I don't."

I do. The house was perfectly ordered. A refuge from an untamed world. Was that the kind of house the Captain had asked McComb to design for him? Was it that different from Nicky, who wanted a refuge from Hollywood?

She looked at her placid father. Had Veronica told him anything, even a hint? She thought of what Hadley would say. "If Veronica spends any more time in your head, at least charge her rent." Her father broke into her thoughts. "You will keep me posted, of course, of any developments." He half-smiled. "And do be careful."

Chapter Twenty-Six

"Casual," said Wren. "My father said he and Veronica were just casual. That was his word."

"And no hint that she shared anything with him?" asked Hadley.

"None. I gave him a chance. I mean, I warned him that Veronica was involved. I didn't say how, though."

"So, no lever."

"No, unfortunately, but it wasn't a waste of time by any means. My father thinks I'm right. He agrees that houses can lead to something like this. We are on the right track."

"That's good," said Hadley. "But is this going to help us with Veronica? One way or the other, she has no reason to cooperate with us."

"Perhaps," said Wren. "But we're going to take her on in the house. It's why it happened. And it's why she's going to work with us. Look, if nothing else, Veronica knows the power of a setting."

"The house." They stepped off the launch onto the ground, and Hadley looked up at the mansion. "Yeah. You may be right."

There was a celebratory air on the island. The director was happy with what they had, and the location filming would likely end that day. It was back to L.A. for everyone. Saffron was skipping around talking to people, and Cal was in a huddle with Nicky.

"Cal seems to be applying himself to his job again," said Wren. "He's won Saffron and doesn't have to spend all that time pursuing her. He's trying to stay on the good side of his boss and father-in-law." Cal gave a final nod to Nicky and then jogged over to Veronica, and they put their heads together.

Wren sighed. "Look at that. They have to keep it all together. It's a group event, as I said. I never saw that—with the Turnbulls or Nicky and company. Let's try to grab Veronica now. Before someone else is attached."

Veronica was out of costume, in a casual pair of slacks and a matching blouse. She caught Wren and Hadley walking to her and smiled.

"So glad you're better," said Wren.

"Thank you. I admit it was terrifying, but as the method acting people say, I'll use that someday. Anyway, I'm glad we're wrapping up. I want to give you some final hugs. I'm going to miss you, but we'll meet again when this house is complete. Also, there's going to be a big premiere party, and I already made sure Cal put you on the list."

"How is he doing, by the way?" asked Wren.

"Oh, I know I make jokes about him. But he's going to be a good husband, and he's been very loyal to Nicky, and loyalty is in short supply around here. You know, Saffron really likes you two. You're like the cool big sisters. I'm thinking about what Cal said earlier about toning it down with Saffron on the crime. She has a new life here, and we're all going to be living here together." She smiled wryly. "More or less. Anyway, a chance to heal and move on. She's had a rough life."

Wren steeled herself for the speech she had prepared and rehearsed with Hadley. "Listen, I know we didn't exactly get off on the right foot—for which I blame myself. It's been just me and my father for some time. I'm an only child—sharing doesn't come naturally to me."

Veronica laughed. "Say no more. I wasn't very kind myself."

"Let us make it up to you. If you have time this evening and don't mind a studio apartment, Hadley and I would like to have you over for dinner." She hoped her beating heart wasn't showing through her shirt.

Veronica looked at her without emotion. Wren would have trouble anyway, but no one could read this actress if she closed down.

"You know what? I would like that very much. Thank you. Can I bring wine?"

"Thanks, but I don't drink," said Hadley.

"You're wise," said Veronica. "It ruins the complexion."

* * *

"I ought to write a cookbook—the cramped gourmet," said Hadley. "How to cook in a small kitchen. I can't wait until we're in our new place."

As Hadley attended to the stove, Wren slipped up behind her and gave her a hug. It surprised Hadley; Wren wasn't a hugger.

"I want you to know," said Wren, "that I realize that I sounded a little hesitant about moving in together, but now I am frustrated with having to wait until next month. I feel silly delaying. I'm sorry for that. I'm one hundred and one percent in."

Hadley turned around and smiled. "It's okay. You are who you are, and it's good that we balance each other. I'm glad you're reassuring me you're fully onboard, but it wasn't necessary. You may find it hard to read me, but I can easily read you. Still, don't worry. You're the house-whisperer in our relationship." She turned back to her cooking. Wren kissed her on the back of her head and set the table.

Veronica showed up five minutes late with a box from Sugar Sweet Sunshine.

"I know," said Veronica. "But we're almost done filming, so if I slip a little above my ideal weight, I'm okay until the next project. By the way, I was very pleased that the Con Ed workers outside your building were big fans of my Captain Blake role and was happy to take selfies with them. They promised to see my film with Nicky. Anyway, lovely little place but I'm glad you're getting a chance to move on."

"We'll have a real kitchen," said Hadley. "Of course, we have a professional kitchen I use for my business, but to have a real kitchen for us...."

"Yes," said Veronica. "I can see that. I was thinking about the kitchen at the Turnbull House. You're the expert, of course, Wren, but I've heard those were the warm places, and I'm guessing that little island is really unpleasant in January. Did everyone just hang out in the kitchen? That oval room was nice, but how warm was it?"

"You're right," said Wren. "Here, have a seat. Can I get you anything? Hadley made her patented low-sugar lemon iced tea, plus her homemade hummus and veggies."

"Lovely." Wren got them drinks and sat on the couch with Veronica.

"About the kitchen—yes," said Wren. "It's funny. I'm a terrible cook, but I love kitchens. I think Saffron does too. She understands the family aspect of the house—there's a reason we use the term 'home and hearth.' Some look at the Turnbull House and think of its beauty. Saffron looks at it and sees a home."

"I'm glad. I wonder just how warm that hearth is going to have to be to keep them warm through their first winter here. But Nicky and Saffron grew up in Idaho and I grew up in New Jersey, so maybe everything will work out. Poor Cal is from California—he'll be cold. Say, either of you two been to California?"

"San Diego, briefly," said Wren.

"A couple of weeks in L.A. and a couple of weeks in San Francisco," said Hadley. "I was told I had a good time—I don't remember."

"Well, you'll be my guests in Los Angeles," said Veronica. "I know it inside-out."

"Saffron seems to think that Hadley and I will be your guests at the Turnbull House." She looked closely at Veronica as Hadley poured herself some iced tea and joined them at the table.

"Wren." Veronica leaned over and put her hand on Wren's knee. "I know you love that house. If it were in my power, I'd hand you the deed when you were done on it, and you two ladies could live there the rest of your lives."

Like Katya and Verity, surrounding themselves with that house, drinking tea in that oval room evening after evening, sitting in the shade of the house on summer evenings until the sun set, until Manhattan went dark.

"For us?" asked Wren. "Not for you and Nicky and Saffron and Cal?"

"Wren," Veronica said again. She sounded like her father; he'd talk to her just like that. Maybe in their short acquaintanceship, Veronica had picked that up. "You've seen Saffron. You've seen Nicky. He's unsophisticated and uneducated, but he is by no means stupid. He wanted a couple hundred acres out West, and I don't blame him. He doesn't fit in that house, and I'm not judging him for it. That pair won't even make it through the first winter there. This house is a bright and shiny toy."

Hadley caught Wren's eye: *later. There will be time later, after a nice meal.*

"Dinner should be ready now," said Hadley. "You're going to love it."

Veronica smoothly turned the conversation to all the places in Southern California she'd like to show them. "Not all the tourist stuff. I have friends with lots of fun houses—nothing like what you have on the east coast, Wren. Fantastic restaurants, Hadley. All kinds of people..." She was a good storyteller, Wren would give her that, and the good food helped make everything merry.

Or was Veronica just playing the role of a storyteller? With an actress at Veronica's level, the line was very thin.

Hadley trusted only one shop in Manhattan for her coffee and had worked with them to create a custom blend. She served it with the fruit tarts Veronica had brought.

"Yes," said Veronica, "trust me. Southern California in winter. Our little Saffron will hop into a bathing suit, and we'll all have fun in the sun. She'll get used to Nicky's lovely house there. It's not Turnbull House, but it's very nice."

"Saffron told me it was more of an HQ for friends, supporters, and fans of Nicky Tallon than a true home," said Wren. "The funny thing is, she grew up without a real home, so I tend to trust her. Now you were saying about Nicky—he and Saffron see the house as a bright and shiny toy. You may be right about Nicky—you know him better than I do." She forced herself to keep her tone even as she watched a small smirk on Veronica's face. "But I am telling you that Saffron loves the Turnbull house. I've watched scores of people, maybe hundreds, look over houses. And I know. This isn't just a toy. Not for Saffron. And that is why there is so much death here. Two murders, one attempted murder."

Veronica's eyes flickered back and forth between her two hosts.

"You're not going to let go of this, are you?" Veronica shook her head and grinned. "I don't know if there's a code among architects or chefs. But despite our bickering and jealousies, there is a tight bond among those of us in film. I didn't want to say it earlier, but Beebee Jenkins had been augmenting his income and keeping his associates happy by supplying various drugs. One of his customers, and sometime business partner, was the dear departed Thalia."

"Lieutenant Howard told us, but not that you were the source," said Wren.

Veronica shrugged. "If nothing else, this will get Howard away from us and onto another track, back in L.A."

Wren gave Hadley a quick look.

Veronica just looked at Wren, who wondered if the actress could see her heart pounding, smell the sweat.

"You're not worried about someone trying to kill you?" asked Wren.

"They're trying to kill Saffron. And not succeeding. Anyway, with the shooting wrapping up, we can protect her better."

"No. You can't. I'm paying you a compliment when I say you know why."

"Wren. Can I ask what you're talking about?" asked Veronica. *Oh yes, you're a brilliant actor*, thought Wren.

"I'm talking about homes. What people will do when a residence like the Turnbull House is on the table. This isn't about some wood and glass monstrosity overlooking a private beach in Southern California or an Idaho trailer park, or a great big ranch in the Wild West. This is about one of the most extraordinary homes ever built in this city, in this country, and what people will do to have it or to make sure someone else doesn't have it."

"Well," said Veronica. "I didn't know you had it in you to be so…passionate."

"When it comes to buildings, she's all in," said Hadley. "She once called a client a 'pompous bourgeois vulgarian.' I was there."

"I'm sorry I wasn't," said Veronica. "So the bottom line is that our little Saffron is still in danger. Supposedly from whatever drug cartel Beebee and Thalia have been involved with."

"I have no idea if Beebee and Thalia were involved with drugs. Whether they were or not has no bearing on this. You know what this is about," continued Wren. She took a breath. "And for Saffron's sake, it's time to end this. I insist."

Veronica just let the silence sit there. Wren suddenly felt she had eaten too much for dinner out of anxiety and was going to be sick.

"It's already done," said Veronica. "There aren't going to be any more killings and don't give me a speech about justice for Beebee and Thalia. And don't waste your time worrying about me. I was lucky. And now I'm in control. You need to know there's much more weight on the scales of justice than those two."

"Oh my God," said Hadley. "You delivered that exact same line as Captain Blake in Bronx Precinct. Nice!"

Veronica glared at her—then laughed. "Oh wow, with the pair of you double-teaming me, I'm never going to get out of here alive. All right, guilty as charged. I'm a great actress, but I can't make up my own lines—I'm not a playwright. But the point remains. Let it lie, Wren. For everyone's sake. I can take care of myself. Things will be fine going forward, I assure you. I was careless, but I'm not naïve."

"I won't argue the morality point," conceded Wren. " My profession is rooted in physics and earth science. And I know you can't look me in the eye and tell me there will be no more murders. You, and Nicky, and Cal, and Saffron all want what you want. And when that house is involved, I find it hard to blame any of you for what you've done. But you can't really think it's over. You're too smart."

Veronica just stared again, but then turned away. "Christ, Wren. Manipulating people by flattering them. Maybe you could get a job as a Hollywood agent. What if I just walk out of here?"

"Maybe she can't persuade you to come clean," said Hadley. "But Wren knows what happened to Captain Turnbull. It's all clear to her. It's all about this house now, not people. You've seen how persuasive she can be. If she can't persuade you, there's still a chance she can persuade the lieutenant today's murders weren't just about a drug deal gone wrong."

"It will take a while," said Wren. "But architects are patient. I'm not letting go of that house either. My name is not on the title, but I think of it as mine as much as did McComb. And that goes for the people who are involved with it."

Veronica sighed and stood up. "Thank you for a lovely dinner and the stimulating conversation. I really mean that. I'll call you tomorrow, and we'll talk further. I'll tell you one more thing—I'm two decades older than you two and see a lot more gray than black and white. Think on that. And that's all me, not Captain Blake."

Wren stood to show her out.

"I'm sorry," said Wren.

"No need to apologize."

"Thank you. And can I ask—do you, did you, care for my father?" She forced her voice not to waver.

Veronica rested a hand on Wren's cheek. "Silly girl. I only slept with him so he'd make me mistress of that really smashing townhouse you grew up in. Too bad he's still in love with the memory of your mother." She looked over Wren's shoulder at Hadley, winked, and slipped away.

Wren just stared after her. "I'll help you clean up," she said. "But first, I'm going to curl up in a fetal position on the couch."

Hadley laughed. "Fair enough. I'll sit with you." Hadley wrapped herself around Wren.

"I have never felt so drained. I want to move with you to Paris where no one knows us and live a La Boheme life. I'll restore old houses, you'll cook, and as we age, we'll cultivate a reputation among the local children as those strange American ladies who are probably witches."

"Ooh. That sounds very lovely. We'd like it there very much. They could put you to work fixing up Versailles. But as you well know, we'd run into the same things there we run into here. It'll be even worse there, because the homes are much older, and France is...full of French people." They both giggled.

"Thank you," said Wren. "You're right, of course. And we're stuck here for now with this. I haven't any idea of what just happened here. Did I reach Veronica? I can't tell with normal people, and she's far from normal. Still, I think I appealed to her vanity that she couldn't reverse directions now."

"Oh, you reached her, Little Bird. Her vanity is her Achilles' heel. The real question is, what is she going to do? If she says nothing, can she make peace with herself? I don't know her well enough. I doubt if anyone does."

"I bluffed, but can we really make a case if she doesn't open up? I'm not sure, now that Veronica has put Lieutenant Howard on the scent of Beebee's drug ring, that we can pull her back again to the house. After all, these were fentanyl murders, so maybe it was the truth, and Beebee really was into drugs with Thalia. But I still think that's a side issue. It's too much. I'll call the lieutenant tonight, though. In fact, I'm going to do it now before I lose my nerve."

Wren was half-hoping for voicemail so she could just leave a message instead of having a conversation, but it wasn't to be.

"Hello, Miss Architect," said a weary voice. "I half-thought of blocking you, but our little partnership is going to be dissolving soon anyway, so what do you have? Be brief." Wren knew about the drug connection, and that she wasn't supposed to know it.

"I hope you've made progress," she said. "I know Saffron has been especially anxious. Have you been able to tell if it's about the house?"

"No, and I can't say anymore. Do you have something?"

"I don't want to confuse your investigation—"

"Yes, you do," said Howard. "But proceed."

"Okay, I do. I want to tell you that even though the film shoot has wrapped, work will continue on the island for some time. I'm going to meet with Nicky, Veronica, Saffron, and Cal tomorrow, before they return to California. It will be a while before they will be able to see it again."

"Fine. You don't need my permission."

"I know. But we'll be discussing the Turnbull murder and the ways I think it served as a pattern for the current murders. For what it's worth, I think Saffron agrees with me. And so does Veronica."

"Okay," said Howard, eventually. "I hear what you're saying. And I appreciate it—I really do. You're planning one of those mystery book wind-ups where the detective gathers everyone together, and someone breaks down under the weight of evidence?"

"There is someone who can stop this. And I'm hoping my discussion will persuade them to do so." It was silent for a while.

"That's not what I expected you to say. Wren—be careful. You may be stepping on the toes of someone who has nothing to do with this but could be very unhappy at other secrets being revealed. Hadley coming too?"

Yes—she'll be continuing to provide food for my work crew anyway."

"Stay near her. She looks pretty sensible. Have a good evening."

Wren put down her phone.

"I got half of that," said Hadley. "I see I came up?"

"Yes. She wants you to be my bodyguard."

"I never leave my home without pepper spray," said Hadley. "So she's nervous but doesn't entirely believe you?"

"Maybe she'll give me the benefit of the doubt anyway. It really must be about the house, and she'll have to accept that it could take a long time to prove that. And meanwhile, the bodies could pile up. Look at that tight little group—somebody else will die."

"You're right," said Hadley quietly. "I wish…" She said nothing for a few moments. "But you're right."

Chapter Twenty-Seven

I t will work here, or not at all, Wren knew. She had gotten used to the many rooms she had worked on over the years, square and rectangles, even an octagon once. They became familiar quickly. But not this oval room. It was fresh each time. Did McComb have a sense of the mathematics of the oval, of the way it would work with the human mind?

The film people were gone. They would continue to maintain the launch service for Wren, Bobby, and his crew. Nicky, Veronica, and the other actors would be flying back to California in a day or two, but for today they'd be saying goodbye to Turnbull House until it was finished.

Veronica had sent Wren a cryptic text early in the morning: "I'll do what's right." What would happen would happen, Wren thought.

Bobby greeted them when they disembarked. "It's been really quiet here with all the film people gone," he said.

"I guess you get more of a sense of what the island is like," said Wren. She turned to her guests. "Very quiet and empty."

"We're working on the second story, on the left, near the balcony. It's touchy enough, but wouldn't you know it, a city construction inspector had to show up today. I don't think he knows a Philips head from a two by four, but we'll give him what he wants and hope he doesn't come back."

"A waste of his time," said Wren. "My father told me when I was a little girl that no one ever finds anything wrong on a Fiore site. Anyway, we'll talk again before we leave."

Inside, Hadley put out some food and drink. Wren had found bits and pieces of furniture from around the house to make the oval room reasonably homey for the six of them: Wren and Hadley. Nicky and Veronica. Cal and Saffron.

They had all come over together on the same launch, so there was no chance to talk to anyone privately.

"I don't need any excuse to visit this place," said Nicky. "But tell me again why you wanted us for a last look before we head back to California?"

"It's the history of your new home," said Wren. "Houses like this are funny that way. You can't get away from the history. Houses affect people the same way they did then and do now. And you need to know that to allow for that as you make a home here. I've already given you some of the story. Now I want to give you the rest."

She looked at her audience. Everyone was curious, but Wren could tell that Nicky and Saffron knew what she was telling them was *important*. She had been wrong, about both of them. Unsophistication wasn't stupidity, and she should've known better.

"Oooh...what are we finding?" asked Saffron. "Do we know more about what happened to the Turnbulls? And we can make our peace here?" Saffron turned to Veronica. "See—if we can fix it, we can stay here, right?" Veronica just smiled. But Saffron was right. That was a shrewd question, and Wren wished she had a better answer.

"Perhaps we can...fix things," said Wren. Another presentation. Hopefully, the last one. At least this was about the house, only about this magnificent home. She could handle that.

Wren looked at Veronica but saw nothing.

"Aside from some servants who weren't really involved, we had four residents living here long term," said Wren. "When we started, we had five, but one of them, the man who commissioned and paid for this house, died early on. And we were left with four: His widow. His sister. And his two senior servants who married each other. Plus, the child, of course. We may want to know *who* killed the Captain. But the real reason is *why*. Someone wanted control of this house more than anything." Saffron wanted to say something but was forcing herself to be quiet and listen.

"We thought it was Jack," continued Wren. "It could've been so he could be master of this house. Because Abigail pushed him to do it. But I don't think so anymore. Dr. Leopold, who examined the Captain's remains, said he was killed by someone about five-foot-ten. Even today, that's tall for a woman. But we saw some furniture designed especially for a tall woman. Furniture Abigail would have used on a daily basis. And another thing: she controlled the interview with Coroner Bedlow, who investigated the murder. Abigail was in charge. You know, I often wish I had a time machine to go back to when the homes I worked on were built to see how people lived in them. But we can only guess, especially when it was so long ago." She took a breath. "We think that Abigail killed the Captain. He wouldn't have thought twice about a woman—especially a maid—sneaking up on him. We talked about how important it was to be chatelaine of this house. What is interesting is that although the Captain left behind a wife and sister, it was Abigail who desperately wanted to be chatelaine. And she succeeded."

Nicky was trying to figure out how this changed things, if at all. Saffron thought deeply about it as Cal comforted her. Veronica gave away nothing.

"Why?" asked Saffron. "Why did Abigail kill the Captain? Just to be in charge of the house?"

"We don't know what else happened here," said Wren. "Katya was injured, and Abigail seems to have used that to spin a story for Coroner Bedlow about Katya being abused, as she had a broken arm at some point. But Dr. Leopold tells us that an injury like that is much more likely to be an accident than an attack. Abigail, at work again. I imagine that the Captain was not a pleasant man at all—warmth and kindness were not the attributes that marked a commercial sea captain of this era. But he was a strong man, and I doubt he was stupid. So I don't think Abigail could've done it on her own...." Wren looked over her audience to make sure they heard that. "...so we have to assume that her future husband Jack, as well as Verity and Katya, were in on it too. What we can take away from this is that Abigail was going to be chatelaine. And everyone agreed with this. What is interesting is that only Abigail had the sheer nerve to actually do the deed."

"What does this mean?" asked Saffron. "We just know that they all hated Captain Turnbull, and now Abigail would run things, with her husband, for

Verity and Katya and Katya's baby. Is that right?"

"It appears so," said Wren. "It might've seemed more obvious for Abigail, as a servant, to take over the caregiver role alongside Katya, who was expecting a child. But I imagine it was Verity who took over that role. They were related by marriage and Verity didn't have a husband herself—we have no record she ever married. Abigail kept things running. It was a job Abigail *wanted* and ultimately killed for. For the house, yes, but she was the de facto leader. They were family of a sort, and she did it for them, at least in her own mind."

"Well, you folks have done a terrific job," said Nicky. "Architect, caterer, and now it seems like you have a crystal ball in your bag. How about that, Saffron? Hell of a history in this place. I'm glad to know all this, but I'm glad we can make it all right again. Be a family here."

"I agree. In fact, I don't think we need to spend too much time on this," said Cal. "I'm not sure what the point is. We're going to make new history here, like Nicky says, never mind what happened here, what we *think* happened here, two hundred years ago." He gave Wren a sharp look, which didn't surprise Wren at all. She had been right.

"I just feel bad about what happened here," said Saffron. "I was hoping we'd find out what happened and...I don't know...save someone."

"Unfortunately, life is not a fairy tale," said Wren. "Things end badly sometimes. There are no obvious good guys or bad guys, especially after all this time. Was Abigail just power-hungry? Or did the Captain really need to be killed? Even if we had been here then, it might've been hard to see."

Wren watched Saffron's face crumble and felt terrible. It was like hitting a child. But she wasn't a child. She was a grown woman with a husband.

"I'd like to make it right after all this time," said Saffron, looking down. Then she turned to Veronica. "Can't we stay here? Can't we be a family here?"

"Sure, hon," said Nicky. "It's like I said." Cal nodded vigorously.

"Look," said Veronica. "We can visit from time to time, but everyone here has to grow up. We can't lock ourselves away here on this empty island. I told you that last night and I'm saying it again. I know you love it—and so do

I. But you're a grown woman with a husband, and you have responsibilities. Abigail did not neglect her responsibilities, and neither can you. Our home is in California. This is an occasional vacation spot when we need to get away for a while. That's all."

Saffron looked like a four-year-old whose ice cream had just been snatched away. *Indeed, that was always the way with her...thinking of her as a child. But she was a woman, a married woman.*

"But I thought..." she turned to Nicky. "You told me..."

"Come on, Veronica. The airport is practically around the corner. We'll have fun here in between shootings. I told Saffron we could invite our friends and just hang out ourselves. Why the hell not?"

"For God's sake, Nicky, grow up. Everyone here has to grow up. I've been doing this longer than any of you—I was making films before I could have a legal drink, and it's time all of you became adults. We have jobs and responsibilities, and we can't just walk away. All right?"

Wren saw Saffron's eyes get wet. Nicky just looked confused. But Cal was the interesting one in this. He was beyond confused—he was shocked. And by the end, he was enraged. Wren could see that much. You couldn't be an architect without dealing with clients who were enraged that you couldn't overrule the New York building code—or the laws of physics.

"Look, I know you're upset," said Veronica, softer now, but still with steel in her voice. "I'm going to ask all of you to trust me. This house is fantastic. It's magnificent. But in case you didn't notice, it's on a *goddamned island.* Don't forget that people went insane here two hundred years ago from being so isolated and ended up killing each other. You think you're different? You'd all go stark raving mad if you tried to live here full-time."

"But this was going to be our *home,*" said Saffron, breaking into real crying and burying her face in her hands, with great gulping cries and tears pouring between her fingers. "You promised!" Veronica shook her head while Cal tried to soothe his wife. Nicky continued to look absolutely befuddled, glancing from Veronica to Cal, trying to figure out who could tell him what was happening.

Veronica was brilliant, Wren realized. With a halfway decent script, almost

243

anyone could be halfway believable. But with this…Veronica had entered the role so completely that Wren became frightened. *What else had this woman made me believe?*

Saffron suddenly slipped away from her husband and ran to Wren, throwing her arms around her. "Wren, you understand, this is supposed to be my home. Tell her we can live here forever. Tell her."

"Sweetie, I'm sorry. Nicky is my client, and who lives here and when is not something I control. But the home will always be here, and it will always be special. Anyway, it's going to be months before it's ready for you to move into anyway. So nothing changes for now."

Saffron sniffled. "Okay. But I want to live here. I *really* want to live here."

"I know," said Wren.

"Uh, Veronica? Can we talk?" asked Cal.

"Later," said Veronica. "Later—okay?"

"Look—I just wanted to give a presentation here about the house's history," said Wren. "This is out of my purview."

"We could all use some fresh air," said Veronica. "My dear Saffron, I am very sorry I upset you." Her voice was now full of honey and cream. "Wren is right. We'll have this house *and* California. This will be our sort of—vacation home. Nicky, I think Saffron and I are going to take a walk around the house and cool off."

"It's Nicky's house," said Wren. "But it's my worksite."

Veronica gave Wren a brilliant smile. "You won't mind, will you?" she said.

"There's a beautiful view from the second-floor balcony," said Wren. "Bobby and his people won't be working there now, but he'll be on that floor. Tell him you're there and you have my permission."

"Come on, Saffron. You'll feel better."

"Hadley, why don't you go with them, too," said Wren.

"Yes, come too," said Saffron. She grabbed Hadley and linked her arms with both women, and they headed off to the staircase. Like a child, Wren thought, quick to tears and quick to get over them.

Cal watched his wife walk away, then turned to Wren. "I asked you not to upset Saffron," he said.

"She wanted the story of this place. I gave it to her," said Wren.

"Oh hell, Cal. Who cares after all this time?" said Nicky.

"They seem to upset her," said Cal.

"By the time we move in here and get our stuff in here, she'll have forgotten all about it. And I'll bring Ronnie around—she's just a little skittish after the attack."

"You're partly right," said Wren. "There is something very special about homes like this, the good and the bad. I don't believe in ghosts, but something led to murder here, and two people connected to this house today have died. It's not a coincidence."

Cal glared at Wren—but she forced herself to look right back at him. She thought of Veronica, Saffron, and Hadley on the floor above. *Hadley was smart. She was sharp. Nothing would get by her.*

Cal decided there was nothing to be gained by challenging Wren. He turned to his boss—his father-in-law—and forced a laugh. "Nicky, you know what it's like dealing with your fellow artists, and Wren is an artist too. They see things in...special ways." Wren may not always be good with people, but she knew when she was being patronized. "Anyway, it's all been taken care of," said Cal with a careless wave. "I'm in touch with the lieutenant. That ass Beebee was dealing drugs on the side—we're all clean on this. It'll just turn out to be a narcotics thing."

"Thanks, Cal, I appreciate it." He slapped his assistant on the knee. "And I'm sorry about Veronica's little speech there. We're keeping the house in California, but we're going to be spending plenty of time here."

"It's what Saffron wants," said Cal.

"What do you want, Nicky?" asked Wren.

"You know, Wren, everyone says I'd be cutting myself off from everyone—I thought at least Veronica was onboard." He gave that smile that had melted millions of hearts and shrugged. "Anyway, maybe everyone was right. But I come from a place where I was cut off from most people, and so did Saffron. Even now, in California, I feel cut off from most of the people I meet anyway. So why the hell not live here? I'm sure Ronnie will agree after a few weeks of thinking it over, right?" He seemed to want a response—perhaps agreement.

"Whether it's an old house or a new one, architects like it when their clients understand their houses. And you certainly understand this one," said Wren. *With a flash of embarrassment, she realized she had misjudged her client. It wasn't the first time. And as much as she'd like to reassure her father, it probably would not be the last.*

At least Cal seemed to be pleased by the compliment for his boss.

"Say, Wren," said Nicky, clearly looking comfortable. Wren had a brief, unpleasant thought that maybe he felt more relaxed without women like Thalia and Veronica breathing down his back. "I hear you and your Dad live in a really nice townhouse in Brooklyn. I bet it's beautiful, you and your Dad both being architects."

"It is lovely," said Wren. "You can visit if you have a chance. My father likes showing it off."

"I've heard what you said, how houses affect people, so I'm wondering how your house affected you. If I'm not being too nosy." And then grin again! Cal was looking closely at Nicky, making sure he wasn't saying something he shouldn't.

"My father and mother made it very warm. It's funny—my father designs very modern houses, but our house is more traditional. It is a comfortable place. I felt the comfort of people who had lived there before. And our family made it comfortable."

"I heard your Mom died when you were a teenager. That must've hurt. I'm real sorry, but I'm glad you have that nice house. And your father."

"Thank you," said Wren softly. Nicky looked around.

"I'd like to make something nice here, cozy, for all of us. I know Saffron needs to heal, and now so does Ronnie. We can do it here, I'm sure. Can we make this a healing place, Wren?"

"You can make any house like that," said Wren. "A one-room log cabin or a French chateau. As I said, I will advise you on furniture and decorations that go along with your taste and with the house. That's what it will take to make a house a home." And the right people. But she didn't trust herself to say that without her voice cracking.

CHAPTER TWENTY-SEVEN

"That's great."

"We'll have plenty of time for that. But let's see what Saffron and the rest are doing—see if she's calmed down. Come on up—we can see the view from the balcony, too, before we have to go back to the city."

Nicky and Cal stood, and they followed her up the winding staircase along the hall until they came to double glass-paned doors that opened onto a little balcony. If anything was going to happen, it would happen now. It would happen in this house, just as, when there was no time left, it happened to the Captain. You didn't get an infinite number of chances. Wren hoped her hands weren't shaking as she opened the door.

Hadley was standing on the other side, glancing at the two women, but pretending to be absorbed in the view to the far left. She was craning her neck over the railing to the right. Veronica turned briefly—perhaps a reflection or the sound of shoes on the bare wood floors had caught her ear. She saw Wren and knew time had run out. She suddenly leaned over the railing herself to get a good view. The physics were dangerous—she was a tall woman, and it wouldn't take much to topple her. Saffron grabbed Veronica's shoulders and gave a shove. But it was misplaced. What had sent Thalia toppling down those steel steps in the nightclub was the wrong method for a railing. Veronica quickly braced herself on her arms as the smaller woman pushed, but that was the end—Hadley moved fast and grabbed Saffron by her collar. Saffron lashed out, but Hadley was ready: her ever-present canister of pepper spray was in her hand, and a quick blast felled Saffron, choking at her feet.

Veronica was still gasping as Wren pushed through the doors. She vaguely heard Cal and Nicky behind her, but no one knew what to do. And then a strange man in work clothes vaulted from Bobby's scaffolding onto the balcony. He wasn't one of Bobby's crew, though; Wren knew all of them. It must be the building inspector. But why—

The "inspector" pulled out a badge. "Detective Nathan O'Shea, NYPD. I work with Lieutenant Howard. I heard, but I couldn't see. What happened here?"

"Saffron tried to push Veronica over the railing when she thought no one was looking," said Wren. "She was trying to kill her again, just like she had killed Beebee and Thalia."

Chapter Twenty-Eight

Things got awkward quickly. Hadley grabbed Saffron to take her to the bathroom to wash out her eyes. Detective O'Shea started to object, but Hadley didn't listen—she had plenty of experience ignoring the police. He followed them, still talking. Cal was talking quietly on his phone, and Nicky clearly was confused. Veronica just cast a sardonic eye on the whole scene.

After a few minutes of silence, Cal said, "I'll see if she's okay," but Wren said, "No, not yet. They'll be back soon."

"I don't understand," said Nicky.

"Let's at least make ourselves comfortable," said Veronica. They re-entered the oval room. Veronica and Nicky sat next to each other on a couch, and she put an arm around him. He reached up and touched her hand.

"What the hell is happening?" Nicky asked.

"It turns out Wren was right. It's about the house," said Veronica.

Saffron came back looking…sad? Angry? Wren couldn't tell. O'Shea had cuffed her.

Hadley sat her down on the other couch and sat next to her. Cal jumped out of his chair and sat on her other side, leaving O'Shea standing awkwardly behind them. He looked like he wanted to do something, but finally just said, "Lieutenant Howard will be here shortly. We can't discuss anything until she gets here."

It was only ten minutes on a police boat, but to Wren, it seemed like ten hours as she glanced from one face to another. Why had Howard sent a detective undercover? *Of course*, thought Wren. Of course. *Lieutenant*

Howard knew I would solve this and wanted to make sure an officer was on hand. She knew I was right. She knew it was about the house.

O'Shea looked relieved when Howard stalked in, followed by other detectives and uniformed officers.

"What happened?" she asked.

"Saffron Scott tried to kill Veronica Selwyn," said O'Shea.

"That's his opinion," said Veronica. Wren watched O'Shea's face fall; even the supposed victim wasn't going to cooperate with him. Howard just rolled her eyes and pulled up a chair.

"Has she been read her rights?" asked Howard.

"Yes, ma'am," said O'Shea.

"Take her away and make sure she's not alone. No one speaks to her until I can question her with her lawyer."

"I've called Zach," said Cal.

O'Shea led her away, and Saffron only looked down. Howard waited until they were gone.

"I guess we're going to have to get the real story," she said. "Wren, any chance you can make it quick?"

"No," said Wren.

"Oh, hell. Look, this isn't a group project anyway. Let's go somewhere private."

"No," said Wren again, feeling as if she had stepped outside herself. "It has to be in this room, this perfect oval room. There's an adjoining parlor with some extra chairs for everyone else. Just you, me, Hadley. And, of course, any of your people."

"Thank you so much," said Howard. Her sarcasm was good, but her father was still better."

"Now, let's get going." Her officers led everyone away. Veronica took Nicky by the hand, and he followed like a little boy, and Cal followed in their wake. In a few moments, Wren, Hadley, and Howard had the room to themselves. Wren closed her eyes and organized her thoughts.

"In 1805, a servant—a housekeeper—named Abigail Bloodworth murdered her master, Captain Thomas Turnbull. She did so with the knowledge, and even support, of the other senior servant, her secret fiancé Jack Llewelyn, and her two mistresses, Katya Turnbull—the Captain's wife—and Verity Turnbull—the Captain's sister."

"So what was the problem?" asked Howard.

"He couldn't fit in here," continued Wren. "That's my guess. This house speaks of order and peace, and harmony. I'd like to think there was once a part of him, a part of everyone, that could appreciate that. But that part of him had been beaten out at sea, a harsh life beyond our imagination. I think the other residents of the house here were in love with it. They would go on to spend years here. But not the Captain. I can see him being miserable here, making everyone else miserable. And so, they killed him. And Abigail was the one who had the brains and courage to pull it off."

She glanced at Hadley, who smiled and raised an eyebrow. Howard leaned back and crossed her arms across her chest.

"It sounds like you're defending her," Howard said.

Yeah. I'm sounding like a psycho. "I don't know if Abigail was a heroine who saved her mistresses or a selfish, scheming bitch. But I know she wanted to be in charge of this house and of the people in it, she wanted the power over it, to be *chatelaine*. And she got it."

"Okay...it's about the house. I get it," said Howard.

"Fair enough," said Wren. "We're all about the house. We throw around the word 'timeless,' but this home is exactly what that word is about. This residence, this room, is as astonishing to us as it was to the Turnbulls two hundred years ago, and I can guarantee whoever is living in it two hundred years in the future will find it just as amazing. Saffron knew that. I can tell you that *intellectually*, but she knew it *instinctively*."

"What does this have to do with the Captain's murder?" asked Howard. Wren saw she had caught the lieutenant's interest, but she was still doubtful about the connection.

Wren gathered herself. "I don't want to sound fanciful, but in a sense, Saffron is Abigail. Saffron was raised in difficult circumstances, and Abigail, from a servant class, was no doubt born poor too. The Turnbull ladies were happy to let Abigail have her way—we see how they let her manage the murder scenario and run the household. Nicky was letting Saffron have her way here. And both women were willing to kill for the right to be chatelaine. Beebee didn't want Nicky to live here. Thalia would try to drag Nicky away, and considering how pliable he was, she might've succeeded. We overthought the motives. It was actually very simple. It was just Saffron killing anyone that got between her and the house. And the power that came with the house."

Howard nodded. "All right...but how far does this go? Did Nicky and the other insiders know, the same way the other Turnbulls knew?"

"I think so," said Wren. "Again, not because I know people, but because I know the house. Cal, Nicky, and Veronica liked this house, maybe not as deeply as Saffron, but they could all see themselves here. I think Cal knew pretty early on, but I can't create a timeline for you. He loves Saffron, but he's also pretty smart. I'm guessing he wanted to tie the knot because of...I think the term is spousal privilege? He wouldn't be able to testify against his wife, right?"

"Yes, there are some protections there. That makes sense. And Nicky Tallon?"

"If he had known, we'd all have realized that. He frankly isn't good enough an actor to have faked ignorance," said Wren.

"Yeah, I can see that. And Veronica Selwyn? I'm getting the sense she set up Saffron to trap her, but now seems reluctant to testify against her. She knew. And she is a good enough actress to fake anything. What's her story? I'm sensing there's more to her."

"She's a cipher. I don't know what she did or why. But I can tell you she loves the house," said Wren, "but beyond that...." She shrugged.

Howard laughed. "You're a terrible liar, Ms. Fontaine."

"I know," said Hadley. "Wren has always been a good girl and doesn't have much experience lying to the police."

"Yeah. How about you, Ms. Vanderwerf?"

"Oh, I'm an expert." Howard found that funny, while Wren just sat there, trying to look *cool* but suspecting she was only managing *prim*.

"All right. We'll file Veronica under 'cipher' as you suggest. A special friend of the Fontaines. And Nicky. And if she helped you flush out Saffron for reasons of her own...I guess that's just a loose end."

Howard stood and gave a look around the room again. "I've seen people killed for the damnedest reasons. But looking around this house—I can believe it. I can almost sympathize." She left Wren and Hadley alone in the room. Wren swiveled around and lay down with her head in Hadley's lap. The minutes went by, and neither said anything.

"Did I do the right thing?" asked Wren. "You are the only one I can trust to give me an honest answer."

"So basically, you want to know if you should've not only let Saffron get away with murdering two people and almost killing two more, but keep your fingers crossed she won't do it again to the next person who, in that scrambled-egg mind of hers, proved a threat?"

"Thank you," said Wren quietly.

"I think Veronica felt the same, in the end. Even though Saffron tried to kill her, she was willing to gamble she'd pull herself together once in residence here. And Veronica didn't like Beebee or Thalia anyway," said Hadley. "But she knew it couldn't go on, as much as she'd have liked to just let Saffron get away with it. For her sake and Nicky's."

"I'm not sure," said Wren. "Veronica connected the dots a long time ago. But I think at the end, it wasn't about justice for Veronica. She was afraid Saffron would eventually decide to kill her no matter what—and finally succeed."

Hadley laughed. "Still not going to give Veronica the benefit of the doubt on anything, are you?"

Wren smiled back at her. "All right. I have some biases. Anyway, I have to say, I'm tired of them. I'm done with the Hollywood crew. Not my scene, as the kids say."

"I don't blame you."

Zach had arrived and was talking to Cal and Nicky, with Howard standing by.

"Wren—" said Zach. *Oh Lord, I really want this to be over...* "My client would like to talk to you."

"I...I don't think Lieutenant Howard would allow that," she said, looking pleadingly at the detective.

"One of my officers has to be there, but go ahead," said Howard.

"Aren't you afraid she'll say something incriminating?" asked Wren, hearing the desperation in her voice. Zach gave her a look: *Oh my dear, that ship has sailed.*

Hadley gave her a kiss on the cheek, and Wren followed Zach to the room. He knocked, and a uniformed officer let them in.

"You have about ten minutes," said Zach, and then left Wren with Saffron. The room had probably been some sort of pantry. At the far end, Saffron sat on a metal folding chair by a table from the 1950s. The officer stood by the door and looked bored. Wren took a seat. Saffron laid her manacled hands on the table.

"I was pretty good, wasn't I?" said Saffron. "Although, to be fair, some of you were easy. You, for example. You're right. You aren't good with people. And Nicky was a piece of cake. But I even fooled Hadley, who's pretty sharp, and also Zach and Veronica. Yes, Veronica was the hardest. She eventually caught on, of course."

"Before or after you tried to poison her at the restaurant?"

Saffron laughed, but there was no humor—it felt like she was laughing because it was expected. "Oh, Wren, you don't get enough credit for being funny. It was kinda amazing that to keep it all together, Veronica didn't turn on me until it became clear you were figuring it out. Then she turned in that super performance like she was going to sell me out. I didn't realize it, but she is one of the greatest actors."

"Why did you want to see me? To apologize?"

"No. I have nothing to apologize for. I just wanted to tell you that that part wasn't fake. I genuinely like you, and I appreciate how genuine you were with me. You never spoke down to me. I know that I'm going away to prison and will never see this house again, or you either, probably, but I wanted to tell you that I really like you, and I know you like me too."

It was a hot day in a windowless room. Wren felt the sweat pouring out of her, like she was a sponge being squeezed. What could she say back: "I like you too." But Saffron didn't seem to expect it.

"Can I ask why?" asked Wren after a long quiet minute. "I mean, you had so much without..." She couldn't bring herself to finish the sentence.

"Without killing people? I suppose. But you know what my life was like. Actually, you don't. I had nothing until I connected with Nicky—with my father. I had absolutely nothing. I guess the shrinks will say I became obsessed with never letting anything go, no matter how big or little. And I really wanted this house. A place where I could be in charge, chatelaine as you say. I love that word, by the way. Just like Abigail. Not like with all those hangers-on in L.A., and boy, did I not want to go back to Idaho. No, it had to be this house. But you'd know about that too, just how spectacular this house was." Her voice was flat. Wren realized. No emotions at all.

Wren stood, but leaned on the table, because her legs felt wobbly. "Is there anything else you wanted to tell me?" Saffron, like the Saffron of old, gave it serious thought.

"No, I think that's it. I appreciate your coming."

"Can I ask..." started Wren. "About Cal..." Again, she couldn't finish, almost wished she hadn't started.

"Oh, you want to know if I really loved Cal? You know, he's pretty sharp too. He began to realize it almost as fast as Veronica did. But he still loved me." She sounded genuinely surprised at that. "I asked Zach if I could have my mandolin in prison, but he wasn't sure."

"Goodbye," said Wren. And when that didn't seem enough, she said, "'Goodbye' comes from the sixteenth century. It's a short way of saying 'God be with you.'"

A smile, but again, it seemed staged. Was it always that way? "I said you were just about the smartest person I ever met. And I meant that too."

The officer opened the door for her, and Wren welcomed the breeze.

Fortunately, the first person she saw was Bobby, and his down-to-earth presence was a tonic.

"What the hell?" he said. "What in the ever-loving hell is going on here? A fake inspector, police everywhere on my worksite, and I heard that kid Saffron is being led off in handcuffs. My crew and I are going to need a bonus for this. Jesus Christ."

Wren laughed in relief. "Our very troubled clients," she said and took a deep breath. "For now, we still have to do the work. We still have a house to renovate." She suddenly felt energy come back. Yes, she still had the house. She got up and slapped Bobby on the shoulder. "Come on. I want to take another look at those floors and walls with you, and I'll explain our loopy clients as best I can as we walk. I may have actually gotten a handle on them." She turned to Hadley and gave her a quick kiss. "We'll have dinner together later."

"Of course, Little Bird," she said. "Umm...you look a little pale. I won't press you about what went on in there, but...are you okay?"

It took Wren a while to answer, but Hadley was fine with that.

"'The Sound and the Fury,'" said Wren.

"Aren't we too far north for Faulkner references?"

"A reference to the servant Dilsey, a matriarch—who held everyone together through tragedy. The last three words in the book: 'Dilsey. They endured.'"

Chapter Twenty-Nine

A month later, Wren and Hadley moved into their new apartment and held a small housewarming for friends and family. Everyone stuffed themselves with the wide array of Hadley's food as they contemplated Wren's artful design and decoration, the tricks used to make the best use of the space.

Bobby came with his wife, Rosa. Lavinia had also come with Angela and had told Wren she hoped to have a quiet talk later.

The evening wound down around eleven, and Wren's father offered to give Angela a ride home, as she had been up early performing surgery.

"Lovely evening. Good luck to both of you in your new residence," said Ezra. "One final word, dear daughter. You understand homes better than anyone. Even me. But don't forget homes are works of art, not personalities. Whatever problems Saffron—and Abigail—had in their minds were theirs and theirs alone. Not the house's. Good night and keep me posted on your progress." He gave her a kiss goodbye.

"Was that a compliment or an insult?" Wren asked Hadley a minute later.

"That was your father being your father," said Hadley. "Anyway, he's wrong. Houses are living beings. You taught me that. But he's right about you understanding homes."

Soon, Wren, Hadley, and Lavinia were alone in the apartment with cups of espresso.

"So, my dears. The weeks have flown by, and the papers are full of Saffron et al."

"I'm in touch with the attorney, Zach Landau," said Wren. "He's my de facto client now. He told me that Saffron is surrounded by an army of lawyers and psychiatrists as they prep for the trial. Anyway, Zach confirmed we're to finish the house. He told me Nicky and Cal will live there. Probably Veronica too."

"At the end of the day, it's really all about being chatelaine," said Lavinia.

"Yes, the house," said Hadley. "Wren and I believe it's about the house. But Ezra thinks it's about two crazy ladies two hundred years apart."

Lavinia laughed. "Oh, I love Ezra, I really do, but he's off base here. I'm with you, ladies."

"It's an orderly house," said Wren. "It's a harmonious one, and that encourages people to want to…order their lives…to be at peace." She shrugged. "But they have to *want* it. A house can't *force* people to behave differently."

"I can see that," said Lavinia. "Maybe that's the way to present it to your father."

"Wren is still having issues," said Hadley. "The whole Veronica thing is still messing with her."

"Not entirely fair," said Wren.

"But partly so," said Hadley. "Look, Veronica fell for your father, but she stayed to mess with you. You knew she knew about what Saffron was doing but didn't trust your feelings because she had set up house in your head. Veronica kept thinking she could keep Saffron under control, not realizing just how crazy she was."

"It's okay," said Lavinia. "I can see Veronica being a master manipulator. But I've known your father since you were a little girl, and he'd give guest presentations to my city history classes. He loved your mother very much, Wren, and I don't want you to ever doubt that. No matter how many Tony winners he takes to bed."

"Thank you," said Wren.

"And speaking of love affairs," said Hadley. "I'm still trying to figure out Katya and Verity. They were apparently content to leave everything to Abigail and her new husband, Jack. Were they busy with other things…Do you think…?"

Wren and Lavinia laughed.

"I would like that," said Wren. "That would tie everything up neatly and make it clear why the Captain was extraneous. We'll never know, though. And we'll probably never really know Saffron—genuinely insane or coldly calculating? I'm not a shrink, but I'm guessing there's a thin line there. Or what was going through Veronica's head. For now, I'm sticking with what I know…the home."

"Why?" asked Lavinia—only Wren suspected her professor already knew the answer.

"Because once again, I was so lost in how homes can affect people, I forget how people can affect homes. For whoever lives there, even if it's just Nicky, Cal, and Veronica, they can turn the house into a place of love. Houses have personalities, but it's how people react to them that make all the difference."

"You're right about that," said Hadley. "Look around—you made this New York apartment a place for love in just a few weeks. Think what you can do with that masterpiece, my fellow chatelaine."

"Oh! That reminds me," said Wren. "I have housewarming gifts for each of us."

Wren ran into the bedroom and came out with a small box.

"I'm so curious," said Hadley.

"Me too," said Lavinia.

Hadley opened it. "Oh!" She held them up.

"Antique chatelaines—two of them, belt hooks for us to put our keys as mistresses of our home," said Wren. "Someday, we'll have keys here for our dream home."

"But if people make the home," said Hadley, "it already is a dream home."

A Note from the Author

The fun part of writing a historical mystery is blending fact and fiction, but it's only fair to the reader to reveal which is which. Turnbull House and Turnbull Island are both fictitious, as is the Turnbull family. There are a number of islands scattered around New York City, but the island in this book isn't based on any of them. However, the architect, James McComb Jr. was a real architect and was responsible for both Gracie Mansion and Alexander Hamilton's house. Except for a few briefly mentioned historic figures, every character is fictitious.

Thanks to my family for putting up with my odd author hours, typing away at all times. None of my books would've happened without them. Thanks also to Verena Rose and all the wonderful people at Level Best Books for their help, enthusiasm and wise counsel. As always, my agent Cynthia Zigmund proved essential in bringing my stories and characters to life.

Finally, a special shout out to the Gracie Mansion Conservancy for an entertaining tour of Gracie Mansion, which gave me a sense of how the Turnbulls might have lived.

About the Author

R. J. Koreto is the author of the Lady Frances Ffolkes mysteries, the Alice Roosevelt mysteries and the new Wren Fontaine Historic Homes mysteries. His short stories have appeared in *EQMM, AHMM* and multiple collections, including the *2020 Bouchercon Anthology*. Over the years, he's been a magazine writer and editor, website manager, PR consultant, book author, and seaman in the U.S. Merchant Marine. Like Lady Frances Ffolkes, he's a graduate of Vassar College, and like Alice Roosevelt and Wren Fontaine, he was born and raised in New York.

SOCIAL MEDIA HANDLES:
  https://www.instagram.com/rjkoreto/
  https://www.facebook.com/RJKoreto/
  https://twitter.com/rjkoreto

AUTHOR WEBSITE:
  www.rjkoreto.com

Also by R. J. Koreto

The Greenleaf Murders

The Alice Roosevelt series

The Lady Frances Ffolkes series